The Counterfeit

TRACY WINEGAR

OMNIFIC PUBLISHING
LOS ANGELES

Omnific Publishing
1901 Avenue of the Stars, 2nd floor
Los Angeles, CA 90067
www.omnificpublishing.com

First Omnific eBook edition, March 2015
First Omnific trade paperback edition, March 2015

Library of Congress Cataloguing-in-Publication Data

Winegar, Tracy.
   The Counterfeit / Tracy Winegar – 1st ed.
   ISBN: 978-1-623421-98-4
   1. Civil War — Fiction. 2. Historical Romance — Fiction.
   3. Union Troops — Fiction. 4. Female Soldiers — Fiction. I. Title

10 9 8 7 6 5 4 3 2 1

Cover Design by Micha Stone and Amy Brokaw
Interior Book Design by Coreen Montagna

Printed in the United States of America

Chapter One

"I've come a long way to meet you," he said with a pleasant, false smile. It was the sort of smile you measure carefully, when meeting a stranger and not yet sure of his intentions. "I understand you have an unusual story to tell."

I waited for him to prepare himself for the interview, as he shifted in the chair and pulled papers from his leather case. He straightened the papers by tapping them against the table, and then he laid them out, neatly, precisely. I realized he must be a thorough type, which was not reflected in his finely tailored yet rumpled suit. Perhaps it had been freshly pressed when the day began, but now, after spending hours confined to the passenger car of a train, it was a wrinkled mess. However, his boots were polished to a high shine, and his mustache was neatly trimmed and combed, two things that attested to his attention to details. Finally, he took out his bottle of ink and pen, cleared his throat, and gave his attention to me.

He adjusted his glasses and checked his records with a detached and cool manner that led me to believe he had little interest in me. I wondered if he had read my case, or if he was just now looking at it for the first time. Perhaps he had grown used to such interviews. This was his job after all. One case was much like another to him; I was nothing more than a tick on his list of to-dos.

"You understand correctly, Mr. Franklin. Where shall I begin?" I asked, tucking my hands into my lap, trying to appear nonchalant, although my back was ramrod straight and I held my head up and at an angle, clearly indicating I was on my guard, if he cared to note it.

He was a young man. I realized he must have been only slightly older than I was when I went to war. This was something that made me feel both superior and discomfited all in the same moment. I had life experience over him, and yet often youth unwisely feel as though they know more than their elders. It would put me at a disadvantage if he felt no deference toward me. At least we were on my territory, in the dining room of my own home, surrounded by the things I was intimately familiar with: my grandmother's china cupboard, the table my father-in-law had hand crafted, and the candlesticks my mother had left me. This was where I felt most comfortable.

"Wherever you would like," he replied.

I had thought about what I would say for some time but now reconsidered as I looked at this young man. He looked as if he wasn't attentive but only committed to doing his job. He looked as if meeting me was not worth the long trip by train and boat from Washington. I had a great deal riding upon him, and yet I was too proud to allow him to see the effect he had on me.

"It's best to begin at the beginning I suppose," I said with a non-committal shrug.

"It is my aim to take an accurate account of your story. It really is up to you what you feel you should share and what you deem worthy or notable."

"I will share what is pertinent for your review, and if my account should wander into the private…Well, I'll do my best to keep private things private and only tell the important information. But I suppose that won't keep me from remembering it all as it was."

"I'm sure it would be difficult to separate the two," he said with a touch of indulgence.

I was amused by this, although it irritated me at the same time. How could I make him truly listen? What could I possibly say that would get his full attention?

"Difficult indeed," I agreed. "You see, I had a secret that consumed me. It was a secret that haunted me in daylight and dark. Some days I believed it would be such a relief for someone to discover it. Other days I lived with the terrible fear they might."

"And the secret was?"

"Mr. Franklin, you should know my secret," I replied demurely. "Have you not read my file? You must know that I lived and fought in the war as a man. But as you can see, I am a *woman*."

The young gentleman sat back in his chair with a small smile upon his lips, as though amused. Perhaps I had broken down a wall and formed some channel of communication between the two of us.

"I did indeed read your file. Fascinating stuff. I'm hoping it was worth the trip."

"I certainly hope so too," I said with a laugh.

"Can you tell me how this all came about?"

"It's very complicated. I had my reasons, although now those reasons seem foolish — the silly whims of a rash girl. Age does much to teach patience and temperance, Mr. Franklin."

Shortly I settled upon the beginning…Caleb's death. Like following the gurgling path of water until you find its source, I knew that was where I must start. My memories drifted along, caught upon the tide of those waters, and I remembered Caleb with the same tender swell and softening of heart I always experienced when I thought of him. Even now, after many years of having him gone, I could sometimes feel his influence over me. I still ached from missing him. After all, his life and death did much to form who I was, who I am.

Chapter Two

Caleb was sixteen, full of promise and eager to live life to the fullest. There was nothing he feared, nothing he couldn't undertake with that zeal evident on his countenance, like a babe wears the innocence of new life. He was called Caleb, after the man Moses chose to send into Canaan as a spy. It was Caleb and Joshua who brought back news of Canaan to Moses, a true account of the land of milk and honey. Only the two of them made it from Egypt, and then through those torturous forty years in the wilderness, to finally see the fruits of their labor fulfilled when they at last arrived in Canaan.

My brother Caleb was the pride of my father and mother. Not that they didn't love me, cherish me, treat me with all of the kindness and warmth parents could afford their own child, but Caleb was without a doubt the favored of the two of us. He was remarkably able at just about anything he set his mind to. I was quiet and never very much good at anything, while he had a gift with speech. He could charm and sugar talk with the best of them. He was captivating, charming, and attractive. How could anyone help but like him?

As I compared myself to Caleb, I summed myself up quite neatly with one word. I have thought on it long and hard and dwelt on it many an hour, and that one word would have been *mediocrity*.

I was never much good at anything. As I was educated in the things a woman, a wife, would someday be required to know, I am ashamed to say I only grasped it enough to be adequate. I was plain in looks to the degree that I was forgettable, average in height and weight. I was a girl who would never be the focus. No, not me. I was the sort who would easily get lost in a crowd.

The only thing I was good at, my one redeeming quality, was that I was not afraid to work, and I always worked hard to be better, to be worthy. I persisted at those skills which did not come easily to me, like a fish persists in swimming upstream. The current endeavors to keep it from progressing, and yet it manages to struggle along, to finally make its objective despite the challenge. Likewise I was set upon finding a way, as unconventional as it might be, and I persevered until I was able to master a skill.

But Caleb, he was something special. He radiated light and everyone was drawn to him. Just as the sun draws the very planets into their orbits, so did Caleb. It was no secret to me that he carried me. He made sure everyone knew I was his sister, and accordingly, I was to be included and treated well. It was as if he allowed me to borrow some of his light. However, it only worked if I was in his literal and physical company and under no other circumstances.

I did not like being insignificant, and consequently could usually be found by his side for fear I might disappear completely without him. If it was burdensome to Caleb, he never let on. I always thought he got all the best there was, all of the goodness that could be afforded, and then when I came along a year later there was simply nothing left to endow upon me.

I suppose my parents couldn't help but show a good measure of pride in him. My poor mother felt her pride in him was the cause of his death. She felt it was God rebuking her for loving him so very much. She saw it as an unbearable punishment when he was taken from us.

I don't know that I shared her view. For didn't the Good Lord endure a similar pain when they crucified his son upon the cross? He himself knew something of the suffering and anguish of losing a child. This is when I learned, or came to understand, that you can study all there is to know from the Bible, you can go to church meetings every chance you get to hear the teachings of the preacher, who I suppose knows all there is to know about God and his ways, but you only really know if you believe when you are faced with something as awful as a child's death. The testing is in experiencing.

I think my mother believed in God. I do. But she didn't have the kind of faith to allow her to move past Caleb's death, to know for a surety that Caleb made it back to a land of milk and honey. That he goes on in some other place. When Mother was holding Caleb in her arms, holding him like a baby even though he was a big grown boy, I was there. I saw the life spirit move out of him. I saw when his body was only a body and no longer Caleb. She could not let him go, would not leave his side. She didn't understand it was just his shell, like a crab that had given up its old armor and moved on to a new one.

Father pried her away from him. The doctor had to give her something to stop her weeping, to keep her from harming herself. Ever after, she was not the same mother I knew. It was as if she and Caleb left at the same time. Only she was here, and he, I hoped, I believed, was Canaan bound.

Father said it was because she had suffered so to bring us into this world. Father said she was told not to have children. You see, she bore three before she had Caleb and then me. Three beautiful babies all born to her in the spring and then taken from her shortly thereafter. Their graves were all lined up neatly with simple wooden crosses to mark them. Three sisters with the names of Adeline, Ellen, and Molly. Mother was my age when she lost her first. Only seventeen. How difficult it must have been for her to put a baby in the ground.

She was very ill each time she carried one of those babies. So much so that the doctor said she might die if she continued to try to have a child. Father said it was because she had walked in the valley of the shadow of death, and it was such a struggle for her to bring Caleb into this life, that it was too much to watch him leave it.

My father was a wise man, a man of learning and living. If anything good came of Caleb dying, it was that I discovered I wanted to be strong like Father. I would not be the kind to give up, to cease living, as my mother had.

Maybe that is what gave me the notion to leave. After all, there is no strength in sitting at home and waiting for your fate to find you. I was weary of living like that. It turned out to be much easier than I thought it would be to abandon my former self. As I said before, I'm ordinary in every way, which was to my benefit in this instance.

I did have pretty hair, which, when Caleb was alive, my mother would coax into curls with the torn rags from an old petticoat. I didn't have the wherewithal to tend to it myself, so it was a bit liberating to take the sheers and clip my locks off near the base of my neck. I hesitated over it, the one thing of beauty I possessed and here I was preparing to destroy it, to hack it off and discard it. It fell to the floor in shocking silence. After the first stroke, I waited. But the world did not end. No one rushed in to intercede. The moment of doubt and apprehension over whether I should do it or not had passed without incident. What was done was done so I proceeded with the butchery of my hair, dropping it carelessly into a pile which added up quickly.

Once I had taken that first cut, I knew there was no going back. When I finished it was short and choppy, close to my scalp and as light as down. It felt as though my head had nothing to anchor it to my shoulders. I thought it might float away without the weight of my hair. I ran my fingers over my scalp several times. It was a strange sensation, one I was sure I would never get used to.

No one had touched the camelback trunk, a shrine to my dead brother, since the day my father had packed his things away. At first I could do nothing more than run my hand along the smooth cool edge of the curved top, wondering if I dared defile it by opening the trunk. I sat with my legs tucked under me on the floor before it for some time, but eventually I found the nerve to unfasten the lid and plunged in. As I rifled through it, they were just things to me, shirts and britches and boots Caleb once wore. Just things. Until I came upon his pocket watch. A lack of winding had stopped its arms at the numbers two and seven, as if time itself had stopped with him gone. I took a moment to wind it, to set the arms right. And I knew it was wrong of me, but I took it. I took it with me, in the breast pocket of his coat.

He had been dead nearly two years. But his clothes still hung on me like they would a scarecrow's frame in the act of protecting the fields. I felt this might be a good thing. If they were too tight, it would give me away. I'm not as well-endowed as some I know, but I do have telltale breasts and a slight roundness to my hips. With my hair gone, dressed in his clothes, his hat pulled low on my brow, I was transformed. I looked totally and completely different, nothing at all like my former self.

Now here was the part no one knew. This was the secret I carried with me, that threatened always to be exposed. I was a girl, just a girl. I didn't wear fine dresses or tortoiseshell combs in my hair. I didn't sit in the parlor and play beautiful music on the piano under the watchful eye of my mother as my love came to call on me on a Sunday evening. I was not part of the ladies' relief effort, rolling bandages and toiling over knitted gloves and scarves and hats. I did not train my hand to stitchery or tatting fine bits of lace to accent the edge of a piece of linen.

No. I was not a proper girl. They did not call me by the christened name of Serena Elizabeth Ann Stark which I was given as an infant. They addressed me as Frank. No one in that sea of men and boys knew I was Serena. They believed I was one of them. They believed me to be a man, as they were.

You may ask yourself why I masqueraded so. What would drive a girl such as me to become Frank Stark the soldier?

And really, there is only one answer to that question. Only one motivation for my unconventional deception. Not for duty, or honor, or love of country, no, not one of those noble notions which might compel someone else to do as I had done. My inclination to join up was much more selfish in nature, and imprudent in its broader sense. You see, it was for the love of a boy.

Chapter Three

Sampson Barlow worked in timber. His father owned the saw mill and was a well-to-do, influential citizen in our town. Sampson was a friend of Caleb's when Caleb was alive. That is how I grew to know him. Although he never paid much attention to me. He was always polite. But really he didn't notice me. I was merely the little sister of his good friend.

He was called Sam for short, which I thought was a good and fine name and seemed to lend to his strength of character. Sam. Doesn't it sound strong and dependable? I had been helplessly in love with him from my earliest recollections.

Once, when I was only ten or so, I was alone near a stream. Many of the streams in Richfield feed into Schuyler Lake, which sits impressively in the southeast corner of town. And being a child, with no notion of what was proper, I took off my best shoes, pulled up my skirts, and waded into the shallow depths at the edge of the water. In spring thaw those streams could be dangerous, but this was a calm summer day. Unfortunately, just moments into my exploit, I struck the tender part of my foot upon a rock, then lost my balance and fell forward.

Not only was I soaked through, but my bonnet came right off, and went floating away like a paper boat set on a current by the young children who raced them down the fast spring waters. I didn't know how to swim and the thought of going after it was far too frightening for me to even attempt. Soaking my feet was one thing, but I didn't dare venture beyond for fear of drowning.

I thought first to try to fish it out with a stick I found in the moist soil on the embankment. My frantic attempts were in vain. The bonnet taunted me, bobbing just beyond my reach and drifting further. I sat on the bank, my knees drawn to my chest, my head in my hands, crying and wet and frightened. I had given up, but did not have the stamina to head home and confess my crime.

Who should come along just then, but Sam Barlow, a good two heads taller than me and with his strangely colored eyes, more hazel than any other color I could describe. Maybe most boys would have walked on by. Maybe they would have ignored a silly girl sitting near the stream crying. But Sam came up next to me and stood looking down upon me.

"What's wrong, little girl?"

At the time it didn't dawn on me that he was calling me little girl and I was only a year younger. Nor that he did not call me Serena because he did not recognize me as Caleb's little sister without Caleb there. I couldn't even form the words to tell him that my best bonnet was floating away, and my mother would be plenty upset over it. I just sat there like a ninny, tearfully lamenting my loss.

Sam looked out over the water and surmised my distress. "Is that your bonnet there?" he wanted to know.

"Yes," I sobbed. "And I can't reach it."

He sat down next to me on the grass and worked to get his shoes off. He took off his shirt and without another word he dove into the stream, swam out like a frog with his legs bent and then straight, bent and straight, until he secured the bonnet by its ribbons, and towed it back to the bank. When I saw what he was doing, I stood up and leaned in toward the water, eager for him to come back. He popped up, wiping his face with his hand as he offered me my bonnet.

He could not have been more of a gentleman to me. Here was a grown boy who had taken the time to help a silly little girl of no consequence in a moment of distress. It thrilled me that he had treated me with such consideration.

Funny how a girl has romantic notions from the time she is old enough to observe the tender intimacies of her father and mother, the way they speak over dinner with their hands brushing one another's, or in a fond embrace before they part in the morning. A girl day dreams and fantasizes over any small gesture a boy quite innocently offers, even if that gesture is meant only in kindness and not in love. And the boy only thinks of her for a brief moment's passing, while she spends long hours envisioning their life together and how fluidly her name will roll from her lips when coupled with his last name. So I was looking to Sam in adoration and with the new beginnings of an infatuation I have not broken to this day, and he was looking at me as the silly little girl who was too helpless to even retrieve her own bonnet.

I watched him from afar for nearly seven years with the same longing. But there was no real interaction between the two of us after Caleb died. For two years I silently observed how he opened the door to a lady when one was present, how he played with his little brothers out front of the school house when he went to fetch them after his day's work. I watched him play baseball with his friends, using wooden slats from the mill as a bat, like he and Caleb used to do. I saw how he labored at the mill, cutting wood and loading it onto the wagons with such effort that the sweat dripped from his body, soaking through his shirt, wetting his hair. I knew he liked lemon drops from seeing him buy a few at the mercantile, and he read books about faraway places and adventures, which was evidenced in the selections he carried about in the crook of his arm.

I suppose that is what compelled him to enlist. What young man doesn't dream of adventure? And what better way to attain it, than by agreeing to fight in a war? Don't get me wrong. I'm sure the convincing and persuasive Abraham Lincoln, with his words of encouragement, had something to do with it too. Our country was at war. There was no one but men and boys to defend us in the treacherous fight the Rebels brought upon us. But over a year into that fight, many were beginning to wonder if it would ever end. Sam turned eighteen a few months before he enlisted. There was nothing holding him back now.

I was in town the day Sam enlisted, just outside of the Mayflower Post Office, as I hung back and peeked round the corner. He didn't seem like he was excited or smiling over the prospect. His face was grave, his eyes sorrowful, as he added his name to the list. There were other boys who seemed all too eager to join up. They were talking about what a good time it would be, how grand it would be to get out of this place where nothing ever happened. The tiny town of Richfield appeared a prison compared to the excitement of war.

It broke my heart. Because I had loved him ever since the day he had rescued my bonnet from a watery grave. While I never had the benefit of actually speaking to him in the last two years, I could watch him from afar. I could still be near him. But with him gone… It struck me that perhaps I would never see him again. What if, as he signed *Sampson John Barlow* in his somewhat clumsy handwriting, he was simultaneously enlisting and signing his life away?

Why, like all the other women and girls, did I not just accept it? Why did I not just promise to write, cut a lock of my hair and give him a likeness of myself on tin so he might carry it in his pocket? What possessed me to undertake such a foolish endeavor? But all I can say in my own defense is that when I saw him sign that paper, I could not let him go. He was still alive and his heart still beat. I had to resign myself to the fact that Caleb was gone. There was nothing humanly possible I could have done to save him or to bring him back. But Sam? Sam was not sick. He was not destined to die from a fever that even the celebrated Richfield Springs could not cure. He was to live a long and productive life, become a beautiful old man with silver whiskers and a hearty laugh. How could I ensure that I would not lose Sam like I had lost Caleb?

Chapter Four

I cried. I cried all the way home, feeling terribly helpless after I saw him signing the muster role. When I came home my eyes were swollen and my face red. Crying leaves me in an unsightly state. My father found me in the yard and attempted to comfort me.

"What's the matter, Seri?"

"Nothing, Father," I lied. "Nothing."

"But, well now, you've been crying," he told me. The way he spoke to me was so filled with empathy and kindness that I nearly began to cry anew. There is something about Father with his tenderness and his many mercies toward me and others that softens me, makes my heart hurt for him.

I couldn't dispute I'd been crying. It was obvious enough. To do so would have been laughable.

"I've just come from town."

"Yes, from town…"

I scarcely heard him, I was so distraught. But he was patient and waited. I do so wish I had such patience, his patience. But there was nothing of his long-suffering in me. Patience was a thing I felt must be endured not acquired.

"There were a lot of men from town joining up," I told him.

He still seemed confused. After all, how could all of those men, practically strangers, affect me so deeply? It was none of our kin, no one near and dear to us. He had no way of knowing it was someone near and dear to *me*. As much as I loved my father, this was not something I felt comfortable confiding in him. I'm sure he was like most fathers in that he didn't want to know his baby girl, his Serena, was growing up. And I, like most girls, found such discussions with a father painful at best.

"Why has it got you so upset?"

"I don't know," I lied again. Somewhere along the way, I had become a very proficient liar.

"If not for your mother…"

"Yes, Father, I know." He didn't have to say it. I knew what he wanted to say. If not for Mother, he likely would have joined up too. This made my heart hurt more, and I was unable to hold the tears back any longer. He put his arm on my shoulder and gave me a little squeeze. After a moment's pause I said, "Father, I have heard about a training facility in Washington, D.C., that is recruiting women to be nurses. They train you there in Washington and then place you in a field hospital to help care for the wounded."

"What's this about?" Father seemed surprised.

"They are taking young women to be nurses for the army, on account of they need the men to fight." I saw his misgivings and hastened to add, "It is a very reputable program."

"Respectable women don't do that sort of thing, Seri," Father replied. "Besides what happened to you wanting to teach? I thought…"

"I haven't given up on that. It's just that I want to do my part too, you know. They could use girls like me, and after the war is over I could always finish my schooling so I can teach. Sara Shoeman says she is signing with the Nurses Corps." He still looked doubtful, so I changed my approach. "I just need a change, Father. I want to get away from here for a while. Sometimes I feel as though I can't breathe."

"And leave your mother? She…well, it would break her heart."

"Mother isn't even aware of me. She hasn't spoken a word to me in two years," I snapped. I immediately felt sorry for my words when I saw his reaction. I would have gotten a similar response if I had slapped him in the face. "Father…" I could not stand it. Seeing him so broken and thinking of Sam leaving for far off places was all a bit too much, and it brought my tears on again. Father took his handkerchief from his pocket and sympathetically offered it to me.

"Oh, now, girl…" It seemed ever since Caleb had died, my father never finished the words he began. As if he might say the wrong thing, he would start a sentence only to have it run out on him midway and abandon it there. I fleetingly wondered where his words had gone. Perhaps they were keeping Mother company in her lonesome place.

I had pity upon him. I wiped my tears away with his handkerchief and reconciled myself to the fact that I was hurting him. I was being difficult. That's really the last thing I wanted to do. Father was already hurting enough for everyone.

"I'm sorry, Father," I said. "I don't know what came over me."

"Let's get us some supper. I'll bet Mrs. Dilly has got something good waiting for us. Things always seem better when you've got a full belly," he confided. He stood up and helped me do the same, guiding me back to the house with an arm around my shoulder.

We came through the door, and Mrs. Dilly straightaway put on her ratty old shawl, which I was sure had been crocheted in the early days of her youth, now long gone in distant memories. She headed for the door, ready to go home and work on her laundry. "She's in the rocker next to the window," Mrs. Dilly told Father in a quiet whisper, as if she didn't want Mother to hear her talking about her. "I thought the sun might do her some good."

Mrs. Dilly was a widow and poor as a church mouse. She took laundry in from some of the families in town to try to make a living. When Mother took sick, I stepped up to care for her. Weeks went by and she grew no better. We began to accept that this would not be a short term problem, but a long term inconvenience, and would have to be dealt with accordingly.

Father wouldn't hear of me giving up on my studies. He had only gotten to the third grade himself, and he had always regretted it. He insisted I continue with schooling, and Mrs. Dilly agreed to take care of Mother during the day in exchange for meals and two dollars a month. It wasn't much, but to someone who had nothing it was something. Mrs. Dilly was grateful for the opportunity, and we couldn't have survived without her help.

"Thank you, Mrs. Dilly," Father said. She nodded solemnly, because that was the sort of person she was, solemn, her mouth always set in a hard line, her eyes forever squinting in concern, and she headed for the door.

Father went to Mother, stooped down so he was at her level and said, "Home again, home again, Rebecca." She seemed to be staring out into the open space beyond the window. Her gaze did not waver when he spoke to her.

He washed up as I set the table. Then he carried Mother to one of the chairs, tucking a towel into the collar of her blouse. I watched him extra close as he fed my mother stew from a spoon. I watched him coax it down her throat with the patience of Job.

"Come now, Rebecca. Come now…just a bit more," he whispered to her, as if he were talking to a small child. Mother took a bite. "There, there. See. It tastes good now, doesn't it?"

Before bed he brushed her hair. It was long and quite beautiful although I had noted she was beginning to gray around her temples. Still she was a striking woman, despite her current condition. Just as her head was laid upon the pillow, Father gave her a dose of laudanum to block the thoughts from her head, to make her sleep a dreamless one. He did this every morning and night.

I thought it ironic that he would readily give it to her at all. It made us so miserable. But it made her happy. And that's why he did it, because he wanted her to be happy. Even if it meant erasing her, smudging her out like soap and water washes away a trace of dirt, he wanted nothing more than for her to be happy.

I lay awake that night, wondering over his sacrifice. There was nothing of him left either. Everything he was, all that he had within him had been given over to her. Yes, Father was in a self-induced trance as well. But it occurred to me then perhaps that was what love is — being willing to give up one's self in order to care for and be with another. The idea seemed so splendid in the dark that it overwhelmed me, kept me thinking on it. And I thought I should be willing to give up myself to take care of Sam. But a battlefield is no place for a girl. It's not as if I could offer my services to him. I doubted he even knew I was alive.

That's when I struck upon the idea. I can't say it occurred to me right off, but gradually the plan formulated in my head. If I was a boy, if I could enlist, I could work alongside him, and fight along next to him. I could protect him and keep him safe. And then I would know where he was, what his fate was to be without the agony of waiting months on end to find out at the same time everyone else would. What would it be like to be close to him, to have him rely upon me in all things? If only I was Caleb…

And that is how I came to be a counterfeit.

Chapter Five

I left several days later, with Caleb's clothes and watch and not much else to call mine but some brown bread and cheese and apples. I left a note for my father. I didn't want him to know exactly what it was I planned on doing so I lied to him. I said I would be going to Washington, D.C., in order to become a nurse. It seemed infinitely more pleasing than telling him I had dressed as a man and was headed off to fight in the army.

Dearest Father,

You know that I love you more than anything, and that I care deeply for your opinion and blessing. When I spoke to you several days ago about becoming a nurse, you did not wish for me to pursue such a course. But, Father, I had already made up my mind to do so.

The past several years have been difficult for both of us. And I feel a great sense of guilt over leaving you in this manner. I don't wish for you to be alone, and I certainly don't wish to cause you distress. But, Father, only try to understand why I feel such a deep desire to leave. I wish to get experience and see the country. I wish to try to put Caleb's death behind me and continue my story beyond the limitations of Richfield, where I am constantly reminded of that terrible heartache. I wish to support the fine young men who have joined the army to fight for a noble cause.

I feel eventually you will come to understand my reasoning and appreciate that you have raised me to be a woman of independence with my own mind and my own will. Do not be cross with me, for I could not bear it. Know that we will only be parted for a short time, and then I will return to you, changed for the better, having learned about and experienced the world.

I will be leaving with the men of the 121st, our good men from Richfield, and should arrive at Washington, D.C., within several days of my departure. There I shall train for only a short time before I am to take up duties in a field hospital to which they will assign me. Please hold off on writing until I have further information on my assignment. I love you, Father. Always you will be in my heart and in my prayers.

Your Loving and Devoted Daughter,
Serena

I was certain it would console him some that I would be with the boys from around here, the boys we knew well. Richfield was a small town known for its cheese, and the springs of course, but not much else. Likely Father knew every man on the enlistment roll from here and possibly a few from the surrounding towns as well.

There was a moment of doubt, when I thought I should not leave. I experienced a tightness in my chest, like heartburn. A wave of guilt swept over me at the thought of abandoning Father. But I wanted what I wanted so badly that I talked myself out of those feelings. After all, I was doing no good for him or Mother anyway.

I struck upon the idea of sending most of my pay home. A man could make a pretty penny bartering his life, much more than a woman could make at woman's work. It ought to help with expenses around the farm and with Mother's medicine. Perhaps my service in the army would be more beneficial than staying behind. But really these were things I told myself in order to ease my guilty conscience.

I signed the letter with my name "Serena" for what could be the last time for a very long time. I folded a nice crisp line in the note and left it on the table, where he'd be sure to find it. I suppose it was a cruel thing to do to my poor father, leaving him like that. But in the excitement of my resolve, I did not weigh things carefully. I did not understand how my actions would surely hurt him.

I was on my own, without a horse. We only had Gus now, and he was old and needed at home. There seemed little point in taking a horse. I was not joining the cavalry, merely the infantry. Where I was going I would be walking. I met up with the men early the next morning after having slept some in a pile of hay just outside of Camp Schuyler. The newly organized camp was for the purpose of assembling enlisted men and training them. But on this day it was the departure point. There were those who seemed eager, those who seemed nervous, but everywhere there was a thrilling energy. I tried to stay to myself and say nothing. I didn't want anyone recognizing me. From the large gathering of men, I felt confident I would be lost in the throng.

As fate would have it, Mr. Haney laid his eyes upon me and looked me over quizzically almost from the moment I arrived. I could not look back. I looked away and hoped he would too, sure that my discomfort was evident to anyone who should care to be watching. Reed Haney was maybe a few years older than my father, though still a bachelor. He was graying at the temples, thin frame, but sturdily built. He and his brother were blacksmiths, sharing the responsibilities of running their business in town. I had never had much cause to visit with him, but I knew who he was.

When Mother was still Mother she told me a tale of how he had fallen in love with a very pretty girl called Flora. Flora was never one to withhold laughter or a smile. She had beautiful red hair and the most perfect figure Mother had ever seen. Mother said Flora Wright was a friend to her younger sister, my Auntie Cassandra, and so she knew the story well, for she was there to witness much of it herself. Mr. Haney was an incurable romantic, she said, who had professed his unending love for Flora and had asked for her hand in marriage. Flora consented, with the blessing of her father, of course. But as the wedding preparations began to get underway she contracted diphtheria, as did Auntie Cassandra and Mother's younger brother Bertram.

The doctor warned Mr. Haney he should stay away from Flora, for he himself could get ill. He would not listen. He went to her, although she was not expected to live. Mr. Haney grew very sick himself because he had ignored the warning to stay away from his true love. Sadly, Flora died. So did Cassandra and Bertram. Mr. Haney did not. He lived. Mother said his was not the only heart broken by diphtheria that fall in Richfield. There were many who felt the pain of loss, including my mother when she lost her younger sister and brother, but none more so than Mr. Haney.

When Mother told me the account of his shortened love affair, it had seemed so perfectly romantic and sad all at the same time. It was the stuff a young girl dreams of, a tragic death, a lover pining away for the only girl he will ever love, unable to find anyone to rival her. It was the way I hoped I would be loved someday. I could not see him without thinking of his misfortune.

Well, sure enough he said to me, "You look familiar."

I shrugged. "Don't know you," I said quietly.

"What be your name?" he asked.

"Frank," I told him. Then I acted as though I were busy with my satchel, taking great pains as I tightened the latches. He continued to openly look me over.

"Frank what?" he persisted.

"Frank Stark," I said, unable to think quickly enough to come up with a different last name from my own. I never did do well under pressure.

He smiled and nodded his head. "Makes sense now. You looked so familiar but I couldn't place you. You belong to Matthew Stark of Richfield somehow?"

To hear Father's name turned me clammy and cold all at once. Perhaps it would be over before it had even begun. And really it would probably be best. I couldn't speak immediately.

"No need to be bashful. Speak up."

I cleared my throat a few times before I nodded my assent. "He is my uncle," I lied.

This got the attention of a few of the others. Mr. Haney extended his hand and I shook it. "Good to meet you Frank Stark. I'm called

Reed Haney," he said. He turned to the other curious onlookers and told them loudly. "This boy is nephew to Matthew Stark." I shrunk deep into myself, my shoulders curling in on me, my head dropping so that my hat nearly covered my face.

Sam stepped forward now and shook my hand too. "I was good friends with your cousin," he explained.

"Caleb?" I asked with shy eagerness.

"Yes, Caleb. I am Sampson Barlow, but most just call me Sam," he informed me.

"I am Frank."

"Hello, Frank."

I nodded my head again, but not knowing what to say, kept silent. Being so close to him made my stomach queasy. That he was even speaking to me at all gave me emotions I'm not sure I can clearly explain. It was then I realized my deception would take a heavy toll on my nerves. If I was to decide this was a bad idea, it would soon be too late to back out.

But I didn't back out. Just being this close to Sam was worth any trouble I might get into for my trickery. I was frightened, yes. But I wanted to be near him so desperately I concluded I would rather die than stay home and wait for another outcome. Besides which, the thought of going home to the stillness filled me with dread. I didn't want to go back. I wanted to move forward.

He looked quite dashing in his best britches and coat with a pistol tucked into his belt. His father must have given him the pistol. His dark hair curled just a bit over his ears and he was clean shaven to boot. It seemed he had taken great care with his appearance on this morning. Likely he wanted to impress.

Once all the men had congregated there was no going back. I was Frank Stark, Matthew Stark's nephew, Caleb Stark's cousin. The men from Richfield and myself were now part of the 121st New York Volunteer Infantry Regiment. We were only a small part of what comprised Company H. From Richfield we would march in the heat of late summer to report to Fort Lincoln in Washington, D.C., under the command of Colonel Richard Franchot. All in all there were just over a thousand men in our regiment: thirty-nine officers, nine hundred and forty-six enlisted. The Colonel made a rousing speech, after which Captain Ramsey of our own Company H accepted a flag given us by the citizens of the town.

From there it seemed a splendid parade as we marched to the railcars where a train was to take us to New York City. The band played "When Johnny Comes Marching Home Again" in a fast upbeat pace with drums beating and fifes ringing as Colonel Franchot led the way, looking as if he thought himself the most noble of characters with his expression full of self-importance. A large group of supporters, comprised of friends and relatives of the newly enlisted, trailed along behind, still not ready for the festivities to be over. I saw Sam's parents, his brothers, and sisters crying over him as they sent him off.

"Please take care!" his mother called after him. Her children gathered round her to give their sympathy as she dabbed her eyes with a handkerchief and worked to suppress a sob.

Sam bore it bravely with his jaw set firm, although I knew it must be hard for him to see his mother cry so. As for me I was one of the few who did not have a loved one seeing them off. I was alone and I worried over my father. Would he carry on without me? Was I doing the right thing? What would it be like for him to spend his days with no dialogue from another living soul? But it was too late now, wasn't it?

With a sense of trepidation I was pushed along by the crowd and followed the line of men as they climbed the steps of the rail car. I sat in a seat across from Sam, next to the window, and watched the large crowd wave hands and flags at us. The whistle blew and a cloud of steam shrouded the air before the train slowly pulled away. Moments later we picked up speed and left the great field behind.

There were all sorts of things to see as we traveled along the rail. I doubt most of us, myself included, had gone past the boundaries of our own county. A trip to town was a treat beyond measure, but this…Well this was an adventure none of us were likely to experience again. It was a great exploit we had undertaken, sure to hold the promise of thrills we had not yet experienced. Scanning the general mass of men, I wondered how many of the lot were merely soldiers of fortune, here for the adventure of it, and how many had signed up with the realistic expectation they might not return home.

We didn't see it then, but death, that invisible apparition which waits patiently for his moment to steal the breath from you, followed us as surely as the dogs follow the gut wagon. Yet none of us knew then who had been marked, who would survive and who was moving steadily closer to their end.

Chapter Six

Along the way on our journey by train, we saw many people turn out to glimpse us, even if it was only briefly. It seemed to me there were many who were grateful for our service to this country. As the train passed town after town, the good citizens lined up to wave, to cheer us on. Some of the women flourished handkerchiefs or small flags and the children looked awestruck and admiringly at us. Occasionally we could hear their voices mingled together, singing the strains of a hymn or a patriotic tune. On our way to Albany they threw apples through the open windows to us. Some of the men were very pleased with this, catching the apples up and biting into them with grins spread clear across their faces, though I did see a fellow get chucked in the head with one of them and he seemed quite peeved. I caught a few myself and stuffed them in my bag with the other food I had brought along.

We rode the train as far as Albany. What a sight awaited us there. The ladies of the town had gotten together to organize a dinner in our honor. They ushered us to a social hall all done up in draped flags with long tables covered to the floor with elegant table linens and laden with foods and drinks. I don't know as I ever saw such a lavish party back in Richfield. Many of the folks back home were nothing more than common farmers. They may have had a dance every now and again, or a social event, the tables spread with gingham cloth and the simple fare of common folks to eat, but it was nothing like the sort of finery I saw in Albany. I stood uncertain for a moment, because I didn't have anyone to sit with. Everyone else seemed to be in a group, as though they belonged. My heart raced as the sensation of being an outsider overwhelmed me. Sam saw me standing alone near the door. He jerked his head to indicate that I should follow him and said, "Come on, kid."

I took off at a trot to catch up to him and eagerly sat down next to him at the table. I couldn't say I wasn't pleased with the spread, for they had obviously gone to some trouble, but it put me ill at ease to be waited upon. I should have been one of them who served, and here I was being served.

Sam noticed my reluctance and said encouragingly, "Eat up while you can, Frank. Food is scarce where we're going."

To my utter discontent, I noted a lady clothed in fine silk, a vivid green ball gown bodice trimmed in ivory lace, paired with a fashionable skirt which was gathered and flounced. She wore delicate lace gauntlets upon her arms, with her yellow hair done up in an intricate bun with braids and ribbons all woven throughout. She carried herself with an air of superiority, the result of fine breeding, and her pale blue eyes were upon Sam. She kept near him, attending to his every want.

"Have another drink," she insisted several times, topping off his glass with red punch whenever he had a need for it. As terrible and unholy as it was, I hated the unnamed girl. I hated her like I've never hated anyone before.

I had never owned such a dress as hers. Much of what I wore were blouses and simple skirts. Sometimes I wore the old round dresses of calico my mother wore when she was a girl. When my mother was once responsible for doing my hair, it looked fine. But when I did it on my own I simply braided it or wore a hair net or a ribbon. The popular style *Cats, Rats, and Mice* was well beyond my ability, and I was most certainly not capable of executing anything as fancy as hers.

I wondered fleetingly what it would be like to be as sophisticated as that girl. She said things like, "Won't you allow me to fetch you some more bread?" "Can't I get you some more beef? I have an eye for the tender cuts." "Let me top off your glass for you." Things that sounded so genteel seemed to drip from her lips without effort. And Sam, oh, Sam. He couldn't have grinned any broader for fear his face would split in two! I observed him nodding and laughing and his eyes were alight. He seemed quite content to have her adoration poured out upon him.

She went away for a time to get him something more, and I whispered to Sam, "I wish she'd go away for good."

"I don't know," Sam said, unaffected by my attempt at swaying him. "She seems a nice enough girl."

"Yes, I suppose she does. But she seems to be awful nice to more than just a few of the men, you know. I don't like a girl such as she, that carries on with men so as to make each think she has eyes for only one while pandering to them all." I hoped my meaning was clear, that what I was insinuating made him dislike her even if just a little.

Sam chuckled. "Well, now, a girl as pretty as she ought to be gay and enjoy some fun, I suppose," he said. "A good time should be had when one can, in times as troubling as these."

I felt my face burn in an uncomfortable flush when she came back with a slice of pie as big as you please and presented it to Sam. "I have one for your friend too," she said, giving me a much smaller wedge.

I tried to force a smile, although I was sure it was more of a smug grimace. "I don't want any pie," I said flatly, without even so much as a thank you. I knew I was being rude, but I just simply couldn't make myself care. Sam looked at me a little surprised and gave a quick chuckle.

"What's got into you?"

"Nothing," I replied sullenly.

Before we left, Sam went with her to a corner of the room and spoke with her in soft tones with his eyes bright and firmly planted on her. She had her back pressed to the wall, looking up at him with nothing short of desire in her gaze, and he was next to her leaning in toward her so as to make their conversation seem quite intimate, his lips hovering just inches from her ear. It was as if the rest of us weren't in the room and it was only they two. It made me want to run from the place in tears. To love someone so and see him find pleasure in anther girl's company was nearly insufferable. Who was I compared to this beauty? I had left my poor father for this? I wished then I hadn't come. I wished I wasn't there to witness it. I felt like a scorned lover, although I knew we had no such arrangement. As a matter of fact, he didn't even know who I was.

It was with a heavy heart I finished my meal. Eventually all of the men filtered out onto the front lawn, and then headed toward the river to board the largest river steamer in the world, the *New World.*

My only consolation was that we were leaving *her* behind, hopefully for good, because I never wanted to see *her* again, and I certainly didn't want Sam to either.

The *New World* was impressive to say the least. I had never been on a boat so fine as this before. Yes, there were the row boats and smaller vessels at home, but this was of such a large scale, it was hard to fathom such a ship existed until I saw it for myself. It was late in the evening and the stars shone down upon us as if for no one else. I felt alone with nothing but a vast black sky and brilliant candles dotting it all, glittery and flickering like jewels upon a sea of dark velvet. It was a magnificent sight.

After a time, what with all the excitement and rigors of the day, I began to feel weariness set in, and I could scarce keep my eyes open. Sam was kind enough to secure a few of us blankets as they were passing them out. Some of the other men had already settled in and were dozing. This being my first night among them I felt a certain discomfort in the fact that I would be sleeping with a thousand or so men.

"Thank you," I said, as I took one of the wool blankets Sam offered me.

"Think nothing of it," he replied. He sat down next to me and grew comfortable with his long legs stretched out before him. Eventually we slept. I can't speak for him, but I at least slept very well.

What a testament to modern marvels. The *New World* got us to New York City in roughly twelve hours. "I'm glad you insisted I eat last night," I told Sam.

"Yes," he said. "I am feeling the weight of an empty belly too. But we'll eat as soon as we get off the boat and make it to the barracks."

True to his words, we got off of the steamer and marched to the barracks through the streets of New York City, with its grand edifices and more people than I knew existed. There was a wide range of classes, some begging and pitiable, wearing rags and covered in filth, others dressed in the most decadent of fashions with fine carriages and servants who waited upon them. A peculiar combination of coexisting extremes. It took us a short walk to get to the barracks where we were fed. It was after noon by then. I ate as much as they allowed, which in my estimation, wasn't enough. Perhaps I shouldn't have hated the pale blond from last night after all. She, at least, fed us well.

"It seems unnatural to not be at church this morning," I said, for it dawned on me it was the Sabbath.

"Yes, I know. I can just imagine my family all singing a hymn, and the good Reverend giving his sermon with his usual enthusiasm." He paused briefly. "I wonder as to what the subject is he will lecture on today. If I know him at all it will have a generous dose of hellfire and damnation," he said with a chuckle and a wink.

We left the largest city in America, New York City, with its tall buildings and thronging masses, the next morning. We traveled all day on the rail, leaving our own State of New York behind for good. All along the way we saw people congregating and waving and cheering us on and the spirit became somewhat infectious. We reached Philadelphia around dinner time and were pleased to find another fine meal awaiting us. There was bread and butter and beef and cheese and beets. I ate until I thought I might burst. I even slipped some of my meal into my bag with the other food I had taken from home. There has always been something in my nature that makes me prepare for the worst, a sick fascination with the "what may be."

After dinner we milled about, waiting for the next train to take us further on our journey. It grew late and the men grew restless. They were rowdy and loud, whooping and carrying on. A few were wrestling with each other or playfully boxing. Perhaps it was desperation that drove the men to find some diversion. One of the men I didn't know, another soldier, got it in his head to get a melon from a field just over the fence and a short ways off from the depot. I suppose not wanting to be the only one at fault in the matter, he began to rouse the other men, and talk them into following after him.

"Look at them melons," he cooed. "We ought to have some. We ought to go get one for ourselves!"

This went on for a while. He walked about, inciting the others until he had stirred a group of them up. Soon many of them were ready to go with him. Sam held back, leaning against the wall of the depot with his arms crossed over his chest, observing the scene with his face carefully blank.

"I wouldn't go along with it if I was you," Sam suggested to me privately. "I wouldn't wanna do anything that might get me into trouble. Bad way to start off. Besides, think on the poor farmer who planted them melons."

But later, he and I went on many similar excursions, trying to hunt up food. How was he to know then how we would be driven by such hunger? We were still innocent country bumpkins without an inkling as to what was in store for us.

"I'm with you, Sam. It wouldn't be a kind thing to do after we were received so generously and fed so well here," I agreed.

We watched as a big group of men jumped the fence and ran through the field scooping up a melon, all ripe and brilliant green, into their arms, snapping vines, and then returning at a run. They were like locusts descending, stripping the field of all its bounty. I doubt there was a single melon left for the poor farmer. Likely he got a shock the next morning when he awoke to see what the men of the 121st had been up to, and discovered his crop was completely gone. I was glad I wasn't there to see it myself. Often times things done in the cloak of night seem a good notion until you must view them in the light of day.

Shortly thereafter we boarded the train, a large number of us with melons still in arms. Sometime after midnight we left Philadelphia and arrived in Baltimore, Maryland the next day. Through the long night Sam and I listened to the rumors circulating. It set me on edge, for it seemed we were entering enemy territory, although it was just Baltimore, and still very much a part of the Union. They may have disliked the North, but they hadn't gotten the nerve up to secede with the other Confederate states.

"Expect them to be hostile," I was told. "Them Marylanders can't be trusted."

I was afraid. I wanted to go back. I didn't want to know what would happen next, as my imagination played all sorts of wild tricks upon me. But there was no stopping the train.

Chapter Seven

"They attacked a Massachusetts Regiment a year ago," a man also named Frank, a big fellow we just met, told us. "You can't trust 'em. They're Southern sympathizers. I wouldn't put it past them to attack us too, just like they did them Massachusetts men. I aim to be prepared for anything. That's right, I'll be at the ready."

He was of course referring to the Massachusetts 6th. In April of last year they were headed to Washington just as we were. There were two train stations in Baltimore ten city blocks away from each other, and the regiment was forced to leave one station and walk to the other in order to get to Washington. In the midst of their transfer, they were set upon by a throng of Southern sympathizers. Surrounded in the streets of Baltimore by the violent and unruly mob, the soldiers did their best to defend themselves against the bricks and rocks and debris volleyed at them. No one is sure who began shooting, although the people of Baltimore maintain it was the soldiers and the soldiers insisted it was the Baltimore mob.

Even if soldiers had been the first to fire shots, I couldn't say I blame them for trying to defend themselves. They were in a terrible predicament and surely must have been frightened for their lives. The fact that they were ambushed on friendly soil was a horrible blow to the whole of the North. In the end, four of those Massachusetts soldiers were killed and many were wounded. Some of the mob members suffered a similar fate, which only proved to incite the sympathizers further and create a good deal of animosity toward the Union troops and give them a rallying point to gather behind. The police eventually managed to hold the mob at bay as the soldiers hastened to board their train. They got out of Baltimore none too soon.

Now, there was no going around Maryland to get to Washington, so I'm sure we were not the only men to suffer through such suspense. But it didn't make our anxiety any easier to bear. It was a frightening thought that you might lose your life on "friendly soil" before even having the chance to see combat as did those men in the Massachusetts regiment. It only proved not all Northerners were lovers of Abe Lincoln.

"Colonel Franchot has forbidden any of us from buying anything eatable. They will stop at nothing. Not even poisoning our food," the other Frank told us.

"You don't suppose they would really do such a thing?" I asked innocently. It was difficult for me to imagine anyone hating us enough to do such a lowdown and rotten thing as poison our food. The notion seemed completely outlandish.

I saw Sam and the other Frank exchange a look, which I took to mean they found my question silly and naïve. I immediately felt foolish. I thought I should learn to keep my mouth shut. Better to listen and observe than to say something that would draw attention to myself or make them think I was a half-wit.

Certainly there was a different mood from the other places we had stopped at as we pulled up to the station. It was heavily guarded by Union troops, which lent to a most ominous feel. After all why would we need a guard unless there was a real threat? We got off the train skittish and ready for anything. I don't mind saying I was afraid. I hung close to Sam, my senses on high alert.

With no place to go and in the dead of the night we were forced to wait out in the open in the middle of the road, our eyes darting from side to side, alert for any hint of trouble. I nearly came out of my skin when a cat jumped from the shadows. Sam was startled too, but recovered quickly and laughed with relief.

"Just a cat," he said. Finally we were told it was time to leave. We had to travel from one station to another to catch our next train. It was merely the distance of ten blocks, but there was nothing to speak of for protection, because as of yet we had not been issued arms.

"Just let them try something," Sam said, putting his hand to the grip of his pistol, "and I will give them what for!" I remained close, thinking that if anything did happen he at least had a weapon. We milled about the streets to the wee hours of the morning as the horizon grew to be a dull gray in the distance, when we were finally told we could climb aboard the train. I could hear a collective sigh of relief as we pulled away from the depot and left Baltimore behind.

Exhaustion began to take its toll again once I realized I had been up every night for nearly three nights. But my sleep was restless and I came fully awake when we pulled into the station in Washington, D.C. They ushered us from the train and we spilled out into the station, funneling through the massive crowds of people. Sights I'd never seen met my eyes, and I cringed at the harshness of it. They were using the depot to transport injured men, fresh from battle, to hospitals there in the capital. To see their empty eyes and their dirty faces, some maimed, some who would never use their broken limbs again, was disheartening to say the least. They lay about on litters, moaning, crying out, crimson red splashed generously over the whole scene. We saw right from the start what we were in for. I looked upon their wretched appearances with a foreboding that made me physically unwell. I developed a headache, my stomach hurt, and I could feel the saliva in my mouth turn thick and vile. No matter how I tried, I couldn't seem to swallow.

Sam's expression mirrored the appearance of many of us, I was sure. He looked lost, as if he were wondering if this was where he was supposed to be or if he had gotten off at the wrong station. I wanted to go to them and help them, but I also wanted to run from them and never look back. Acknowledging their conditions was conceding that this was real. We were headed into a fight that could affect us just as sorely. We hurried through the cramped space and then waited again for further orders.

For two hours we lay about without a shelter from the sun waiting to find where we were being sent next. The only good that came of it was Sam was there. I suppose he felt some pity for me and endeavored to take me under his wing. He watched me pull my stockings from my feet and grimaced sympathetically. I had not taken those boots off in three days now, and my feet were hurting something awful.

"How many sets of stockings have you got, Frank?"

It took me a moment to realize he was speaking to me. I silently berated myself for not remembering *I* was Frank. He was saying my name. Not some others. "Who me?" I stuttered.

He grinned. "Yes, sir, you."

"I got two pair," I said, as I picked gingerly at the milk white skin covering the blisters rising up in angry bumps where my feet had rubbed against my boots. It made matters worse that those boots were Caleb's and he had worn them in all funny. Good for his feet, but not so much for my own.

"You might ought to think about doubling up on 'em. See if it don't help some," he suggested.

"I'll try," I told him. I put my stockings back on, gathering them up between my thumbs and fingers, starting with my pointed toes and stretching them up over my feet and legs, when I noted he was watching me with a curious expression.

"You put your stockings on in a peculiar way," he said.

I attempted to remain calm. "I do?" I said, with an indignant edge to my voice.

"You ever been away from home before?" he wanted to know.

"No. Never," I admitted. "New York was certainly a sight to behold," I added, trying to divert the conversation to something safer.

"How old are you, Frank?" He was watching me closely, his face appeared skeptical. I suppose he was trying to discern whether what I was about to say was truth or not.

I was thinking hard. If I told him seventeen, which in very deed I was, I doubted he would believe me. I was too thin and too short to be a *boy* of seventeen. So I told him, "I'm sixteen."

"You sure?" he asked in amusement. "Cause you seem younger than that. Your voice hasn't changed yet neither."

"Sure it has," I argued. "You never heard me before. It's lots deeper than it was." Even as I said it, it sounded foolish to my ears. Sam burst out laughing. I could feel my face burn hot with shame, and I dropped my head in a sulk.

"I'd say you was more like fifteen, if that even," he guessed.

I waited a long time before I said, "Don't know, maybe you're right. Fifteen, sixteen, it's nearly the same."

"You're too young to join up," he said.

"There're boys younger than me in the fight," I argued.

"Maybe so, maybe so," he said with a nod. "But that don't make it right." He paused for a moment, then cleared his throat and said, "What about your mother and father? What do they think of you leaving home and all?"

"I don't have a mother and father. They're both dead and in the grave," I lied. It came out so quickly I surprised even myself.

Sam felt bad, I could tell. Nothing can cast away the eye of suspicion like guilt. At the mention of being an orphan you are exonerated almost at once. "I'm sorry to hear it. Both gone. It's a terrible thing for a boy to be on his own in this world."

"It isn't so bad," I said, trying to make his remorse less of a burden upon him. "My father died when I was just a babe. Never knew him that I can remember anyway. And my mother, she was taken last spring from me. But she was a good mother and I have no doubt she's with the angels in heaven."

"Isn't there anyone who should care to speak to you on your behalf to tell you it's not wise for a youth such as yourself to run off to war?"

"I've got no kin to call my own…but my aunt and uncle of course," I added hastily, remembering Father and Mother and how they played into my lie just in time. "And my uncle had no say in my coming. I'm old enough to decide for myself what I should and shouldn't do."

"Well, now, Frank, I see you can take care of yourself. But I miss my own family something terrible, and I have a brother just your age. If you should need anything, you can count me as kin. You are Caleb's cousin, so you just as soon are mine. And you'll rely upon me in all things."

My heart nearly beat right out of my chest. What a man was he! What a good and tender heart he had. I so hated misleading him with my deceitfulness. This, coupled with his vow of allegiance to me and the blisters on my feet, made me feel weepy. I had to swallow hard to keep from crying. Boys don't cry. I looked away quickly and hoped he hadn't noticed it.

"You may do the same of me," I told Sam earnestly. "It's not my wish to be a burden and perhaps I may prove useful to you as well."

"It seems we've struck upon an agreement between gentlemen then," he declared. "And as such, we must shake on it." He extended his hand to me and we shook resolutely.

We made Fort Lincoln on September the third and were promptly issued a smart new uniform with hat, an Enfield rifle musket, a haversack, which was a canvas bag for carrying equipment such as a cup and plate and spoon, a woolen blanket, a shelter tent, a sewing kit, knapsack and a canteen, and a little pail for cooking and fetching water. My uniform was a deep blue with yellow piping, which was how I was to be discerned as infantry, and was stiff from being brand new. It was strange to me, the thought of these things being mine. Actually, it was a bit of a thrill. After all, I had never owned something outright I could truly call my own. All things previous to this had been provided by my father.

Fort Lincoln was built directly upon the Baltimore and Ohio railroad line. Newly constructed in the summer of 1861, it looked brand new. There was the main building, of course, but then it was surrounded by countless white tents as far as the eye could see. The Fort was to serve as the outer defense of the city of Washington, D.C., if the enemy should ever make it this far north. Already we heard rumors of threats of attack upon the Fort.

We pitched tents and made arrangements as to who should sleep in which one. I said nothing when they were going through this process, but I did stay very close to Sam, so I might be in his tent. I did not want to risk being stuck with someone else. The thought of sleeping with men was horrifying, but the thought of sleeping with men who were total strangers was simply unbearable.

They divided us into squads, groups of ten men, and then sections, and platoons, and so on and so forth. I was in a squad with Sam, the other Frank—Frank Garner, Mr. Haney, Rueben Morrell, Vern Stapleton, Marcus Carvey, Gaston Shriver, James Roberts, and Orson Penrod. I will endeavor to give an accurate account of each.

Frank Garner was a big man, which I believe I have before mentioned. The other Frank was maybe in his early twenties and had only been married now for six months. He seemed to be a jester, and always ready to laugh at anything remotely amusing. I took to him right off. I could see he was the sort you would want to have backing you in a fight. He was rowdy and lively, but immensely entertaining.

Mr. Haney, of course, I have also previously mentioned. Solid, dependable, mild mannered, and easy to get along with, he was another of my favorites from the group. I was glad I had luck enough to be in his squad. The story my mother had told me of his previous suffering had endeared him to me. I felt as if I already knew him, although he was still a stranger to me.

Ruben Morrell…Well, I am not sure I could put words to him and adequately describe his personality. He was a man who changed as surely as the tides of the sea. One minute your friend, the next a mortal enemy, and then back to friend again, all before the setting of the sun. Depending on the situation and the players, he might be one way, and then again he might be another. He wasn't a bad sort, but neither was he good. I got along with him. However, I did not count him an ally. He was not to be trusted but instead tolerated as best you might.

Now, Vern Stapleton was the worst sort. He probably grew up hiding behind the barn torturing animals for the fun of it. Yes, I can see his gleeful and malevolent grin as he's at the task of tying tin cans to a poor dog's tail or worse, and thinking it is some fun. I didn't need to know him well to know he was not a gentleman. The look in his eyes said it all, dark and calculating, always summing up his prey. For that was what everyone was to him, something to be preyed upon. I didn't like him, and I don't know many who did. But rather than be the one he picked on, they undertook to be his friend instead, so that he had many a chum.

Marcus Carvey was good at most everything, but he didn't delight in his abilities. He was probably in his thirties, his face tan and his frame strong from many an hour working out of doors. He was confident but not cocky, and he was very much unlike Ruben in that he had formed his opinions and they did not sway based upon the whims of others. He was another you would consider good to have in a pinch.

Gaston Shriver I did not ever know too well. He came from a nearby town, and although he was in the same company as us he stuck to himself. He seemed an unhappy sort, not the kind I would seek out as a friend. He was perpetually shrouded in gloom. He looked at the world from a pessimistic view. He liked to complain even of the smallest things, always rolling his eyes and sighing deeply.

James Roberts was as backward as they came. I wonder if he had ever been away from his own farm before this. He was simple in his manners and speech but was a decent fellow. And although he was eighteen like Sam, he seemed more like a child than a grown man. It was an innocence he bore on his countenance that made him seem so. He said very little but was pleasant to have in one's company all the same.

And then there was Orson Penrod, the unfortunate man. He too was young. His father had pressed him until he had given in and enlisted. What purpose his father had in doing so, I will never understand. "It will make a man of you," Orson told us he had said.

He was a fearful, apprehensive boy. I suspect he may have had some sort of a nervous condition. Simply not cut out for the rigors of war, the tragic Orson Penrod, and oh, how Vern had some fun with him.

It was a somewhat miserable situation, me in a tent with these nine other men as my bed fellows. After all of the goings on of the day, we were sorely disappointed when we received one loaf of bread to divide between all of us. At night it was difficult to sleep. Not only from the hunger pinching my belly, but also from the sleeping conditions, which left much to be desired. There was snoring and rolling about and scratching in places that would make a lady blush. I certainly didn't care for it. What's more, on chilly nights, the tent flaps were shut and the stench of stale sweat and flatulence made me positively ill.

Imagine my horror when we were instructed to sleep in a spooning position, lying on our sides with our knees drawn up, the man behind you with his knees pressed to the back of yours, all in a row, like a set of dominoes fallen over. Not only was the purpose of this arrangement so we could all fit in the tent, but also to keep warm. I made sure I was on the end, claiming that being pressed between the group would make me ill.

"I don't do well in tight spaces," I told them. "It makes me sick to my stomach." This was a good story to tell, because no one wanted to be stuck next to a potential vomiter. I secretly relished having Sam at my back, with his body close to mine and yet managed to stay away from the others at the same time. I thought it was pretty smart of me. After all I was getting what I wanted out of it and still managing to avoid the unpleasant parts I wanted nothing to do with.

For nearly three days after our first day there we suffered through with no rations to speak of. Everyone was in a foul mood over being so hungry. They grumbled fiercely over it. I was glad I had brought a bit of food along with me. But I was afraid they would find out and be angry with me. I was not about to divvy up the food I had kept in my bag with all of those men, and mostly perfect strangers to me. I thought if they should discover it they would simply take whatever they wanted and I would be left with nothing. Under these conditions I wouldn't put it past them to take it forcefully. They were hungry. But so was I. I alerted Sam to my stash privately when no one else was around.

When I told Sam about it he said, "That's good. But don't go telling anyone else. They're all so hungry they might try to take it from you." I was glad we saw eye to eye upon it because I was thinking the exact same thing.

"I won't tell anyone else. It's just for you and me to know," I assured him. We got through the lean time by dividing my apples and bread and cheese and the food I had taken from my meal in Philadelphia between the two of us, eating the items that would perish quickly first.

I was thinking I had it pretty good, all things considered, when I found out I was to undergo an examination to see if I was fit to serve. This was something I had no idea I would have to do, and I went into a full on panic. The dread that came over me was real to the extent it made me sick to my stomach. My mind went over it and over it. How could I get by without being discovered and protect my reputation? How would I keep the fact I was a girl a secret?

Chapter Eight

Given my lack of previous experience with such things, I had no notion of what was to come. I had seen a doctor maybe twice in my life. Once when I broke my leg falling from a horse when I was eight, and once when I was sick with the measles when I was thirteen.

We were all told to make a line, as we filed in a long procession and waited to go through the tent door into a great room. The room was outfitted with tables and cupboards filled with gauzes and medicines, which I noted as I looked over the place while waiting to be examined. I could feel the sweat wetting my shirt as I suffered through it. Every so often they would call for another group to go back. I watched them with a growing desire to hastily leave and never look back.

The line began to dwindle as they took a dozen or so men in at a time. As quickly as the line was moving, it felt like slow torture to me. My face was screwed up in agony. I shifted impatiently from one foot to the other and wrung my hands. At one point Sam, who was standing in front of me, noted my distress and tried to give me comfort.

"It won't be painful," he assured me. I knew that remained to be seen. It could be very painful if I was found out before a room full of men. If they asked me to take off my clothes I was resolved to run right then and there and suffer the consequences later.

Sam and I went in to the tent at the same time. We stood idle for only a brief moment, my eyes flitting about the room apprehensively. Finally one of the doctors motioned to me and a few others to come over to him. To my chagrin he chose me first out of the lot as we stood in a short line before him. I hesitated, looking from side to side to make sure he was talking to me. I saw it was indeed me he wanted, so I stepped forward slowly, feeling my heart beating hard and painfully in my chest. I felt as if I couldn't swallow as I trudged toward him. I must have been too slow for his liking.

"Hurry along," he scolded me. "There's little time for dawdling. I'm a busy man."

His irritation with my pace did nothing more than put me nearly over the edge. I felt as if I might break down and cry. I stood in front of him, uncertain and self-conscious.

"Got good eyes?" he asked me.

"Yes, sir," I mumbled.

"Speak clear now, so I can hear you."

"Yes, sir," I said, louder this time.

"Open up that mouth of yours," he commanded. I'm not sure if it was just my perception or if he truly was an imposing figure. He was a large man, with impressive height and weight. His voice was loud and deep. Each word that came from his mouth was like a bass drum resonating. I tried not to jump when he spoke to me.

I opened my mouth, and he took me roughly by the jaw and peered in at my teeth. After wrenching my mouth this way and that he announced, "Good strong teeth." He took up a pencil and a list on paper. "What's your name?"

"Frank Stark, sir."

He wrote this down. "How tall are you?"

"Five feet and five inches, sir."

"How much do you weigh?" he wanted to know.

"I couldn't say, sir," I answered.

He looked me over, then did his best to estimate. "One hundred and twenty pounds give or take, I would think." He made a notation next to my name. "Gonna have to fatten you up, son."

"Yes, sir."

"What about your hearing?"

"I hear good, sir."

"Let's take a look at those feet," he ordered. I took off my boots and showed him my feet. He took a look at my bare feet and then nodded his approval. "Besides the blisters, they seem fit. Well, I suppose you're cleared to fight for Abe Lincoln then," he told me before he was on to the next man. I wasn't going to hang around and wait for Sam. I got away from there with all haste, afraid the doctor might call me back for further inspection. I waited for Sam in the tent where it was safe.

"It wasn't so bad then, was it?" he asked.

I laughed with relief. "I suppose not."

"And now we are on our own time. What should we do?"

We trained much of the day, learning to take orders and battle commands, which I found very much confusing, but late afternoons and evenings were empty hours, free to pursue our own interests. There was so much to see in Washington. The place was alive with activity. I was dying to see it, wondering if I would ever have such a chance again.

"I have a notion to go walk around the capital and see the sights," I told him.

"I don't know if they'll let us leave the fort," Sam said. He thought about it for a moment and then suggested, "Might not be wise to ask permission. We'll go and if anyone should say something to us we'll ask forgiveness then."

And so we went without a word to anyone. It was Sam and I, of course, for as I had been a constant presence with Caleb, now I was also with Sam. Reed Haney and the fellow named Frank Garner, the man who warned us about Baltimore on the train, and James Roberts came along with us too.

It was so grand a place compared to Richfield, the streets stretching on and on with beautiful town homes and countless businesses. The people we passed in the lanes dressed as though for a great social event, the ladies wearing beautiful gowns and bonnets that had to have cost a pretty penny. They didn't wear the simple skirts and blouses we worked in at home. There was a constant rumble of carriages upon the streets. The noises were difficult to get accustomed to. There was color and light and movement everywhere we ventured and an infectious excitement was palpable.

We saw the Capital Building. I was disappointed because there was scaffolding marring the face of it. There was work being done to add a dome. I could see that once finished it promised to make the immense building all the more grand. I couldn't even begin to imagine what the inside must look like. Once we finished there we drifted toward the White House.

"Can you imagine living in such a splendid home as that?" I asked as we viewed the president's home with its massive columns and rows of windows softly glowing. It was down a great lane lined with trees and lit with street lamps.

"I bet Abe Lincoln himself is probably sitting down to dinner this very minute just inside there," I commented.

"You better believe it ain't a bit of tough meat, a hard biscuit, and some beans." Reed laughed. "Or worse yet, nothing at all. What do you suppose he's eating tonight?"

"Roasted beef and blood pudding with some brown bread and fresh butter," James guessed, his mouth practically watering from the thought of it.

"A turkey as big as a hog with all the trimmings," the other Frank offered.

"Eating a sight better than us anyway," Reed said.

"Seems a small comfort for a man who must bear the burden of running a country," Sam observed. "He must be sorely encumbered by the business of sending all those boys to their deaths." Sam was such a thoughtful sort. When he said that, we all felt a terrible remorse for having spoken such resentful words about the president.

The other Frank wore a mischievous grin. "Well, you know how to ruin a man's appetite," he joked. The rest of us, including Sam, laughed heartily over it.

Later the five of us, out of curiosity, stood on the walk just outside of Carroll Prison. It was a large old brick house converted over to a jail, with several chimney stacks and a scattering of sparse and naked trees out front. The prison was right off the road and sitting just next to the sidewalk. Some of the men back at the Fort told us the famous spy Belle Boyd was here. She sounded like a girl who did not lack in spirit. She had somehow managed to sneak a Confederate flag in to her cell, and although they searched her room in hopes of finding it, they had been unable to. I wondered where she was hiding it.

I could not imagine being so bold after hearing the tales of her renowned exploits. Everyone spoke of how she had somehow smuggled important intelligence past enemy lines, and in the midst of a terrible battle no less. This was her second time being imprisoned, although she was only eighteen. They said she possessed such beauty that she was able to easily make men, who were otherwise impervious to weakness, part with information of great importance. It was rumored that she was close to General Jackson himself. It sounded so exciting, so sensational.

I lamented over the fact that there was nothing resembling Belle Boyd in me. She was a woman of daring and bravery, and I could only wish I were. But then I thought on how, this very minute, I was in disguise, playing a part which was nothing like my former self, and I took comfort in the fact I had had the pluck to pull it off.

"What do you suppose she does with all that time in a prison cell?" I wondered.

"For all we know, she might be looking out her window right back at us this very instant," the other Frank observed.

"I heard she's got the finest ankles in all the South," James added with a hint of awe. James was a bashful, backward type, so when he mentioned the girl's ankles I was somewhat surprised and horrified at the indecency of it.

"That's not what the papers say. They say she isn't a handsome woman at all and that she wasn't particularly smart either," Sam told us. I could see he was amused with our interest in the subject. He was intent on rattling those of us who were fascinated enough with her to care.

"Just goes to show you the papers don't know everything," the other Frank said.

"So you think she's got to be the most beautiful woman there is, then, Frank?" Sam questioned.

"No girl is as pretty as my Nell," he answered. He still had the moon eyed look of someone newly in love. I liked him very much for it. He was a joker, yes, but one without malice, and his devotion to Nell was so charming.

I took to him right off because, although he was loud and big and rough around the edges, you didn't doubt he was true through and through. Besides, he proved to be of great entertainment value. Not only did he have a way of telling a good yarn, but he could also play a mean fiddle. Both of these qualities were an asset, in my opinion. The evenings and nights could grow so long, but spending time in his company, with the distractions he provided, made it vastly more tolerable.

"How we going to tell you and Frank Stark here apart?" Sam asked out of the blue.

The other Frank was well over six feet tall and a good two hundred pounds or more. He had a thick beard and dark hair generously covering his arms and chest like fur. I laughed at the thought that we were in any way comparable.

"It isn't so hard to tell us apart, Sam," I pointed out.

"Well spoken, Frank," Sam agreed. "But I was referring to your name. I say Frank and both of you take notice all at once."

"He's Big Frank and I'm Little Frank," I said.

The other Frank burst out laughing loudly with an enthusiastic guffaw that set his belly to shaking as he pounded me on the back with his massive paw of a hand, nearly making me lose my balance. "I like that. Hear that boys? I'm Big Frank." From then on that's what we all called him.

When we got back to the fort we settled in for the night, as usual, only to be awakened in the dead of night, roused after only a few hours of sleep, to learn we were to leave Washington immediately. I was glad for the chance I'd had to see the city with my own eyes, knowing I might never be back.

We were to head south to Maryland and who knew if we should ever return. We were told to leave everything not absolutely necessary behind. I had my satchel with all of Caleb's things in it. Sadly I had to leave it behind at Fort Lincoln. I tried to figure a way to keep it, but knew there was nothing I could do about it. Everyone was saying we wouldn't be gone long. We would be coming back. Despite the promise we would soon be returning to the fort, we did not. And so I never reclaimed his things. I kept only his pocket watch.

I knew my mother would take it very hard when she discovered Caleb's things were gone. I wondered how I could've done such a thing to her. What kind of person was I? First, leaving my father, and then taking what precious little was left of my brother and leaving it behind so thoughtlessly? I felt terrible about it.

Washington at my back, marching four men abreast into the morning, the reality of what I had done washed over me anew. I realized I might very well be marching to my death. Then too, detection may be just a moment away. What would I do if I was found out? How would I explain what I had done?

Before we left I held back, thinking perhaps I could get lost in the throng and find a way to accidentally be left behind. But then Sam called me to attention.

"You coming, Frank?" he asked, as though we were best pals.

44

Chapter Nine

I hastily collected my gear. "Coming," I said, and fell into step with the others.

Being at the fort for only a short time, it was with regret I left it. I may have been hungry, I may have been over crowded with a lot of men in my tent, but it felt somewhat safe, even with all of the threats of possible attacks. We marched from Washington to Maryland, there to reinforce Major General Fitz John Porter.

"I shouldn't like to be one to complain," I told Sam, "but it's terrible hot." And indeed it was. The heat during the day was unbearable and the cold at night was just as sore.

"You aren't the only one to note it, Frank," was his grim reply.

Along the way, in the heat of the day, there were many men who became unwell, throwing up, growing so weary they scarce could walk, but still pressing on. It was close to midday when Sam and I saw quite a few of the men from the regiment fall out of rank, collapsing to the side of the road, sick from the sun and tired out beyond their ability to go on. If I hadn't wanted to prove to Sam I wasn't an encumbrance, that I was strong and able to endure it, I might have stopped to sit for a while myself. Thankfully, in late afternoon we were allowed to stop for the day.

We went to make camp, and that's when it sank in that we had no tents, no blankets, no comforts of any sort. The heat of the day receded and wore into a cold and chilly night. It was misery. We lay upon the hard ground, shivering without a blanket. For once the idea of having the body heat of all those men in the tent as we did at Fort Lincoln was appealing. Somehow sleep came, because I was so tired I simply couldn't keep my eyes open any longer. The following day was disappointingly much the same. Marching in the heat of the day, sleeping in the cold upon the ground at night, and more ailing men unable to go on.

Sam scrounged around and came up with a shelter made from branches stripped of bark, anchored into the ground, which he then covered with brush. He shared his shelter with me, and it helped some. I thought I would probably perish if it was left up to me. I would have never thought of such a thing.

"Can't believe they would have us leave everything behind so we might suffer without the benefit of even a tent," he grumbled. "It seems like poor planning to me."

"I don't suppose Colonel Franchot knows much of war strategies," I put in. "Being a political man does not qualify him in leading a regiment."

"Just so, Frank. Very smart of you to observe it," he praised. When he said it I felt a pride that made me tingle from the tips of my toes to the top of my crown.

Now, you may wonder how I went undetected as a girl among all of those men. As a general rule, men are not shy about anything of a private nature when they think there is no woman present. They do their business right out in the open. When I had to do my business, however, I took to the woods alone and found a solitary spot away from the others, on alert for the duration of it. I grew very good at being very fast.

They joked and teased about it saying I was too modest, and I was a secretive sort. They thought I was odd, yes, but most girls don't go around in men's clothing, playing at being a soldier, and so they didn't suspect me. Maybe if they had seen me in a dress, they'd wonder as to how they ever thought I was a boy. It helped that they believed I was raised by my mother, without the influence of a male, thanks to the story I concocted about my father dying when I was only a baby.

Here was something else to my benefit: the men slept in their uniforms, even their boots, at night. Not only did it provide extra warmth, but also they must be up and ready at a moment's notice. On the really cold nights, they wore their overcoats as well. We marched as light as possible and so we didn't bother with carrying night shirts or extra clothing. It would only add to the fatigue we already endured in carrying our rifles, knapsacks, provisions, ammunition, blankets, and haversacks.

They did strip down to bathe, at times in a general mass of naked men, a great herd of them heading for the water. I avoided the scene, steering clear of their bathing area completely when they made their plans for washing known. When I bathed, I waited until it was good and dark and then slipped away to some secluded spot. Some of the men didn't care to bathe at all. Cleanliness was not a priority for them. No one thought to ask any questions as to why I didn't go wash with the rest. In these ways I managed to elude detection.

Over the next few days of marching Sam grew sick. His nose was running and he was coughing something fierce, sounding like the bark of a dog. With nothing but his sleeve to wipe his nose on, he seemed miserable. Still, he was lucky compared to some. For sickness and disease seemed to be spreading rapidly through the men who were now living in such poor conditions and in such close proximity to others who were unwell too.

More than half of us were seriously ailing, some unable to continue on, on account of being so gravely ill. It was easy to become downhearted, remembering the great sendoff we were given compared to the current situation. We all began to murmur against the difficulties we were forced to bear. Sam didn't utter a word of complaint, though. No, not he.

"It is a hard thing to think you were before your home hearth only a short while ago, and then to be here now like this..." he said to me. "But it only makes the suffering worse if you dwell on it."

"You don't think of home at all, Sam?" I wanted to know because I thought on it an awful lot. I was not from a wealthy family, but I did miss the small comforts home offered. Just the memory of a bath before the fire, a privy house, the hot food from the grate, and a bed of down feathers and quilts to keep me cozy at night made me so very homesick.

"Thought on it enough to know I don't want the fight anywhere near there. I'm right glad it's a march that takes us away from home and not to it."

When we reached Hallstown, Maryland, and after some discrepancies about exactly where we were supposed to be on account of Colonel Franchot's apparent lack of understanding concerning chain of command, we hooked up with the 2nd Brigade commanded by Colonel Joseph Jackson Bartlett. We were fighting with the 5th Maine, the 16th New York, the 27th New York, and the 96th Pennsylvania regiments. I was relieved to have come to the end of our long journey. I looked forward to some rest, and sleeping in a tent again.

It was with a great deal of joy that we were finally issued shelter tents, coats, and blankets again. It seemed slow to come, after living under such terrible conditions for several weeks, but what a pleasure it was when we were again beneath a warm blanket on a cold night.

The other regiments of the 2nd Brigade were all seasoned soldiers who had seen many battles. Some of them greeted us warmly, mainly the men from the 5th Maine, whom we felt a great kinship toward. But there were those who resented us right off, mostly the 96th, without even being given a chance to prove ourselves. They believe us to be the weak link, afraid that we would be the cause of their demise because we hadn't had any experience with fighting yet.

One evening Sam nearly got in a fight with one of them. As he was passing by to bring some water back in a pot for dinner, this other fellow intentionally bumped into him. Sam was plenty put out by it, I could see, as the water from his bucket spilled all over his coat. He briskly brushed the water away with his hands, visibly working to hold his anger in check.

"Excuse me," he said, managing a hard smile. Then he tried to go on his way.

The other fellow barked after him, "Let it not happen again you fresh fish, paid hireling, trash."

Sam could not take the insult. He stopped in his tracks with outrage on his face. He slowly turned on the fellow and called him out, "What did you say?"

I suppose the fellow was not expecting Sam to stand up for himself, because once he was face to face with Sam and others had taken notice, he didn't seem near as arrogant. It grew quiet and everyone waited to see what would happen next. A few were anxious to possibly see a fight.

"Well, you heard it," he replied, this time not so cocky.

"Say it again then, to my face and not my back," Sam insisted. "Say it and I'll bust you up." His words were cool and far too calm.

"A green lad such as yourself ought not to challenge someone who's seen the fight a time or two," the fellow growled.

"And a more wizened and experienced man such as yourself ought to have learned some manners by now," Sam retorted.

"You'll learn your place soon enough," the fellow countered.

I had witnessed the whole scene from a distance, and had finally worked up the courage to come to Sam's side, so he wouldn't be standing alone. I was frightened, but I wasn't about to leave him without a friend to back him up. Everyone else seemed content to watch, which made me a little angry.

"His place is fighting alongside his comrades in arms," I added. I grew worried with how this all might end and looked for something to say that might smooth things over. "Aren't we all fighting for the same cause?"

The other fellow chortled with contempt. "A boy not even weaned from his mother's tit thinks to counsel me now," he grumbled, then turned away dismissively from us and walked off.

Sam stood where he was for a moment, then turned back toward the tent and began walking. I took up next to him.

"What's the matter with him?" I asked. Sam stopped abruptly, losing more water over the lip of his tin pot.

"I can take care of myself," he said. "I don't need you butting in and trying to do it for me." It was the first time he seemed even remotely cross with me. Although he didn't say it sternly, I felt sick. There was a pounding in my head simultaneously accompanied by the dropping of my stomach. My face fell in remorse.

"I know it, Sam. I only meant to be a comfort to you," I explained. I didn't think I could stand Sam being angry with me.

He must have seen the distress his words had caused. He nodded his head reassuringly and said, "Come on then and let's get some supper."

While he didn't intend to be malicious about the incident, it took me several days to get over feeling ashamed, to grow comfortable with him again. I tried to say as little as possible. I hung back from the crowded ring of men that pressed in around the fire. Eventually he made a marked point to include me and by the end of our conversing with all the others I felt as though he had let it go and we were back to being friends again.

Right off Colonel Bartlett tried to bring our unseasoned regiment up to snuff. I wasn't the only one who had never handled a gun. Some of the men from the other four regiments who had some experience with war and knew what would be coming to us were assigned to instruct us. But there wasn't enough time to teach us sufficiently. For it was just over a week later we saw our first conflict. September eighteenth opened our eyes to a great and awful day. It is said to be the bloodiest single day in American history.

Antietam.

Chapter Ten

Should I live to be a hundred, I will never be able to erase the days that followed. I recalled once, in my youth, coming upon a dead cat to the side of the road. Its eyes were opened and its mouth agape as it lay sprawled upon the ground, expired from some unknown reason. It frightened me so that I didn't have the stamina to pass it and left the road to walk nearly a mile out of my way in order to avoid it. But there was no avoiding the carnage I was forced to witness as I watched the battle unfold before me.

There was a certain amount of anticipation among us all on the eve of our first battle. Not knowing what it would be like, I thought perhaps it would be a lark, something to experience for bragging rights, because I heard the others really talking it up and making it sound so grand. "We'll send them back to their mammies with their tails between their legs! We'll whip 'em good!" I heard them say.

But once it was upon me, once I saw the horrors of it, well, I'm fairly certain that many besides myself wanted nothing more than to go back home. While it spread out like a bad dream before me, I tried to talk myself out of doing just that.

I recall the night before the battle, how having finished our meal, we sat around the campfire talking and visiting. That was when I noted some of the other men from the seasoned regiments had their sewing kits out. The kits had been issued to us along with our other provisions back at the fort. Shaped like an envelope, they were cloth bundles that unrolled to reveal pockets with a few buttons, a small pair of sewing scissors, some cards of floss, and a few needles and straight pins tucked within. The men had taken up a needle and thread and were concentrating with squinted eyes next to the fire on their handicraft.

"What are they doing?" I asked.

"Don't know," Sam said with a shrug.

"Hey, what are you all doing?" Big Frank yelled over to them.

One of the men from the group got up and came over to talk with us. "There's going to be a battle soon."

"We are aware," Big Frank acknowledged.

"Just making sure they know who we are. In case."

"How?" I inquired.

"Sewing our name into the lining of our jackets," he explained.

"What for?" I asked, still confused by his answer.

"Dead men don't talk," he replied with a satirical smile. Then it dawned on me. If he should be killed, his name would be imprinted in brightly colored thread into the lining of his jacket. I shivered at the thought of it. Dead men don't talk…

Colonel Franchot was set upon us being in the fight. He wanted to prove himself to be a great war hero, and he wanted it badly. I suppose it was his hope we might be thrust into the heart of the battle and come out fighting savages, sending the other side running, so everyone would sing his praises. He went about like a pouting child, fairly begging to be included. After watching him for some time, I began to conclude that Colonel Franchot was a somewhat pompous and vain man. But I attributed it to his being a political man. Fortunately there were those more wise and knowing than he was that took charge. In the end we were held in reserve and not part of the actual fight on account of our lack of training and inexperience. I heard one of Franchot's superiors lecture him on how sending us in would be like sending a calf to slaughter. So, all that day we stood at the ready. And the waiting was sore.

At one point we came under cannon fire as we waited there at Crampton's Gap. Some of the men who had been writing letters or playing at cards ditched their endeavors and ran for cover. Each time a ball whistled by I grew jumpy and irritated. I don't know if we were in any real danger, but it felt like torture being exposed to the cannon that way.

I, at least, was able to make it through without branding myself a complete fool. Not so for poor Orson Penrod. The noise rattled him beyond his ability to cope. The unfortunate fellow wet his pants when a ball came too close for comfort. His face was filled with humiliation and despair. I thought for a moment he might cry, which would have only made it worse. I was filled with compassion for him, wishing there was something I could do to alleviate his suffering. No one mentioned it, because we were all just as frightened, and felt some empathy for him. All but Vern Stapleton, who tormented Orson at every turn and brought it up every chance he could. Vern began calling him "little baby Orson" and asked him if he needed his soaker changed any time a round came close.

I hate myself for not having stuck up for him. But I was afraid of Vern too. I didn't want him to turn on me and do the same as he did to Orson, so I kept my mouth shut. I did nothing. I knew deep down that I was just as guilty as Vern for not doing anything to stop it. What a coward I was. We all were. We did our best to ignore it, but we shouldn't have let Vern treat Orson that way.

From our vantage point we could see some of the battle below. It was strange to watch friend and enemy clash together in a conflict that somewhat resembles insects, as a line of them crawl over one another. I couldn't believe I was there watching it all. My insides were in a constant turmoil waiting to find out who the victor would be.

As we hung back, drawn up in the rear and waiting for further command, the activity below us was all movement and frenzy. We saw Union troops marching in and we saw wounded and dying coming back, the litter bearers having no time to rest as they carried men from the battlefield. Thanks to the effort of our men the Gap was held and the Rebels retreated. It was then many of us got our first peek at a Confederate soldier. A whole slew of them were captured and taken prisoner. We being in the reserve were there when they were brought back, to be held there until further accommodations could be made.

Not knowing any better, Sam and I and several others from the 121st came up to watch. Those Confederates looked to be in bad shape, skinny and frail. Some didn't have on proper clothing, some were without boots, their heads bare. As much as you would have liked to hate them, it was a hard thing to achieve when you saw the state they were in. One of our men was more curious than the rest.

He came close and offered a drink from his canteen. The Rebel accepted it, and seemed grateful.

"It's been a sore fight, and I surely could've used a drink," he said in thanks to the man.

"You fought well," another consoled him, for the Rebel looked poor and downright fragile, and I suppose he thought to cheer him. As much as we had hated him in an abstract way, it was difficult when we saw an actual man, pathetic and broken in the flesh. Looking at this fellow I didn't know how anyone could be angry with him.

"And yet I am a prisoner," he lamented.

Two boys by the names of Clinton and Adelbert grew bolder still. "What made you want to invade Maryland? You had to know you were facing more Union than you could beat."

The Rebel closed his eyes and rested his head in his hands. I'm not sure what he was thinking at that moment. Was he looking for the words to appease us or was he attempting to get his emotions in check? Strange that he was only a man and not the monster we thought he would be.

Finally he said, matter-of-factly, "We were made to fight."

Another one of the prisoners who sat near and was listening, agreed. "We were starved out. It was either fight or die."

"And who knows what we fight for anymore," the other whispered, as if he were haunted by this reality.

"They didn't seem all bad," I observed when I was talking with Sam after we had left them.

"Men, just like you and me," he said.

"It seems a shame," I replied.

"Yes, a shame."

"What will become of them?"

"They'll be sent on to Baltimore as prisoners," he informed me. "It is a sad thing, Frank. But you shouldn't think on it. You can't think of how they are just men and how much like us they seemed. That will be your death."

"Yes," I said. "Yes, I mustn't think on it."

The battle raged on throughout the day and into the night, before it finally came to a messy conclusion. We were spared the fight but not the horrors of it. And after such a terrible loss for both sides McClellan let Lee go. Just let him go. Some thought it folly. Some said if McClellan had pursued him instead of losing his courage the war would be over and we could've gone home. As it turned out we were to chase him deep beyond into Secesh territory.

We did not fight, but in some ways I felt our responsibilities were far worse. Our duty, in the aftermath of the battle, was to collect and bury the Rebel dead. We had watched the battle of Crampton's Gap from a distance, but the view of Antietam's field was more horrific even still. Stretched out before us on a carpet of grass lay more men and horses than could be counted, all killed in one battle. The bodies lay heaped for miles around.

What was once a spacious cornfield, planted with care in the spring, was cut down by bullets, and bodies were scattered across it. The gently rolling hills strewn with shade trees and swathed in tall grass, once a picturesque scene, was now the sight of such slaughter I could scarce trust it to be real, although I was seeing it with my very own eyes. A fence ran along the length of Hagerstown Road and it seemed there were a great number of the bodies piled there. A small white church called Dunker's Church, of saltbox construction, was pristine and seemed untouched but for the blue and gray soldiers lying before it, until you drew near and saw the damage done by the fighting. The picture of the aftermath of the battle was eerie beyond anything I have seen or shall ever see again.

"God himself upon his throne must shudder at the sight of it," I said, looking over the expansive field.

"There is nothing of God here today," Sam said softly.

I knew he was right. War is never in God's infinite plan. The things men do to other men in the name of God must surely make him sorrowful indeed. That day was a day that saw many a man's soul home to the heavens where they came from, their lives cut short by unholy violence. I, like many others, was somber as the desolation spread before me.

We first dug out the trenches, laboring with shovels and picks until our pit was big enough to lay the men side by side and three or four deep. My upper arms burned from it and my hand was so overworked, I couldn't hardly grip the shovel. Finally my arms began to shake when I tried to transfer the dirt from the ditch.

Then we worked on retrieving the bodies, placing them in rows, and stacking them on top of one another. The digging was the easy part for me, as back breaking and laborious as it was. Having to put my hands upon a dead stinking body, to lift it, stiff and bloodied, to its resting place, was the truly awful part. They called the place where we had dug the trenches *Bloody Lane.*

I emptied my stomach when Sam and I came upon our first body. He was probably about our age, shot through with a ball right in the center of his throat, with a look of fear frozen upon his face. Some looked peaceful, as if they were sleeping. He did not. The apparent panic he had experienced in his last moments in this life was not only sad but made you feel the same dread just to look upon him. And it wasn't merely the sight of him, but the smell of him too that had sickened me, made me retch, my whole body heaving uncontrollably. There is nothing like vomiting in front of the man you love to make you feel cruel chagrin at its worst.

"You all right?" Sam asked. I nodded my head and went to help pick the body up once more, but had to turn away and be sick again. A third time I attempted it and that time I might have vomited up my guts, it was such a violent heaving. Ashamed for my weakness, I was more than a little upset I had done something so embarrassing in front of Sam. But he didn't seem to be repulsed by me, but rather had a great deal of sympathy. He wore a grimace, showing me he thought the task was disagreeable to him as well, but he succeeded in keeping himself together.

"I think I can manage it now," I told him. I took the feet and Sam took the shoulders and we carried the body to the trench we had dug and dumped him in.

The aberrant way the bodies were positioned, the looks of agony upon their faces, unnatural color upon their skin, no soul left in their empty eyes — it was all terrible. Their blood had flowed by the gallons into the soil and awful, rotten smells permeated the stale air, a smell that seemed to infuse itself into my skin and hair and clothing. That smell would come back to me at the oddest of times, like rotten meat and privy and foul sulfur all mixed in one. Oh what a vile smell!

Although my stomach was empty I still continued with dry heaving for some of the bodies in the worst condition. I tried to breathe through my mouth, even tucking the lower half of my face into my shirt with no results. The thing that kept me going was to think of it as a task, to say *one more is in the hole, and now I must go for another, and soon it will be over.*

We came upon a fellow who, by all accounts, looked as if he were yet in the heat of the battle. He was kneeling on one knee and had been killed as he was in the act of pulling himself up to look over the fence he was hiding behind. His head was still upright, his clothed body with canteen, knapsack, and all seemed untouched, just like he had been frozen there, as if time were standing still for him like old Rip Van Winkle in his slumber. An eerie and unsettled feeling swept over me, for it was against the laws of nature to see him crouched there. It gave you the feeling that you were off your head, a trick of the brain.

One of the surgeons came running up to us and told us to get back, to not touch him, a command I was glad to obey, for I was loath to touch him anyhow. The surgeon then pulled a small sketchbook and pencil from his pocket and began to write. It seemed as if it was a significant find to him. We left him there and moved on.

I admired Sam's ability to distance himself from all of this. There was a job to be done and he solemnly did it. The only time I saw him affected by it was when he found a man who was pierced through with many bullets in his legs and arms and torso. His suffering must have been terrible for he had in one clenched fist tufts of grass he had ripped from the ground by the roots, and in the other a tin type bent and mangled. As he waited for death to come, he had held tight to the picture of a woman, looking at her as his last breath left him.

Who was she? A sweetheart waiting back home for her man to return? Someone he loved and cherished. She was a very pretty young woman, with dark hair and dark eyes, her head tilted ever so slightly, her gaze staring wide and innocent right back at him. It was the last thing he was to see at Antietam.

Sam's stoic face broke as he looked at the picture thoughtfully and his voice was small when he said, "What must it have been like for him?" Then Sam slipped the daguerreotype into the man's breast pocket before we carried him away too.

I came to count my mother lucky that Caleb was allowed to die in her arms and not on some forsaken field. He was not left to weep in agony with the flies crawling over him as the blood let out of him. It was a merciful blessing. Mother didn't know how good she had it when the fever took him quiet in his own bed. I saw countless boys that day, Caleb's age even, whose mothers suffered a much worse fate. How sorry I was when I thought of their families back home.

One of the soldiers also assigned to burial duties came and told us he thought he may have found a girl among the dead in the cornfield. She was dressed like a man, in a Confederate uniform. He told his superior, who investigated the matter, and sure enough she had died as a soldier upon the field of battle. This news spread like wildfire and all of the men wanted to go and investigate, to see for themselves. I was afraid to go, but I didn't want to appear suspicious, so I followed a group of men from the 121st over to where she was.

Like me, she had cut her hair short too. It was a rich chestnut color, and she had a beautiful and symmetrical face, which had not been changed in death. I wondered how the men she had fought with had not recognized her right off. After all there wasn't much that could be considered masculine about her. What was her story? What was her name? I didn't know what place she called home, or what her motivation for dressing as a man and marching with the army was, but I felt a kinship to her I cannot describe. I fought hard to keep from crying.

"Should we put her in the pits with the other men?" someone from the group that crowded around her asked.

"No. She shall have her own resting place," a captain said.

I saw a few of the men with tears in their eyes, thinking on their wives or sweethearts back home, I suppose. One man willingly gave up his blanket, saying he could find himself another. They wrapped her in the blanket and dug a small hole, only for her. Someone had worked at marking a cracker box with the words *Unknown Woman CSA.*

"This is no place for a woman," Sam said. My stomach dipped, giving me a horrible feeling. I wondered what he would say if he knew the truth about me. We watched as she was laid to rest and then we went on about our business.

The whole day was spent in this way and as another night fell, still the bodies were heaped up. We were made to camp out on the field, sleeping among the dead. My conscience pricks me some when I think on how well I slept. I had carried so many bodies, and dug so many holes, that I felt nothing but tired and I slept as soon as my eyes were closed, even though my bedfellows were corpses. I would've preferred my shelter tent, but it was not a possibility, and yet I slumbered quite soundly still. The next night we did the same.

When we finished our duty of burying the dead we were allowed back to camp. I was glad to be away from those fields, where so many lay beneath the ground never to return to family and home. As we sat around the fire that evening, some of the men began to show off the new treasures they had carried away from the dead bodies.

"Got myself some fine boots," said Ruben as he pulled up the leg of his pants so we could see them for ourselves.

"And here is a pair of spectacles," said Vern. "Don't know if I'll ever need 'em, but if I should I have 'em."

I heard similar bragging throughout the camp, from those who had taken personal possessions from the dead. It made me feel an anger I couldn't really explain. What should I care that these men were robbed of property? They wouldn't need it anymore anyway, not where they were going. Still, it sickened me.

"You should be ashamed," I blurted without thinking. "Stealing from the dead." The reaction was nearly instant. The men who had taken from the bodies of the dead were angry and defensive, and those who had not were uncomfortable and didn't want to acknowledge any wrong doing.

"Now, Frank…" Sam began. He was either trying to comfort me, or protect me. I'm not sure which.

One of the others laughed a little. "They can't take it with 'em," he said. "May as well find a use for it."

"Don't you feel at all sorry for it?" I persisted.

"Bully for our side, and down with the rebellion!" Vern cheered.

When I saw how unremorseful they were even after my speech I was all the more upset. I sulked away to my tent and stayed there the remainder of the evening. When Sam came to bed he didn't say anything, just slipped in under his blanket ever so quietly. He must have thought I was asleep and didn't want to disturb me. It was silent for a time but I couldn't hold my tongue any longer.

"Sam?" I whispered.

"I thought you had gone to sleep."

"I can still smell it on me," I groaned.

"Smell what on you?"

"That smell. Can't you smell it?"

"Ah, Frank…"

"I tried washing it off, I did. But I can still smell it."

"It's in your head." His tone was sympathetic, but he was firm in his conclusion.

"Sam, I don't know that I can do this," I told him.

"Do what?" he asked.

"I don't know that I can kill a man." The words hung in the air and I could tell Sam was trying to figure out what he should say to me. "I don't know if I can look at a man in the heat of battle and have the courage to kill him."

"You'll do what you have to when you must, Frank," he assured me. "Everyone has the fight when they are faced with death. You'll do what you have to, to hold on to life."

"What about goodness and decency? Has it all gone then? Has it all gone away to leave us nothing but barbarians?"

"There are some whose hearts are innately dark and have no natural inclination to do good, Frank. Those are the exceptions. Because most of them are ordinary men just like you and me, trying to do the best they can in a very difficult situation. Even those men who stole from the corpses, they might be different under better circumstances."

"It was wrong, Sam. Even under these circumstances, what they did was wrong."

"I don't disagree with you, Frank. On the whole men make sorry company. They only seem to grow worse when they're confined to close quarters with one another. They feed on one another's depravities and are capable of doing unspeakable crimes. The thing is, you can't be responsible for their actions. You can only be responsible for your own."

"But I'm so small. I'm nothing…nobody. I always have been," I whined. "What do I matter?"

"You matter," Sam insisted. "There isn't a soul who wasn't put here on this earth for a purpose, for a reason. You find that reason and you'll make your mark."

I didn't know what to say. What he said was true, but it didn't seem to change my mood. I still felt helpless and overwhelmed by everything I had experienced over the past few days. I wanted to feel better, but I didn't. I couldn't. Each time I closed my eyes I was met with gruesome scenes of the battlefield, and the thought of the men robbing the bodies of the dead. I could smell that smell and I wanted to scream, to cry out, and to beg God to erase the memory of it all.

"I am tired, Frank. Now go to sleep," he said. "And don't think about it anymore. Because if you let it, it will drive you mad."

If only I could take his advice, forget the faces of the dead. If only I could put it from my head and think on it no more. But I was not like him. His admonition was easier said than done. I thought too about how I would at some point be required to kill someone. To put more of them in the grave. Could I do it? Was I capable? I was to learn just how capable when the time came, and it was coming. It was coming…

Chapter Eleven

After that awful battle things radically changed. All of us got a view of the ugly nature of war, and we knew tomorrow it could very well be us in those pits being covered with dirt. I'm not sure if that was the deciding factor for Colonel Franchot, but he quit us, just up and resigned. I looked upon it with mixed emotions. Perhaps he saw how unprepared and ill-informed we really were, and he decided to head back to Washington before he became too involved and couldn't extricate himself. I doubt he was ever made of the right stuff to survive a war, much less lead.

We were thereafter called "Upton's Regulars" after Colonel Emory Upton. Following his dramatic and embarrassing display before the battle of Antietam, Colonel Franchot relinquished his command to Colonel Upton so he might serve as a congressman once again. No one was particularly sorry to see him go. On the other hand, the men had the utmost respect for Colonel Upton, just out of West Point, and I could see why. He was exceptionally organized and made it his aim to know his men well so he might utilize their best skills to the army's advantage.

A native New Yorker, he was much younger than I might have expected, with close set eyes that appeared shrewd and alert, and high cheekbones, which gave him a great deal of character. He was lean and fit in his uniform, an impressive figure. He wore a mustache and neatly trimmed hair on his chin. He wasn't a bad looking man at all. I thought him rather attractive from a woman's point of view.

"Do your best for me and I will do my best for you," he told us all when we met him for the first time before drills one morning. He said it with such conviction that I believed him, and he never gave me any reason to believe otherwise.

Each morning we were called by the sound of the bugle to drill in a spacious field. You should have seen how inspiring it was, all the men in their uniforms, guns propped up tall against their shoulders, all at the same impressive angle, with bayonets catching the sun. Many of us knew nothing of war and had no training in weapons or military strategies. There was a good majority of the men who were as ignorant as me in these matters.

Sam was quite handy with his pistol, but proved to be less so with his rifle. He had practiced with his pistol many a time and hunted at home with his old Hawken rifle, but the Enfield rifle was new to him, and it took some getting used to. As for me, I'd never handled either a pistol or a rifle. Father had a rifle, but I never had a use for it. He and Caleb did the hunting. I hardly knew how to even hold the thing.

"Becoming well acquainted with your rifle will serve you well, gentlemen," we were lectured. "Being good at loading and reloading is fine. But being exceptional is what will give you the advantage over the enemy, and preserve your life."

To begin with, I had little talent for loading and firing my rifle. I hesitated in firing it, shutting my eyes tight as I squeezed the trigger and then flinching at the terrible noise and recoil it produced. The first time I attempted aiming at a target to shoot I was nearly turned off from it for good. It did not come easily to me. Not a bit.

I loaded the paper cartridge and ball into the receiver and moved the breech block back up into place. I held the rifle, as demonstrated, peering down the barrel to take aim. When I pulled the trigger the force of the kick threw me off of my feet onto the ground, as the smoothly polished butt hammered my shoulder with a fierceness that left me completely unprepared. I was ashamed when Sam had to help me up. I tried to act as if I weren't hurt, but I knew my act was not fooling him.

"You all right, Frank?" he asked.

"I suppose I been better," I admitted, rotating my arm to make sure it still worked. My shoulder had already begun to stiffen up and I winced in pain. I couldn't hold my arm right, and once I realized how bad it hurt, I tried desperately not to have to move it at all. I just sort of let it hang there next to my side because every time I shifted, it throbbed terrible.

"Hold the butt tight to your shoulder so it's got nowhere to go. Hold it tight and firm," he said. He stepped up behind me and put the rifle to my shoulder, showing me how I should hold it proper. For a brief moment I forgot about the ache of my shoulder, and enjoyed his tutoring. How heavenly it was to be his sole preoccupation. "See?" he said.

"Must I fire it again?" I asked. "I don't know if my arm can take it."

"It's best to crawl right back into the saddle," he said. "So you don't lose your nerve."

I nodded my head grimly, gritting my teeth as I pulled the trigger. I nearly hollered when the gun bumped my shoulder again. It pained me something fierce. Sam seemed happy when I hit the target, even though it was only to nick the corner of the large plank of wood. To be honest I think it had nothing to do with my aim. It was simply sheer dumb luck.

"That's it, Frank!" he encouraged. "Once you shoot a few more times you'll get a feel for it and be able to correct your aim. You'll see."

"If this is the best I can do," I said wryly, "then I may as well kiss my rear end good-bye."

Sam laughed at my words. "No one is good to begin with, Frank. It takes a great deal of practice and a great deal more patience."

"Patience is something I've always lacked," I admitted.

"Well, for now, when you try to hit a target, be slow and deliberate. Once you've got your aim down, you can practice for speed."

Marcus Carvey could shoot like nothing I'd ever seen. As easy and fluid as if he were doing something as simple as tying a shoe, he would load, aim, reload—hitting the target every time. Colonel Upton used him as an example, calling him before all the men so he might show us what a proper shot should look like.

"Eleven separate motions, gentlemen," Upton called out over us as Marcus Carvey loaded his Enfield. "It takes merely one minute to fire three shots. That includes loading and reloading." Marcus was so fast, I could scarcely count eleven separate motions.

"Your bayonets will do little good in combat. Yes, they look fierce, but it will be the rifle that will serve you best. Take care of them, keep them in working order, ready at all times." It frightened me to hear those words from the colonel. My resolve was to become much better at it and quickly; I needed to become as fast as Marcus Carvey if I stood a chance of surviving. As much as I wanted to be near Sam, I didn't want it at the cost of my life, or perhaps his, because of any mistake I made.

That night Sam came to me seeming very pleased with himself. "Let me have a look at your shoulder," he said.

I was immediately on the defense. "No need. It feels just fine," I lied.

"Come on now, let me see it," he insisted.

I hesitated, feeling put on the spot. If I should decline, he might become suspicious, so I grudgingly gave in and unbuttoned just the first few buttons of my shirt, pulling it off of my bare shoulder so that he might see it. I must admit that it looked very bad. The skin was a deep purple and yellowed around the edges, covering a good six inches in diameter. He gave a little whistle, like he was impressed. I grew embarrassed under his gaze. Sam pulled a small tin of salve from his pocket and tossed it to me.

"Got this from a peddler who deals in herbs," he said. "Mountain Daisy. Put this on that shoulder of yours, and you'll be up to shooting again in no time."

I pulled my shirt back to cover my shoulder, unscrewed the lid and sniffed at it. It didn't smell horrible anyway. I gingerly took some from the tin and stuck my hand in my shirt to apply it.

"Thank you," I said.

"Don't just dab at it, really get a generous lot there and rub it in good," he instructed, taking the tin from my hands as if he might help me do just that. I wasn't about to let him. I couldn't imagine what might happen if he should go to put the salve on my shoulder and discover something more. If it was at all possible, I grew even more nervous.

I must have looked like a complete fool, daintily patting at it. I saw his expression and I thought to myself: *what would a man do?*

"I can do it myself!" I said defensively. Grabbing the tin back from his hands, I dug into the salve with my fingers, and slopped it on in the haphazard way I thought he might do it himself.

"You'll be a new man, now," he assured me.

"What do I owe you for it?"

"Why, nothing," he told me.

"Now I aim to compensate you for it," I insisted. "Just as soon as I get my first pay."

"Really I don't want you to," he said. His tone carried a finality to it. The subject was closed for discussion. I had no choice but to relent.

"Well, I'm grateful." I didn't know what else to say. The fact that he had gone to so much trouble touched me. If he had gotten it from our sutler he had paid a pretty penny for it. The sutler was a peddler who followed after the army with goods to sell. If anyone was profiting from the war it was the sutlers. Our sutler had a wagon full of wares the soldiers could purchase from him, but he sold them at such outrageous prices many of us did without rather than pay the unreasonably high costs he was asking. Oh, the men hated our sutler and all who were like him.

I had to remind myself he was looking out for "little brother" and it was not a sentiment such as flowers or a ribbon for my hair. He was giving a helping hand to Frank and not Serena. This was a turning point for me. I did my best not to look like a pansy fool again. After all, I had come to help Sam out, to be close to him and do what I could to be a cause for good. I didn't want to be a nuisance. I wanted to be a good soldier that could take care of myself. My motto became *What would a man do?* In my head, as I went about my daily tasks, the question would come flitting through my brain: *What would a man say? How would a man act? What would a man do…*

Chapter Twelve

Days were filled with marching, setting up camp, drills and eating, sleeping, waking to pack up so we might march again. This was our routine. Drilling took up a morning block. We parted for a midday meal and then returned for more drilling at two thirty in the afternoon. At five we were summoned to the field again for formal dress parade. Besides that, in my determination to master my firearm, I practiced on my own on the range for another hour or so when I could. It took some time, but eventually I became good at it. It grew to be second nature. It got to the point I didn't even have to really think about it, my hands had grown so used to it they did it automatically.

Finally, I was good at something, really good. And yet it wasn't anything a woman should be good at, I thought with annoyance. There were no bragging rights attached to it. It wasn't something I would be able to discuss with the ladies back home. So the fact I could shoot a target dead center with modest speed was something I quietly relished, and quietly berated myself over, all in the same moment.

Colonel Upton greatly improved conditions in camp. Many of the 121st had fallen to illness and disease. He took it upon himself to clean things up and looked for ways to ensure good health among the men. One thing which particularly pleased me was that he ordered all men to take care of their needs outside the parameters of camp and threatened punishment to anyone who exposed or revealed himself anywhere near our camp grounds. This not only diverted suspicion from me, because now I could go happily to the woods without comment, but it spared me the discomfort of seeing some man do his business right in front of me.

He also set aside Saturdays for washing uniforms and bathing. This was *not* to my advantage. It was a difficult thing to find the privacy to wash myself. I sometimes waited until it was very late in the night to sneak away and bathe. I kept two uniforms with me at all times so while I wore the one, I could mend and care for the other. Most of the men didn't bother with two uniforms. It was more for them to carry, and the less you carried the better. But I felt it was a small price to pay.

It was some surprise to discover what men were really like without the presence of a woman. These were the same gentlemen who would speak with sugared words and would sooner die than curse or rough talk in front of a lady. These were the same gentlemen who exhibited their best manners and would never think to behave disgracefully before a girl. But here among their comrades, among their fellow men, they displayed all manner of vulgar behaviors. They didn't know I was a girl and so they behaved as they would when in the company of other men.

They let loose their flatulence with no ceremony at all about it. They discussed privy habits, and scratched in unbecoming places. One night, sitting around the fire, a fellow made an awful noise in his throat, and then he coughed up a ball of phlegm and spit it right next to my boot. I was horrified but had to act as if it didn't bother me in the least. They discussed women, and some of the talk was not proper or suitable in my estimation. I heard it but refrained from joining in. We were all in close proximity to one another, and there was no way of avoiding being exposed to that sort of crassness.

I thought it ironic how many of them pulled shenanigans that would have left them red-faced and ashamed if they had known I was a woman. I was particularly upset by one of Vern Stapleton's pranks. One evening as we sat around the fire, Vern undertook telling a story—an awful story that left me feeling terribly upset with my insides all in a turmoil.

"Do you remember that girl Sally Steadman?" he asked Rueben. Rueben appeared to be thinking it over long and hard.

"Was she brown haired?"

"Oh, no. She had gold hair, long and curly."

"Maybe," Rueben replied. It seemed as though he didn't want to admit he couldn't remember her.

"Well, you ought to remember her. She was the prettiest girl in Cooperstown. Prettiest girl, I tell you. And she weren't no fast trick neither. A real lady."

"Was she related to Karl Lindman?"

"Why, no. Karl Lindman? No. You really don't remember her?" Rueben didn't answer but from the clueless look he bore it was obvious he didn't. "If you'd known her you wouldn't have forgot it. And you surely wouldn't have forgotten how she went."

"What do you mean?"

"She was sweet on Billy Rand."

"I know of Billy Rand," Rueben interrupted with an eager quality to his voice, as though he were excited to finally relate to Vern's story.

"Well, she and Billy was probably going to get married. He was fixing on asking her. But I tell you any man would have been lucky to have her. They was all of them lined up to have a crack at courting her. Anyway, she was sweet on Billy and had no eyes for no other. One day Billy took her out alone. He took her out for a picnic out by the lake. Had a real nice spread, fried chicken and corn pone, and pie. She really outdone herself trying to impress him. Now Billy thought he would ask her there for her hand, he brung along the ring and everything. Real romantic, I mean a real proper scene."

"What happened?" Rueben asked.

"As they were sitting there enjoying the lake, eating on that food and laughing and carrying on, a timber rattler come upon them. Don't know if they disturbed his nest or what. Big old granddaddy of a snake," he said holding up his hands to show them how big the snake was. "There she sat, knowing nothing about what was to happen, and that snake come up and got hold of her."

"It bit her?" Rueben asked incredulously.

"It sure enough did. And it was the awfulest thing you ever saw. She didn't die right off. No, sir. She suffered terrible while the poison ate through her. Her face was all swelled up, her skin an unnatural color. Unrecognizable by the time Billy got her home. He loaded her up on the cart and tore out of there, trying to get her back to town, back to the doctor, but there was no help for her. She screamed and carried on, she was in so much pain."

"You don't say."

"Terrible shame. The poison had done its work so they had to bury her the next day, her body was stinking and rotting that bad. Boy let me tell you it was ugly."

By the time Vern had finished with his story, he had everyone's attention, including mine. I shivered a little, not only sad for Sally, but also a little sickened by the description of her horrible death. It was dark when I went back to the tent to turn in for the night. I fumbled with my boots, setting them together within arm's reach.

I slid my feet down into my bedroll, pulling the blanket up to my chin. As I worked to make myself comfortable, I felt it. Something thin and flexible and cylinder shaped rolled beneath my feet. I panicked, throwing the blankets away from me as I jumped up, yelling. In my panic I made for the door, but couldn't see which way I was going in the darkness and began running blindly in circles, tearing the tent down around me as I went.

"It's a snake!" I screamed, frantically trying to find my way out of the downed tent, my hands and arms flailing madly. "It's a snake!"

Chapter Thirteen

When I finally managed to free myself from the tangled mess a large group of men had gathered to see what all of the fuss was about. It was enough to silence me, although I was still very much shaken. Sam was there with them, appearing to not know what to make of it all, wide eyed and worried.

"What's got you all worked up, Frank?" he asked me.

"There was a snake in my bedroll," I cried. "Lucky I'm still alive!"

Sam moved past me, working to pick the tent up from the ground. He came across my bedroll, shaking it and probing it carefully until he held up a piece of rope for my inspection. "It's only a piece of rope," he told me.

I looked at all of the faces of the men crowded around, feeling the shame running through me like hot liquid. It was only a brief second of silence before Vern Stapleton burst out laughing and everyone else joined in. He had certainly made a show of me.

"A snake!" he said mockingly.

I caught Sam's expression, his best attempt at suppressing a smile, and the humiliation was complete. Disappointment in him swept over me. I was shocked he would find such cruelty amusing. I thought better of him. But how could he resist finding it humorous? Perhaps I should have enjoyed it too, if I weren't the target.

I stood there uncertain for a moment, and then I walked over to the tent working to put it right, trying to ignore my audience. Once it was erect again, I took refuge in it, doing my best to ignore the continued taunting, until finally their laughter drifted away into the night. I wanted to cry but I didn't. I just shut my eyes tightly and tried to block it out.

When Sam came to bed I had my back to him, and I pretended I was asleep. He never mentioned it again, but I sure got a lot of snickers and laughs from the others about it. I did my best to try to pay no attention to them, but inside I was secretly raging against Vern and Rueben. They were nothing more than cruel tormenters. I hated being at their mercy. I went out of my way to avoid them when possible, but I learned bullies often seek you out when they know you are intimidated by them.

I grew to hate myself for being afraid of them. But I also found myself daydreaming about ways to get even. Only I knew I was too spineless to really do anything about it, and because they knew they had gotten the best of me, they continued to mock and tease me, looking for any excuse to make me the butt of a joke. I always seemed to think of a million things I should have said once I was away from them and stewing over the newest injustice. I never did anything about it. After all, my mother taught me to be a nice girl.

I had better things to think about. There were other thing besides Vern and Rueben that preyed upon my mind in my moments of solitude. The uppers kept us plenty busy, marching, practicing battle formations and such for many hours a day, which was probably a good thing. Because when I was alone with my thoughts I missed my father and worried over his welfare. It may sound terrible, but although I often thought of him, I wrote to him somewhat infrequently. You see, while I was carrying on a lie there in camp, I was also carrying on a lie in my letters to Father. In order to keep Father from exposing me, I told him from the beginning it was nearly impossible to get correspondence while on the march. I also told him it would be best if he didn't attempt writing me, and he should be content with me writing him. It was a hard thing to see others receiving mail from home, and I not get a single scrap. But I felt it was all for the best.

I told Father in my letters that I was a nurse. I told him I was daily called upon to care for the needs of sick and injured men. I told him I was living well and comfortably. I told him these things so he would not worry over me. The only truth to my letters was that I told him I would send money if they would only pay me. How long must a person go on in service without pay? Any other profession I do believe many of the men would have up and quit on account of it. But we didn't even have that option. If you left, you would be hung for desertion. Some were desperate for monies to send to their families back home, knowing they were probably going hungry and deprived on account of having no man and no money to buy what was needed.

By and by things fell into a strangely comfortable routine and we greenlings became soldiers. Even I, the slowest of them all, grew decent at it. And it was a good thing, for who should decide to visit our camp but President Lincoln and General McClellan! The colonel wanted us in our very best condition. We should have our uniforms cleaned and every piece of brass must shine. I went and got my hair trimmed by one of the only fellows who had a pair of scissors, and I did my best to look presentable.

Sam too endeavored to look his best, which in my estimation was not a hard thing to accomplish. The morning of the president's arrival he took extra care with his appearance. I watched him hunched over the small round mirror with his shirt unbuttoned, working quickly but concisely as he swiped the straight edge razor along his jaw line. I never tired of observing him. When he shaved in the morning, Sam did not show the beginnings of a beard again until the next day. It was dark, like the hair on his head. I wondered, flippantly, what he might look like with a full beard, although I preferred him clean shaven. He had such a nice face, why should he want to hide it?

Sam looked up at me with a grin. Mistaking my interest in his ritual for curiosity he said, "Want me to teach you how?"

"No need," I told him. "Don't expect I'll have to for another year or two." I rubbed my fingers over my chin. "Smooth as a baby's bottom." And then I laughed a little.

"Oh, I don't know," Sam said. "I think I've detected a few whiskers there."

I tried hard not to frown. Did he really or was he just saying it to make me, "Frank," feel better about not being able to grow a beard? I certainly hoped I wasn't growing whiskers. I once saw an older woman in town who had quite a mustache, so I supposed it was possible. Although I'd rather have died than look like that woman did.

"Never you fret over it. You've got a pretty boy face, like a cupid. Not ugly that's for certain. The girls like that, when a man has soft features."

"How do you know what the girls like?" I asked.

He went back to shaving, the edge of the razor making the slightest sound as it glided over his skin. "Well, now, I don't rightly know, Frank. The female mind still remains a mystery to me. But now that's what my sister says."

"Your sister says a girl likes a fellow with soft features?"

"Yes." He finished shaving, wiped the razor clean before folding it shut and then taking a small towel to wipe his face.

"If girls like soft features on a man, what do the boys like, would you say?" I asked. I would have given anything to know what he liked in a girl.

Sam shrugged. "I guess it's different for each one."

"What about those girls that follow around after the army. You think any of them are pretty?" We had seen them many a time come and go with some of the men. I knew they were not nice girls, but my curiosity had gotten the better of me at times. Did Sam look at them? Did he like them at all?

He laughed. "Stay away from them fancy girls, Frank. They'll bring you nothing but trouble," he cautioned. He began buttoning his shirt. "Hold tight to that pay of yours and don't go near 'em."

"Some of them are pretty enough," I reasoned, taking his mirror and looking myself over in it. But really I was trying to get at the truth of it. Did *he* think they were pretty? Did *he* like their rouge and curled hair? Or were his tastes of a simpler nature?

"It's their job to be nice. Them girls have got no natural affections. There isn't a thing about 'em that's real. My advice to you is just don't mess with 'em," he cautioned. "Young boy like yourself, no experience with the world don't know no better. Tempting as they may be, it's like I said, they'll bring you trouble. You'd do best to find a nice little lady back home and settle down. These ain't the marrying kind."

"That what you plan on doing?" I continued to inspect myself, noting with some alarm how my face had changed as I peered into Sam's mirror. My round cheeks had thinned and my features seemed sharper, more angular. It hadn't escaped my attention how my body had changed as well. I was nothing but muscle now, and there seemed to be no meat on my bones anymore. I was all sinew, as opposed to the soft and fleshy figure I started out as. The physical rigors of training had vastly changed me.

Sam shrugged in answer to my question. "Can't think on it now," he said. "Wouldn't be fair to a girl to get tangled up with somebody who's likely to die. Maybe when it's all over, maybe then I could plan it out. If I knew I had a future…"

"You haven't got someone waiting at home for you?"

"Heavens, no! Nobody!"

"What about that girl with the yellow hair," I offered, thinking back to the first day we were together and the girl who had served him dinner with such generosity.

"Who?" he asked, still studious in his task of getting ready. He finished buttoning his shirt, tucking it into his britches.

"That girl from Albany."

"Oh, her. I scarcely remembered her. She was a pretty girl now you mention it," he admitted. "But I don't even recall her name."

"Nobody you were sweet on before you left?"

"I had a girl I fancied. Cora was her name. I liked her well enough. Though I didn't ask her to wait for me. She was pretty and all, but I never thought to marry her." I knew Cora. She was a pretty girl with ebony hair and pale gray eyes. She was soft spoken and had the manners of a genteel woman. It peeved me to imagine he might be quite happy with her someday.

"Why not?"

"Why not what?"

"Why didn't you want to marry her?"

He looked at me with his eyebrows drawn together. "You sure ask a lot of questions," he said in a huff, but he answered me anyway. "I don't know. She was a nice girl and all, but she didn't talk much. I guess there's more to it than just thinking a girl is pretty. It was just a lark is all." Sam got a sly look on his face. Maybe thinking he was playing with me. "You, Frank? You got a girl?"

"No! Not me!" From his reaction I might have been too emphatic in my denial. I changed my tone. "I'm too young for such things." This seemed to be the right thing to say because he was shaking his head as if he agreed.

"Suppose you're right," he said. He shrugged into his coat and buttoned it carefully, looking over it to see if there was any lint or anything else that might be amiss. He smoothed his hands over his chest, then set to shining his boots with a cloth. My, but he was a handsome figure. I thought some great artist ought to paint him, put him up on a wall to admire daily.

Shortly we were called upon to congregate on the drilling field. Everyone was eager to get a look at the president. We all wanted to look our best and impress him. The lines of men were straight and each man drawn up to his full height. The sun grew bothersome as time passed and we stood roasting in the heat. I began to lose my enthusiasm for the whole thing. The excitement and anticipation everyone felt earlier began to wear away after an hour or so.

It evolved into a long and tedious wait. Five hours of killing time before we were finally presented in our dress parade. We soon took to sitting about, wondering if perhaps we had been forgotten, until we were finally ordered to get ready again. We hurried to get back into form, falling into rows and columns of men, who stretched out in vast numbers across the field.

I only saw the president from a far off distance, but some of the others got a close up view of him. He wasn't good to look at in the face, but there was a certain draw to him that was hard to define. He was unusually tall compared to everyone else he stood next to. I wasn't sure if it was because he was also very thin, which perhaps made him seem taller than he actually was, or if he was indeed a giant.

He and General McClellan shook some hands, made some speeches, told us what a fine job we were doing. Despite his unimpressive attire, wearing all black and with his hat pushed back off of his forehead, he was an object of intense curiosity. He wasn't at all like McClellan, who made a dashing figure with a natural ease about him. McClellan was a truly handsome man with thick dark hair, parted to the side and combed neatly over. He had well shaped brows that drew attention to his dark and pensive eyes and a mouth shrouded by a neatly trimmed mustache.

He wore a double breasted uniform jacket, deep navy, with two rows of large gleaming brass buttons down each side of his chest. He walked with the pomp and esteem befitting his position, his face properly serious. I could see why his men loved him so and vowed to follow him to death and beyond. Although McClellan had him beat in form, Lincoln was no wallflower, that was certain. His presence lent a feel of enthusiasm which seemed infectious.

That evening there were those who were somewhat harsh in their criticisms against the president. It surprised me a little. My father had talked of him as if he might have the power to walk on water. This was my first exposure to dissension among the ranks, and it left me unsettled. If they didn't care for the president or his policies, then what compelled them to fight for his cause? Then it came to me that I wasn't exactly fighting for it either. I was fighting for something much less worthy and absolutely more selfish in nature.

"Looked no more important than a farmer tending to his crops! Why, he didn't even bother wearing a proper coat. How can he pose as an inspiring figure wearing that?" Reed Haney declared. I admit the president wasn't a fashionable gent, but it took me by surprise that a man notices such things. I thought this was something only a lady might have noted.

"And if he had come all dandied up? If he had worn a tie of silk and the finest coat, would you then have been content?" Sam asked.

"I think I would've thought more of him," Reed consented.

"You wouldn't have. You would've said he was too well dressed and how dare he with a war on and all. You would've found fault with him regardless of what he had worn," Sam replied.

"Well, I could find fault with him, attire be damned," Gaston Shriver said. "Yes, I'm not too happy with old Abe Lincoln just about now. I was perfectly content to fight for preserving the Union, but now he's brought the darkies into it. Them abolitionists have him in their pockets, I tell you!" I assumed he was speaking of the recently released, but not yet official, Emancipation Proclamation that the president had written, and he was angry Lincoln had brought the slavery issue to the forefront.

Big Frank looked as if he might wallop Gaston. "The war may have begun with the Seceshes leaving the Union, but there's something much bigger going on here," he defended. "You've got a people who are owned by another. It's an abomination that must have an end put to it. President Lincoln's used his position of power to give aid to the Negros because they couldn't give aid to themselves." For an uneducated man Big Frank spoke quite eloquently. "It was the decent thing to do."

"Bull, it was never about the slaves until now," Gaston argued. Big Frank shot him a glance that could have killed. I'm not sure if Gaston was afraid of Big Frank or if he thought it best not to say anything more on it, but he didn't say another word.

Marcus smoked his pipe philosophically and said amidst the plumes he emitted from his lips, "I ain't saying I agree or disagree with the president, but I will say he's squashed our chances of going home just like I'd crush a bug with the heel of my boot. Come hell or high water, we're in it for good now. The South can't back out graceful, it's complete and total surrender or nothing. We won't be saying truce and going home respectfully anymore."

"Maybe right. But then it was awful smart of him to make this war about more than just a split between the states. Now he's got something noble for everyone to rally round. He may have prolonged the war, but then he's getting it all on his terms when we win, isn't he?" Sam pointed out.

"Now, I heard it may be another two months at the most and then we'll be going home," I piped up, because that is what I had heard. One of the other men had gone so far as to write home and ask his brother to prepare for his return. The thought gave me some glimmer of hope, until I heard them talking about no surrender and how Abe Lincoln had painted us into a corner. Up till now I was under the assumption this whole thing would resolve itself quickly.

Sam shook his head. "Oh, Frank, they been saying that same thing from the beginning. They say what they must to keep the men's morale up, to keep the fight in us."

"It's a shame how they treat us," Ruben Morrell lamented. "You'd think they'd put more value on us, seeing as how we are the ones they've placed on the sacrificial altar to dispense with as they see fit."

"You think it'll be longer?" I asked, because I wanted very much to go home. I couldn't leave Sam, and I felt sorely for what I had done to my father, and then there was the discomfort and the work of being a soldier which was a great affliction for me to bear. In every direction I was being torn apart. At times I felt my seams weakening, threatening to give, as though I might unravel at any moment. "I heard two months. You don't think it's true?"

"Can't believe everything they tell you," Reed Haney said thoughtfully. I had discovered he was a man who chose his words carefully and only spoke when he felt the need.

I grew frustrated with the situation, and took it out on them. "Well, what can you believe then?" I seethed.

"Don't go shooting the messenger," Marcus said. "All of us would be on the same train back home with you if we could."

"Try to remember you signed on willingly, boy," Gaston said, like he was a bit disgusted with me. "It weren't nobody's choice but your own."

I sat with a lump threatening to come up as I tried to swallow it down, sufficiently chastened. It was true. I was the one who had acted rashly, who had plunged headlong into this charade. Who could I blame but me? I got up and left the group without a word. I sat quietly in the shadows for the rest of the evening, hoping I could disappear completely.

Just as I was about to turn in for the evening, I chanced to hear a conversation that was not meant for my ears. If I were a decent person I would have stopped them and made my presence known. But I was too curious to hear what was being said about me to stop them. It was Ruben Morrell and Sam.

"All I'm saying is he's a queer sort," Ruben was saying.

I could hear the reluctance in Sam's voice, as if he didn't want to get into such a discussion. "Not as queer as poor Orson Penrod. Besides he's younger than all the other men in this regiment. I suppose his inexperience makes him stand apart," Sam reasoned.

"That ain't what I'm talking about and you know it," Ruben said. "He has an odd way about him. He don't fit in with the rest."

"You must understand he never had a father to show him how to behave," Sam informed Ruben. "His mother raised him. And I don't suppose she much knew how to teach him to be a man."

"It's more than that. What's he running off on his own for all the time? What's he so secretive about? I'll tell you what, I wouldn't at all be astonished if we was to discover he was a spy," Ruben hissed.

"Now that's over the top, Ruben," Sam said doubtfully.

"I've heard of it happening. I heard of spies slipping in and out of camp. It's a genuine concern. Notice he didn't show up till we were out of Camp Schuyler? Didn't see hide nor hair of him till then…Did you note that? Do we know where he really come from for a certainty?"

Sam was shaking his head in disagreement. "Bunch of nonsense. I knew his cousins. I knew his aunt and uncle. He only needs to be given a chance. That's all."

And then their conversation faded away into the night as they drifted past, and I could not hear them any longer. I was ashamed and shocked. Could he really think me capable of being a spy? I felt so very out of place among all of these men. Whatever possessed me to do such a foolish thing in the first place? Perhaps if I wished hard enough I would just cease to exist, would dissolve into the ground like the rains from heaven.

It wasn't to be. The next morning, early as always, was the call of the bugle. I got up like I did every morning, then went for breakfast and to drill. The routine could not be ignored and I couldn't change my course now that I was in the rushing waters. Again, the paper boats upon the streams of home came to my mind. I remembered those boats and suddenly felt a kinship to them as I never had before. Being pulled along a current, at the mercies of the whims of the water, with no control over where I would end up.

Finally all of our marching brought us to the Potomac. We were to cross the river just miles from where it all began at Harpers Ferry, when John Brown led an ill-fated uprising against the South. The Rebels burned out the bridge and so we had to cross on pontoons.

I dreaded it for several reasons. First of all, we'd be leaving Maryland to press on into Virginia to chase after Lee and his army. Virginia, our enemy's territory, no longer part of the Union. By self-proclaimed decree they had willingly left the bosom of the United States of America. Second of all, I couldn't swim. Here was a great wide river before me I was told I must cross. The sight of all of those men pressed onto those pontoons made me feel all a-panic. All it would take was for me to go over the side into the depths of that cold and dark water. Just one slip up, one loss of footing, one innocent nudge from someone in the group.

Chapter Fourteen

I suffered with this fear and agony for nearly a week as everyone else was taken across the Potomac in what felt like the slowest of processions. There were a great deal of men to move and our only mode of transportation was the pontoons, which could only hold so many. Perhaps if I could've just gotten it over with. I was beginning to think that maybe it wouldn't be so bad to die of drowning, rather than endure the constant threat of it.

"What's the matter with you, Frank?" Sam wanted to know.

"Nothing," I said.

"Come on now, I can see you're bothered over something," he said as he packed his gear and helped take down his half of the tent we shared. You see, tents are issued in halves. You find a fellow to share his half and between the two you have a whole tent. I thought this somewhat endearing, that the two of us must share a tent in order to be sustained.

"It's nothing really." How could he tell there was anything wrong anyhow? Was I so easily read?

"Bull. Out with it 'fore I have to pin you down and make you talk," he threatened.

I hesitated. Would it be so bad if he pinned me? I didn't think I would really mind so much. But then I dismissed the thought. It was wrong of me to think of it. Surrounded by all of these men, I was beginning to lose my decency; I was becoming one of them.

"I just don't want to have to cross the Potomac," I confessed.

"Why not?" I could see he was careful not to seem too interested, as if he were sparing my feelings by being offhand about it. He kept his eyes on his hands as they arranged things in his sack.

"I can't swim," I told him.

He didn't look up at me, but nodded sympathetically. "Well, now, I can." Something I already knew about him, I thought. "And if you was to go over…and I'm telling you now you won't, but if you was to…I wouldn't let you drown, Frank. I'd come and fish you out if need be."

As kind as it was for him to make such an offer, to try to soothe my fears, I knew he only felt sorry for me. I was the orphan he had taken under his wing, that he had thought to tutor in the ways of manhood. If I ever thought otherwise, the conversation between him and Rueben put any other notions to rest. It hurt a little, feeling like his charity project. This was how it had been from the beginning, and I had just talked myself into believing it could be something more. I was the girl with no name, and he was the boy rescuing my bonnet from a watery grave.

There was one thing he couldn't protect me from though, and that was the other men. Sam couldn't watch over me all the time. And I'm sure they were waiting and watching for the moments when he was gone, and I would be alone. One evening in the dark shadows of twilight, I went out alone to take care of my business, as I usually did. But as I was coming back I was accosted by four men. Two of them I knew: Ruben Morrell and Vern Stapleton. The other two were nameless to me. I could see by the looks on their faces they were wanting to stir up trouble.

I ducked my head and tried to walk past them, but they wouldn't allow me to pass. "We wanna talk to you," Ruben said.

"What about?" I asked, trying to avoid them. I backed away slowly, thinking to put some distance between me and them. But they closed in on me. I found myself with my back to a tree, surrounded on every side by the four of them. Rueben took one of my arms and one of the strangers took the other arm.

I felt a panic run right through me. I was glad I had just relieved myself, otherwise I might have wet my pants. My gaze flicked from one to the other, looking for some hint of compassion among just one of them. But there was no kindness in any of their expressions. There was no hope for me and I knew it. I twisted this way and that, without any real hope of escape.

"I want a look in that sack of yours," he said, motioning to my haversack hanging across my chest.

Vern went to grab it, but I protested. I didn't want to give in to them without a fight. What would it say about me if I was so easily pushed around? Unable to use my arms, I raised my legs and began kicking wildly.

"No! It's mine!" I grunted.

Vern was laughing at me. "Settle down now," he said through his laughter. "Just a peek, that's all." Although he was laughing he was rough as he wrestled the haversack from me and handed it over to Ruben. Ruben shook it upside down, dumping it all over the ground. Then he began to root through it, looking for who knows what. There wasn't much to see. He promptly gave up, tossed the haversack upon the ground with its contents, and then turned his attention back to me. Vern was obviously the ring leader, but Rueben was aching to be part of the action too. He wrenched my arm real good to take my attention away from Vern.

"Now you listen and you listen good, boy," Rueben barked. "Go on now, Vern. Go on and tell him," he said to Vern in a much more tolerable tone.

"We got our eyes on you, Frank — if that is your name. You slip up even a little and you'll be sorry for it. Cause if there's one thing we won't tolerate, it's a traitor. You understand?"

I nodded my agreement, but didn't say anything. I didn't trust myself to. I knew if I did speak I might break down in tears. That would certainly not help my case. I was pretty sure crying would only make them all the more likely to persecute me.

"Come on, boys," he ordered, turning his back and walking away from me. The others began to follow, all of them but Rueben Morrell, who hung back.

"We'll be watching," he said, as he gave me a quick jab to the gut with his fist.

I crumpled to the ground with a groan. I lay there for some time, my nose smelling the smell of dirt and decaying leaves as I remained prostrate, unwilling to pull myself up and move on. I had never, up to this point, been assaulted before, and I was so disturbed by what had just happened to me I dare not return to camp and chance a run in with one of those men for fear of how I might react. Or worse yet, how they might react. I was frightened of them.

Eventually, I mustered up the courage to pull myself together and got up. I put my things back in my haversack and flung it over my shoulder. If it hadn't been clear to me before, and it most certainly had, it was very clear to me now that this sham I was carrying on was a major lapse in judgment on my part. I didn't belong here. I wasn't meant for this kind of life.

The turmoil stirred within me, making me feel anxious, making me sleepless. Should I report it? But no, that's not how men worked. It would only make their hatred of me worse. I must bear it like a man would. After a terrible long night we woke to find it was our turn to cross the river. And one nagging fear was overshadowed by the other. I couldn't think of bullies when I was thinking of drowning.

As it turned out, there was really no need for such fretting. We crossed on the pontoons without incident. I was foolish enough to suppose the worst was behind me now. And then came Belle Plains, a thing that would bring even the strongest men to despair. After crossing the Potomac the weather turned on us. We were to learn just how unpredictable and harsh the elements could be. Only two days into Virginia, there came upon us a terrible storm. The rain fell brutal hard, and then, as the day progressed, transformed to wet, fat snowflakes. Misery followed us as we set up camp.

Chapter Fifteen

Colonel Upton was sorely vexed by our situation. He had it in his head that we should be camped elsewhere. Along our march, early on in the day, he spied a forest of pines and it was his intent to have us return there and find some comfort in the shelter of the trees. When the sleet began to fall he asked his superior Brigade Commander, Brigadier General Cake if we might do just that, and the fellow told him no, we had come too far to turn back now and lose ground.

There we camped on a flat plain near the river, with no shelter to speak of. We were all wet through and forced to endure the night in the mud and freezing rains of a harsh December. Sam seemed angry. He and I set up our tent with little effect. The wind blew so harsh and cold it was as if we had no tent at all. And our blankets had no warmth to them either. We were already wet through to the skin.

"I know you're weary," Sam told me. "But the best thing for it is to keep moving and try to find some wood to start a fire with."

I followed along behind him grudgingly. All I really wanted was to try to get as comfortable as possible and wallow in self-pity. We scrounged up some wet timbers scattered about across the ground. That, in and of itself, was a miracle because there were no trees for miles around. Our breath came out in great white puffs as we labored to pick up any debris we might find that we could use for a fire. He piled these items in my arms and I faithfully trailed after, watching him with no thought in my own head of self-preservation. Without him I would've been lost.

Sam had the idea to go to the mess wagon, and afraid we would be turned away, we didn't ask permission for what he was set on taking. He emptied the remnants of a few of the barrels into the barrels still full of cornmeal and flour and took the empty ones to be broken up. It was on account of his ingenuity we were one of the few to have a fire that night. He used his flint to start the fire, and I was never so glad to see a spark catch and smoke start to rise. A large group of the men huddled with us as we attempted to warm ourselves by the weak flames. The men were so pitifully miserable; no one scarce said a word.

It appeared to me everyone's skin was positively blue, everyone pale and frozen through. Sam had the notion to double up our blankets and the two of us sat beneath them, shivering uncontrollably, our teeth chattering. Now, under different circumstances, I might have welcomed the occasion when I was given a reason to be so close to him. But the despair of our current conditions was such that I couldn't enjoy it even a little. All romantic notions had flown away and my only thought was for survival.

I felt the terrible pain of the cold in my extremities the most, a burning sting that comes just before numbness sets in. My fingers, my toes, my nose and ears, they were all warning me, telling me it was too much, that I was in danger. Oh, the misery. I dreamed of a hot cup of coffee and a warm bed with a pile of quilts. I was no fool. I knew we were in real peril.

"We aren't going to freeze to death, are we?" I whispered.

"No, sir," he said. "Not if I have anything to do with it."

"I'm afraid to go to sleep," I admitted. "What if I don't wake up? What if I shut my eyes and die in my sleep?"

"That's not going to happen," he insisted, although his teeth chattered just as violently as mine.

Chapter Sixteen

Sam's words brought me some comfort, and we managed to sleep a bit surrounded by the harsh winds and the snow and the frigid temperature. I doubt I've ever slept so fitfully. The one thing to calm me during the terrible time was my brother. I don't know why it came to my mind, but I recalled a time when I was nine and Caleb ten. He possessed a quick mind, a curious wit, my brother. Anyhow, he sought me out with such urgent pleas to follow him I dared not ask why because I didn't want to delay him. Besides, I couldn't resist knowing what his eagerness was over. He took me into the barn with his excitement apparent as he motioned with his arm for me to follow. "Come see, Serena," he encouraged me.

Our hens were excellent egg layers. All the neighbors said as much. Every morning it was our job to collect them for Mother. But we always left a few so we always had some new chicks hatching, and in turn they would grow to be egg layers themselves. On this morning Caleb had discovered one of the eggs was hatching and he had come to find me so I might witness it as well.

I had never beheld the marvel myself. The egg was moving about, rocking to and fro ever so slightly, and we sat there in awed silence watching the process unfold. At first it was only the movement, but as we continued to observe the egg began to crack. The fissures spread over the once flawless white oval in just the slightest and nearly imperceptible of fractures. It was a thrill to know there was life in there, and it was struggling to get out.

The tiny chick's beak was hammering against the shell in a desperate struggle to break free from the confines of its casing. Finally, after what seemed like a very long time, its little head peeked through, all wet with its feathers plastered to it, looking wretched and pathetic. It was fascinating to watch, but as the time drifted by I began to grow bored. After initially freeing its head from the shell, the chicken was still struggling to liberate itself. I thought I should help the poor thing along, so I could move on to another pursuit. I reached out my fingers to pull the cracked shell pieces away from its damp body. Caleb quickly grabbed my hand to stop me.

"You mustn't," he said.

"Why not?"

"You will spoil the natural way of things," he told me.

"So?"

"So, you must let the chick do it for herself, Serena. It would be cruel to help her."

"Cruel?" I said disbelievingly. Surely the cruel thing would be to leave it to struggle so.

"If you pull the shell away for her, the chick won't grow to be a strong hen. If she doesn't have to fight to get out it would be to her harm. She'll be a weak thing, unable to be a good egg layer and good for nothing at all. The others will peck at her until she dies. That's what they do, find the weakest of the group and rid themselves of her."

"But she is tired and wet," I told him.

"Yes," he agreed, "and so's every other chick when it hatches too. Don't feel sorry for her; she's learning to survive."

Why did such a memory come to me at that time? I don't know. But then the notion came to me perhaps Caleb wanted me to remember the lecture he had given me so long ago. I was the chick. And as difficult as the struggle was, it was something I had to go through in order to be strong. Somehow I would come out of it all right. I went to sleep with his young face before my eyes, holding the little chick ever so tenderly in his cupped hands, just a piece of pale yellow fluff.

The following morning when we woke, it was our poor luck to find our clothing frozen to the mud on the ground where we lay. During the night it had gotten so cold that our bodies had fused with the earth. I thought it a marvel we were even alive and we hadn't died in our sleep from exposure. Exerting a powerful effort was the only way to get up and break loose from the sheet of ice we had become a part of.

The lot of us were a downhearted crew as we ate at our hardtack over breakfast. We discovered Colonel Upton himself was sleeping on the ground with us. He gave his own bed up for several of the men who were already very sick, so they might rest more comfortably. Following breakfast he called us all together and announced we would return to the grove of pines he had intended on camping at in the first place. He did this at risk of being reported for insubordination because he went against a direct command from Brigadier General Cake. I admired him all the more for caring about us, rather than worrying about himself and what trouble he might get into over his decision.

Hardly able to move my joints as they were so cold and stiff, I helped break up camp, and then we hastily headed back to the forest, some four miles back, where there was wood and shelter from the wind. The moment we set up our tent, Sam was preparing a fire—a proper fire. If it weren't for my empty belly I would've been content. We warmed ourselves by the fire, drying our clothes for the first time in several days. And then I said to Sam, "How do you feel about eating?"

And he said with a cynical edge to his voice, "I'd feel real good about it, if there was anything to eat."

"Well, I have an idea on that. I plan on going hunting."

He smiled. I thought he must like my idea. So we took our rifles and headed off. As cold as it was, the snow was not as wet as the rain had been, and we roamed through the forest, in search of anything eatable. Our footsteps were silent as we tramped over the frozen earth, vigilant for any sign of a living thing. There was nothing but silence between us.

Near a fallen log we saw him, fat and full of feathered plumage. A turkey the size of a very large pumpkin waddled right into view. I gave Sam a tap on the shoulder and pointed to the bird. He nodded enthusiastically. Not a sound was made, not an inch moved. We waited for the perfect moment, excitement coursing through me at the thought of having him.

Ever so slowly the two of us took aim, hoping if one of us missed the shot the other would not. I put my bead on him and waited. Sam fired first, but the ball sailed right past him and lodged in a tree directly behind. The turkey, alerted to us now, took off at a run.

I was ready for him, aiming just ahead of where he was running I managed to hit him square in his plump body before he could get more than a few feet away.

"You got him!" Sam yelled out in jubilation as he sprang up and ran toward the bird. His satisfaction with me made my chest swell with pride.

Cleaning it was a messy business. My father or Caleb or Mother always took care of such matters. Being the youngest and a girl, I was spared much of that sort of dirty work. There were feathers to pluck and innards to dispose of, but we cooked our turkey on a spit just over the fire and waited impatiently as it roasted. Once the smell of it began to drift on the air, we could hardly wait. Our stomachs growled and our mouths watered. If I hadn't had some restraint, I might have eaten the thing raw. It took all day to cook him up right.

"We'll have a slew of best pals tonight, Frank," Sam said with mirthful satisfaction. And the two of us couldn't stop grinning as we cut pieces off and passed it out to the group formulating around us.

"I shot and missed," Sam told them. "Shot and it went right on past him. Well, he took off to run, and Frank here just shot him dead right like that," Sam recounted with the snap of his fingers. "You ought to have seen it. He just fell to the ground and lay there, done in instantly!"

"You came awful close, Sam. You nearly had him," I consoled.

"Close would have left us hungry still," Sam said. "It was Frank. If he hadn't got that bird we wouldn't have this fine feast we have before us now. Living off the top shelf, thanks to him." He handed me a drumstick the size of a fist. I should've been more modest, should've insisted someone else have it, but I was too ravenous to care. I bit into the drumstick, filling my mouth so full I could hardly chew, the juices running down my chin in slovenly disregard for manners. As I gnawed heartily at my meat I was patted on the back and clapped on the shoulder by all around.

I was sitting next to Orson Penrod, who was looking downright fragile. I noted Sam had given him a bigger portion than the others, which I was glad for. Orson seemed so pleased to have that meat. He ate it slowly, savoring each bite. But I couldn't help notice that he kept coughing, which in turn made him gag. I felt sorry for him that he was having such a bad time of it.

Vern Stapleton and Rueben Morrell came up, taking a share of the bird, which I was not altogether happy about. I couldn't completely forget how they had mistreated me. But Vern came up to me and pushed Orson aside saying, "Move over, little baby Orson," so that he could sit beside me as he chewed with his mouth wide open. He leaned in and said simply, "You done good." That was all. Sam was right about the "best pals" thing. I grew angry over his treatment of Orson, thinking I should tell him I'd rather sit next to Orson instead of him, but I thought better of it and let the incident go.

Then Vern went and ruined it further by telling a story about a girl back home. Real ugly talk. "She had a fine form," he said with a wink, showing the outline of her curves by moving his hands in an hour glass shape through the air. "And a man don't like to brag, but she didn't just look good, she tasted mighty fine too," he said, biting into his meat like a savage. Then he began to laugh loud and his half-chewed food was exposed for everyone to see. "Know what I mean?" He winked and then gave my back a good pounding as if he and I were co-conspirators, nearly knocking the wind out of me in the process.

I was sickened by his crude inference but did my best not to scowl. If I could've discreetly gotten up and walked away from him, I would have. As it was I was stuck next to him while he continued on with his bragging. I noticed Sam watching me with the slightest smirk and a raised eyebrow. He knew I didn't like Vern Stapleton and Vern Stapleton didn't like me either. He was having some fun watching me squirm. After a while, I found a reason to beg off and got up and left.

I refused to let Vern ruin the evening for me. I was proud of myself for doing such a fine job on the hunt, and I was completely satiated with food, having been hungry for so very long. I slept so fine that night, with a warm fire before the tent and a belly full of fresh turkey, I scarce heard the bugle the next morning. Sam had to rouse me with a good shake.

That morning we discovered Orson Penrod had expired in the night. He was such a sensitive sort from the beginning, and I don't suppose the bad conditions we were forced to tolerate at Belle Plains did anything to help him. He was not cut out for the burdens of war. Such a pale and sober fellow you never did meet.

I felt a terrible sense of guilt that I hadn't stood up for him, that I hadn't said something on his behalf when Vern was so cruel to him. It occurred to me that my silence made me just as guilty as

Vern was. No one should ever be treated so. No one. I managed to keep my emotions in check until I was alone and could mourn for his loss in private.

We buried him there, in the quiet of the forest among the pine trees. Orson never even saw a battle, and there he was in his grave, beneath the dirt and snow. The irony of it didn't escape me. Neither did the full ramifications of his loss. I thought now I was the prime target for Vern Stapleton's meanness. Without poor, wretched Orson to pick on, he could focus his full attention on me. And just when we had found refuge from the storm, things were to change again.

Chapter Seventeen

They distributed three days' rations and sixty rounds of cartridges to each man, and we were on the move again, bound for Richmond, they said. The consensus was we were headed for battle. The general became bold and set his sights on the Confederate capital. Take Richmond and the war would be over. Lee had other plans. He wouldn't let his prize be taken so easily. There would be a battle, but not in Richmond.

It seemed the army had been preparing for us to come. The roads were laid with logs to make the travel easier. Someone had put in a great deal of time felling the trees and lining them up this way to make corduroy pathways, making the way easier.

In a similar fashion as before, we marched a great part of the day, made camp, ate our miserable dried beef, hardtack, and coffee, slept, and woke up only to repeat it again. If we found a means of supplying our own food, we took it. I didn't like to think of it as stealing, though deep down I knew it was. As we marched other regiments and companies fell in with us, until we were quite an impressive display of numbers.

Some days later we arrived at Fredericksburg, a quaint town situated near the river in a green valley surrounded by rolling hills. It looked like something from a fairy-tale book. When we saw it, it reminded us all of home. It was positioned close to the river, with beautiful homes stretched all along the waterfront. I saw a wheel churning up the water at a two-story mill, and from a distance a tall and proud church steeple pointed upward to heaven. I grew homesick once I beheld it. Preparations for a battle had already begun. Lee had chosen this place to take his stand, and I felt remorse over this being the place where it seemed we would be engaging with him.

This is where we would cross the river. This is where the fighting would be. I worried over crossing another river again. But this time I was not as apprehensive as before. It all went well on the last occasion, so I did not foresee anything bad happening this time either. Besides, there was so much activity and commotion going on there was little time to consider my fears.

I was grateful, for the time being, that I was only a lowly infantry soldier. In order to cross over the river, General Burnside brought in pontoons to form a bridge for the entire body of us to traverse. The engineers struggled to assemble them under fire from snipers who had set up in the houses along the waterfront. Despite the Union's attempt at rooting them out with a bombardment of cannon fire, they continued to take one here and there during the engineers' valiant attempts at laboring to bridge the gap. Soon the cannons began in earnest, firing without ceasing, and the white plumes from the discharge began to cloud the scene in a hazy blur. Some of the houses caught fire and the air became thick with the smell of smoke.

Our cannons did little good. Still those sharpshooters aimed their rifles on the poor engineers. It grew necessary for several regiments to cross the river in boats. Their job was to clean up the town and get rid of all of the Rebels hiding there. We could hear the reports of their rifles as they worked to push the Rebel sharpshooters out of town. They accomplished the task in late evening. But the Rebs had still managed to delay and frustrate the plans of old Burnside.

We set up our camp, Sam and I pitching our tents together, working quickly at something we had become very proficient at. Our camp was just below the river with a bird's eye view of the city and the hills beyond. There was a nervous tension hanging in the air, everyone's hands busy, and everyone's brains racing with the thought that there would be a fight. When? Tomorrow? The day after? It was not for us to say, we only did as we were led to.

The moon was bright that night, glowing like a white hot ember in a sky of ebony black, making it easy to see those passing in the night and all of our surroundings. I sat outside the tent for a good while, in contemplation, trying to take it all in. Shortly the outcome would be known, and I wondered if I would be there to witness it for myself, or if I would be among the ghastly rotting bodies left in the aftermath. As I contemplated these things I fiddled with Caleb's pocket watch, clicking it open, pressing it shut, clicking it open again. Sam came and sat next to me, trying to read my mood, I suppose. He bumped his shoulder into mine.

"You should try to sleep. It will keep you quick and alert for tomorrow," he said.

"I don't know if I can sleep. I think I would just lay there in misery. I'd rather breathe in the night air and reflect."

"Reflect upon what?" Sam asked. He smiled at me as if he were amused by my choice of words.

"Home and family…and what I will do if I come out of this."

"I thought you didn't have any family to speak of," Sam said. His tone was not accusing, but he seemed confused.

I was forced to think quickly. "There is my Aunt and Uncle," I said.

"And your cousin. You still have a cousin," Sam pointed out.

A jolt ran through me, an immediate discomfort that made me feel my stomach jump. I was a liar. I was such a liar. All that I could think to say was, "Yes."

"Were you very close with Caleb?" he wanted to know.

"I was." The sick feeling was quickly replaced, and a sadness overcame me at the thought of my brother.

"You remind me of him at times. Your features are strikingly similar but yours are more delicate than his."

"Yes, well, he was a hard fellow to live up to," I said. I tried to keep the irony from my words. He had noticed Caleb and I bore a resemblance to one another. It was almost comical.

"I know it well," Sam agreed, and his voice had a hint of melancholy to it. "I always wished I were more like him."

It took me by surprise because he felt the same way I did. I always thought Sam was a confident and self-assured person. Not one to compare himself to others. I never would have thought he might feel inferior. Yet, I absolutely understood because I had regarded my brother just as Sam had. I wished I were as clever, as charming, and as talented as he, only to be reminded often through life's hard knocks I was not up to snuff and I never would be.

"I recall the summer before he died," Sam confided. "I don't know if you know about this but we held a tournament in Richfield. It was quite the event every year, with a picnic and dance."

"Yes, I know of it." The truth was I remembered it vividly. All of the boys talked of nothing else but the tournament for months before. Many of them would ask a girl to accompany them to the dance afterward. Each boy chose a color, and his girl wore a ribbon of the same color in her hair.

Caleb wore a sash of deep red bunting and Sam wore a sash of royal blue. I was only fifteen and no one paid me any mind. I certainly didn't get asked by a boy to wear his color, to be his girl. I was only part of the festivities in that I watched it all. But Caleb's girl, Sally Dobbs, wore a ribbon of the same deep red and Sam's girl called Prudence Sayer wore a ribbon of royal blue to match him. Oh, how I envied Prudence.

"We spent all our spare time trying to get ready for the tournament. Any free moment I could find I was riding the course. The object was to run through the course and collect some rings hanging from the trees onto a pole you carried as you rode at a gallop. It was downright difficult." He paused in his telling and turned to me to ask, "Did you ever attend?"

"I may have once or twice," I lied, for I had been to one ever since I could remember. They didn't have a tournament last year, the first year in as long as I could remember. When the war broke out everyone was too somber to celebrate.

"My competitive nature pushed me to practice long hours. I wanted very much to win. It's much harder than it sounds, to get those rings."

I caught myself before I said, *But you did win, Sam. You were the champion that year!* How could I not remember him, smiling triumphantly as he and Prudence were made to sit on two chairs festooned with ribbons and flowers before everyone like a king and queen upon their thrones? But I held my tongue.

Instead I said, "And did you?"

"No."

It was silent. I sat there confused by his admission. I was there. I remember how they crowned him victor, of how his girl Prudence was crowned queen, and much ado was made over the two of them.

I could never forget it. I wanted to be Prudence. I wanted to be his queen.

"Who won then?" I asked, and I truly was breathless to hear what he had to say.

"Your cousin," he said. "Caleb. Caleb won."

"I don't remember that," I told him. I knew in my brain Caleb absolutely did not win. I knew it had been Sam. How could he have failed to remember too?

"Yes, well, he knew how much it meant to me," Sam continued. "But he was just as competitive as I, you know. I mean he trained just as hard, and there was such a big deal made over it. We went through three rounds of running the course. And as we waited for the judges to count the rings we each had collected, Caleb took three of his own rings and put them on my pole."

"Caleb did that?" I said in disbelief.

"Yes. I expect it was enough for him to know he had won. He didn't need the praise. That, and he felt pity for me and knew I wanted it so badly that he was willing to give me the win."

"I never knew it," I said.

"No one but Caleb or I did. His last summer on this earth. I wish now I hadn't gone along with it. His last summer…he should have been crowned the victor. He never had another chance at it. And I've regretted the whole thing ever since."

Was this a confession of some sort? This was a thing only he and Sam knew, and he was telling *me*. I could sense he had carried this guilt for two long years now, before he had finally admitted it to someone. And that someone was me. Suddenly the words I was about to say seemed like a weight upon my shoulders. It needed to be important, to really mean something. I thought very carefully before I replied.

"Would it have made a difference, Sam? Where he is now I'm sure he thinks very little on who collected the most rings."

"I know it shouldn't bother me. It's only that I'd like to say I'd earned it somehow. I wish I could say I'd been a true friend to him too and deserved his loyalty."

"We all lived in his shadow," I said. Because suddenly it dawned on me that Sam must have felt very much like I did about Caleb and his seeming state of perfection. Perhaps he aspired to be like Caleb as much as I had. "I certainly felt as though I would never be as good as him either."

He was uncomfortable. He had made himself vulnerable and now he didn't care for the attention. I could see him shifting, his demeanor transforming. Suddenly his eyes changed and his face changed and he attempted to move the conversation away from himself.

"But you have done well in trying. To be honest, I like having you around on account of you are so much like him."

"You think so?"

"Yes. Caleb was a good natured boy, always agreeable and making the best of a situation. And he was kind and bright. He had a great strength of character. Someday I expect you'll grow to be just as he would have."

"I know he is dead and gone, but still I feel perhaps somehow he's watching over me," I admitted. Sharing something so personal with him felt natural and right after everything he just told me. He didn't mock or belittle as some might. Sam was not the kind. I knew I was safe with him.

"I do not doubt it," Sam said.

"If I shouldn't make it back…" I began.

"You'll come out fine," he interrupted.

"I don't mean to say I plan on getting myself killed. I hope not to be a burden upon you in that way."

"You're no burden, Frank," Sam said with a chuckle.

"Well, it's good of you to say so, but if I should not live through it," I persisted, hoping to get him to take me seriously, "I have written a letter to my uncle. I would be very grateful to you if you would see to it he receives it."

"I will," he said simply, his laughter gone. "And you must promise to do the same for me. I think of my mother and father and Bess, and Jacob, Stanley, and Hyrum, Rosa, and Lilly, and how hard it would be on them if I were to die. I have to do everything I can to make it back to them. But if God should see fit to take me, I would like for you to make sure they receive my pay, if they will ever issue it, and my father's pistol."

"I will see to it, Sam."

"Now you must sleep. As I said, you shouldn't be tired come tomorrow. Fatigue makes you slow."

"I will come to bed shortly," I promised him.

He gave me a brusque pat on my shoulder and then left me to myself. I studied the watch in my hand, Caleb's watch, running my fingers over the smooth case before slipping it back into my breast pocket. Eventually I grew too tired to hold my eyes open. Avoiding sleep does not ensure that tomorrow will never come. So I crawled onto my bedroll and fell off to sleep.

That night as I slept, I dreamed. It was as if I were floating, and the air was warm, and the grass was tall and flowing in waves as the wind stirred it with a constant and gentle movement. There were fat bees lazily flying from one wildflower to the next and the faint glow of sunset as it lends its last golden rays upon the horizon. The trees rustled with that soothing sound they make as the breeze shakes their limbs all at once in a unified shivering of leaves. The whole of it was peaceful and serene. Then to my ears came the faint sound of fife music and drums in the far distance, but I was unconcerned with it, I was too occupied with the beauty of the place. I'd seen it before. Yes, the more I looked around, I knew at some time I'd been here.

As my body floated light and weightless, I came upon a field, and that field, I knew, was where corn once grew. But there was no corn there now. In the shorn down cornfield there was a group of men in a huddle, looking at something, whispering in concern to one another as they stood over it. And at once I recognized the scene. I was at Antietam; I was in the cornfield there, where we had buried so many. I drew closer, curious as to what they were observing. The men parted, as though they were letting me pass so I might see as well. Their voices mingled in shocked and curious tones as I walked through the group. And there was the body of the girl soldier, the woman we had found among the dead. The one we had lay to rest in her own solitary grave.

I leaned in to get a good look, only to be filled with surprise and horror as I saw her face with vacant eyes and a hollow expression. I wanted to look away, but remained fixed upon her with an unexplained curiosity. Slowly a change began to transpire, as her skin rippled, and the color of her eyes underwent a metamorphosis and her face was altered, until she no longer looked like herself. I studied her features, all the while knowing they were familiar to me, but unable to place them right away. Suddenly it came to me. I was looking at myself. The face was mine!

There I lay, dead in the cornfield, being stared and gaped at by my fellow soldiers. I tried to scream, but nothing came from my mouth, because I had no mouth. Her mouth was my mouth and she was dead, empty and hollow, a vessel drained of its contents. I woke with a start, sweating and panicked, gulping air like a drowning man. If I died tomorrow, I thought, I know what will happen to me. I know they will bury me with a marker that reads *Unknown Woman, USA.*

Chapter Eighteen

I lay there fighting the panic, trying to still my beating heart and breathe calmly, but I couldn't erase the terrible vision from my mind. Eventually I dozed off again. And this time there were no dreams at all. But I came awake several times, disoriented by my surroundings, feeling strangely disconnected. It was a terrible long night.

The next morning we were called to the field and marched across the makeshift bridges, the pontoons bobbing and swaying beneath our feet, leaving me feeling unsteady and nauseous. I fleetingly thought of the men who had lost their lives trying to build this bridge I now walked on. It seemed the snipers had been cleared out, because we were able to cross unmolested with cannons clearing the way before without retaliation. I wasn't up for talking and it didn't seem anyone else was either. We were all sober from being on edge.

There were thousands upon thousands of us pouring across the river and onto the banks and fields of the other side. It was a sight to see. I never in my life witnessed so many bodies congregated at once. Artillery covered our advance as we moved from one side of the river to the other. The noise was deafening, and the results a sight to behold as a fire from the town lit up the morning in a vibrant orange glow. While we crossed, floating upon the water, iced over near the banks in the frigid morning, there were hundreds of playing cards, sodden and waterlogged.

"Why are they getting rid of their cards?" I asked Sam.

Big Frank answered for him with a grin. "Nobody wants to meet their maker with playing cards in their pockets."

We set up camp again just south of town. The vast open field was now dotted with white as far as the eye could see where tents and wagon covers littered the place. Sam and I got the notion to go into town and see if we might round up something to eat. Beef and hardtack grows awfully loathsome when you have it day in and day out.

All of the civilians had been evacuated much earlier. Some of the men from the Michigan infantry had been caught under fire as they tried to aid the residents from their homes and out of harm's way. But that was several days ago. Now the place was as quiet as a church. Sam and I walked through the empty streets with the eerie feeling of being in a ghost town, a whole people gone, leaving everything behind where it lay. The unnatural scene made me anxious.

No friendly wave from a front porch. No dogs to chase after you and nip at your heels. The vacant and tomblike windows had no eyes watching from behind lace curtains, no warm glow of candlelight as we approached and passed. It was dark and gloomy, a place where people once lived, and worked, and played all silenced and shadowy, all cleaned out in a mass exodus. We saw other Union soldiers as we went along, but being up to no good they were like stealthy figures dodging in and out of the darkness, keeping to themselves, speaking in loud whispers if they needed to speak to one another at all. I was ill at ease and stuck close to Sam.

Some of the other soldiers got a similar idea as us, only they weren't scrounging around for something to eat. I saw many of them taking liberties they ought not to take with personal belongings. No one was there to stop them and so they were taking everything that wasn't nailed down. The looting was grievous. Some poor family, forced out of their home because of the impending fight, would return thereafter to find that very home stripped of valuables, keepsakes, and personal treasures. Just another slap in the face to an already beaten lot. I'm sure the men knew it was wrong to steal, we were warned against it, but there was no one to prevent them from doing it, and I suppose they figured anything that belonged to the enemy was fair game.

We went through the front door of a fine old house at the end of the block on a wide and spacious street after trying the lock and finding it unsecured. The furniture was well made, and everything within of high quality, but the house seemed to be in a general state of disrepair. One of the walls was damaged by a leak from the roof, the carpets were worn and dusty, and the hinges upon the doors all creaked from lack of oiling.

I wandered upstairs and through the bedrooms. The furniture in most of them was covered in sheets, but one of the rooms had been inhabited recently. I peeked into the wardrobe and discovered a woman's belongings, her gowns, and shoes, antiquated but still quite lovely and of rich fabrics and materials. It was obvious to me a fine lady had owned them. I touched the dresses with envious fingers. I wondered how long again before I would dress as a woman?

I must admit britches are more comfortable and easier to move around in. But they do little to make you feel feminine or beautiful. I considered whether Sam would think of me differently if I was dressed in one of those dresses. Would he think me pretty? Would he be shocked? What a ridiculous question. No doubt he would absolutely be shocked. But just *how* would he react if he discovered his bedfellow for the past four months was really a girl?

Some days I thought I would give anything to tell him the truth, to finally be liberated from the lies I had told. Other days, I grew anxious and apprehensive with fear, certain I would be found out, the consequences of which would be disastrous for me. No decent, well respected woman would do what I had done. Should anyone discover me, the penalties would be far reaching, my reputation permanently and forever shattered.

On the dressing table were bottles of perfume and a comb and brush set made of ivory. I took up one of the bottles and unstopped it to smell the musky sweetness. I dare not dab some at my wrists and neck, but I wanted to. There was a bed, a real bed, stuffed with down feathers and puffy soft. I lay down upon it, the weight of my body sinking into it, and closed my eyes for a moment, spreading my arms out and up above my head, until Sam called to me from downstairs.

"Frank, I found something here," he hollered from downstairs. I hurried down the staircase quickly, not wanting him to know what I had been up to. "There are potatoes and turnips in the larder!" Sam exclaimed. "Won't those taste fine?"

I followed him through the hallway and into the kitchen, where there was a large hearth and brick ovens for baking. This home had a sink with a pump for water and a large oak table which sat right in the middle. Just off of that room was a much smaller room with large wooden bins and shelves. I had never been in such a fine home with a pantry the size of my loft back home where I slept. There in the bottom of the bins were a few shriveled potatoes and turnips for the taking. We scrambled to stuff them into our coat pockets and rummaged around to see if we might find more.

"Looky, looky!" Sam said, pointing to one of the shelves that seemed to me to be empty. I was shorter than he and could not see what he was pointing at. He stood on his tip toes and raked a bottle of peaches to the edge of the shelf with his hand, catching it with his other hand before it went off onto the floor.

"Peaches!"

Sam went back to the oak table setting the jar down and unlatching the lid with a grin as it gave a pleasing thwack when the suction was broken. He fished into the jar with his fingers and pulled out a few slices, handing them to me first. I sucked them into my mouth from the palm of my hands and let them sit on my tongue for a moment, savoring their sweetness as the slices disintegrated in my mouth. Sam did the same.

"Wouldn't they taste fine in a cobbler?" he asked.

"I don't think a cobbler could taste any better," I replied.

We happily finished off the jar together, letting the taste linger in our mouths. I took the jar and put it in the sink and pumped the pump to watch the water fill it up.

"If I ever have a home of my own," I told Sam, "I would be happy if it was even half as nice as this one."

He took the jar up and drank from it, then handed it to me and I did the same.

"Good spring water," he commented, licking his lips and then drying them with the arm of his coat.

He was in high spirits as I followed him while he drifted through the rooms downstairs. Seeing him this way made me feel cheerful too. He took a book off of the shelf, blew the dust from its cover, and then flipped through the pages before he put it back. He picked up a finely carved pipe from the mantel, examined it closely and then sat it down. Eventually we came to the cellar door.

"Maybe we'll find something more to eat down here," he said.

He lit a kerosene lamp he found in the parlor and headed down the dark wooden stairs. They creaked loudly under his weight. I followed him. The floor was dirt, and it was considerably cooler down there than it had been upstairs. He shone the light this way and that, illuminating the dark corners with the glow from the flame.

"What's that smell?" I complained.

Suddenly we sensed movement, which startled us. We both jumped a mile and nearly took off at a run when Sam's light shone on the face of a deeply wrinkled old woman, her thin hair in braids, cowering upon a pallet against the wall. She held up her trembling hands and squinted fiercely from the brightness of the lamp.

She cried out pitifully, "Please, don't hurt me!"

Chapter Nineteen

"Sam!" I called out to him as I tried to meet his long strides, trotting after him down the darkened street. "Sam!" I finally drew up next to him and tugged on his coat sleeve to slow him down.

"What?" he growled. He was agitated and I was only making it worse by badgering him. But I couldn't let him leave. She was waiting down there in the shadows of her lonely cellar, frightened and helpless as a babe.

"She cannot be left alone down there!" I insisted.

He stopped and stared back at the house, silent and gloomy. "Just let me think, will you?" he asked. He was angry. Whether at me or the situation itself I didn't know. He didn't move, neither toward the house nor away from it. I was afraid to speak, but I knew that I must.

"Sam," I persisted, "She can't care for herself. We can't leave her alone."

"There's nothing to be done for it, Frank," he whispered.

"What will become of her?"

"I don't know, but there is nothing to be done for it," he insisted. Yet I could see his weak resolve and I wouldn't let it go. I couldn't. Even if it was by chance we had come upon her, we now had a responsibility we couldn't turn away from.

"She has no way of getting to safety. And what if her house was to catch fire? She'd never make it out alive, Sam. She'd burn right up. Whoever left her down there, they cared more for themselves than for her. She could die down there. We found her, and now we have an obligation to her."

"Maybe so," Sam concurred. "But what can we do about it?"

"We must go back and help her. We must go back and see to it she's all right."

His resolve seemed to be waning, standing there in the street with a troubled expression. Then he turned back to face the house full on and grudgingly headed back. He took up the kerosene lamp he had left on a table near the entrance and went back carefully down the wooden steps and into the cellar. She was still there, dazed and frightened, huddling beneath her quilt.

He knelt down on one knee next to her and said gently, because he didn't want to frighten her, "We don't aim on hurting you."

She broke down in tears, and seeing her that way nearly brought them on me too. "Please…" she said again and again. "Please…"

"Where's your family?" Sam asked. "Why are you here alone?" Even with the stress he was surely feeling he remained kind and spoke softly to her, trying to abate her fears.

"There's no one," she cried. "My servant girl, she said it would be safe down here. But she wouldn't stay and there's no one else." Her despair nearly broke my heart. To be abandoned in her elder years, and in such a thoughtless manner. A lady who was accustomed to beautiful things and a life of ease dumped down on the dirt floor of her cellar seemed truly callous to me.

"Why didn't you go with the others?" he questioned.

"There's no one else!" she wept.

"Sam, she can't stay here," I began.

"I know," he snapped back, not as patient with me as he was with her. "Just let me think."

"Please…Please…" the old woman continued to beg.

Finally Sam stood up. "You grab that end of the blanket and I'll grab this one," he said to me. Then he said to her, "We're going to take you to get help."

I did as he directed. "What do you plan on doing?"

"Enemy lines are not far from here," he informed me. "We'll drop her there. They'll move her on back with the others from town."

"If they catch us, what'll happen then, Sam?" My heart was beating faster than a rabbit's.

"I don't see any other way around it, Frank. If they catch us…Well, I guess we done what we had to." He bent down and picked up the corners of the blanket she lay on, and I did the same. She weighed hardly anything at all. Between the two of us she was an easy load.

We hurried along the barren walks, turning up and up the vacant streets until we drew near the outskirts of the city on the north side. We knew the Rebels were held up there. We knew we were in real danger of being the target of sniper fire. Sam stopped for a moment and laid the old woman down on the ground to catch his breath. I followed suit.

In the dimness of the evening, we could make out the Rebel campfires, just as I'm sure they could make out ours down below. Sam picked up the blanket again, and so I did too. We headed as bold as you please right for the nearest campfire. It was not an easy task with the woman swaying back and forth between us as we trotted up the hilly incline to their camp above the town.

A group of Rebs sat around their campfire in low conversation, getting ready to turn in for the evening, when we came along. One of them was slightly more alert than the others. He saw us coming and immediately took the defense. He pulled his gun up and pointed it at us and ordered us to halt. Sam and I stopped dead in our tracks and waited.

"Well, now, what in the devil have we got here?" he asked.

Sam and I couldn't lift our hands up to show we were not armed; we were encumbered with the weight of the old woman. I didn't say a word and neither did Sam. We waited to be called on to speak. Some of the other men had got to their feet and pointed their rifles at us too.

"We mean no harm," Sam shouted out.

"What the blazes are you doing?" another asked.

"Please, we haven't come for trouble," I said.

"What have you got there?" And the fellow came up to us and looked beneath the covers to where the old woman lay cowering. When he pulled the blanket back and she was exposed to them, she took up crying again, whimpering in a pathetically defenseless way.

"We found her," Sam explained. "Down in the town, down in her cellar."

"Who is she?" they asked.

"Don't know," Sam said.

"She is a Southern lady," I piped up. "And we couldn't just leave her there. She surely would have been caught in the fight if we had."

"We brought her to you, hoping you could get her someplace safe," Sam added.

The Rebel soldiers seemed surprised. One slowly lowered his rifle and then the others did the same. They came forward and took the old woman from us with a great deal of reverence.

"Go on now, before you get yourselves killed and miss the fight that's a-coming," one of them cautioned. "We'll see to it she's cared for."

Sam and I were hesitant to turn our backs to them. We couldn't believe it would be that easy to walk right into the enemy's camp and then walk right back out again without so much as a by-your-leave. They let us go! Perhaps it was just that no one had been foolish enough to try it before. We backed away slowly with our hands up defensively, until we had reached the shadows just beyond their camp once again, and then we took off at a run, not daring to look back. We ran until our sides were splitting and we couldn't run anymore. I had my hands on my knees, bent over, breathing hard, and I looked up at Sam and he looked at me. He was out of breath too, but his lips began to twitch and a slow smiled creeped across his face. He shook his head in disbelief and then his smile faded.

"What just happened?" he asked.

Back in the safety of our own camp, we cooked up the potatoes and turnips and ate in silence. I was sure Sam was angry with me, and I really couldn't blame him. If he was done for good with me, I supposed I would have to pack up and head home. What other choice would there be?

I finally got up the courage to give a weak, "I'm sorry."

Sam pursed his lips, contemplatively. "No, Frank, it is I who am sorry."

"What have you got to be sorry for?" I asked.

"Well, now," he said. "I am thinking the Good Lord saw fit for the two of us to meet up so you could keep me on the straight and narrow. To keep me from losing my soul."

"I don't understand," I said.

"I would've forever after regretted not helping that lady," he explained. "All the days of my life I would've remembered how defenseless and alone she was, and I would've felt terrible guilty for not having done what I could to help her. And I would've always wondered what happened to her."

I was shocked by his confession. "But I nearly got us killed!"

"Better to meet God with a clear conscience than to save your life only to meet him later and have to do penance then," he reasoned. "It is I who owes you an apology."

"You'd have done the right thing even if I hadn't been there," I assured him. "It may have taken you some time to sort it out, but you'd have helped her. I don't doubt it."

"Well, now, you think more of me than you ought. I don't know what I would've done if you hadn't been there. But I'm glad you were."

We turned in that night only to be woken soon after and ordered to evacuate the field. We weren't told why, but all of us took up our things and trotted back over the pontoons and back to our earlier camp across the river. We slept there during the night, and come morning, we marched back across the river yet again, nearly a mile and a half downstream this time at Franklin's Crossing.

We positioned ourselves in a gully. A small river lay just before us and beyond that was the Old Richmond Road. Ahead of us were Russell's Brigade and behind us the 5th Maine, the 16th New York, the 27th New York, and the 96th Pennsylvania. I did not care for the fact that we were with the 96th, and I'm not the only one who felt the same way. None of us liked the 96th. There were still bad feelings from our beginning together after they gave us such a hard time at Antietam. When a person goes into a fight, he likes to know he can rely upon the others who are going into a fight with him. There was nothing to be done for it. Our troops took up cover beneath the river banks of the Deep Run River, made camp all over again, and then we waited.

Chapter Twenty

Many of us woke without being compelled to, our nerves were so on edge. A fog had rolled in, so thick you could scarce see the man before or beside you. It made me jumpy and irritable. We ate a little, and cleaned up after breakfast. A pleasant little creek hurried by and the water was cool and clear. We filled our canteens and bathed our faces and hands in it. Finally our orders came. We were no longer to remain there but take up a place at the advanced skirmish lines with the 15th New Jersey. Everyone rushed to pack up tents and blankets, mess kits, and rifles, and we followed the creek along its course for what seemed like ages until we came to an open field.

In the quiet stealth of the fog we organized ourselves and prepared for what was to come. Following Upton's command we began a march up the road as we advanced toward the Rebels. Right off we came under fire. You could hear the whirr of the bullets coming at us fast and thick and then all around, men began to fall or cry out in pain. Someone was yelling.

"Move out of the road! Move out of the road!"

Sam grabbed me by my coat and pulled me away from the road and under cover of the ditch that ran along next to it. We lay on our bellies and watched as the battery passed us over and moved into position in front. Our cannons fired ceaselessly and theirs fired back. Each time we were to hear their cannons respond I held my breath and wondered if a cannon ball had my name on it, if it was seeking me out from among the rest, if it was my destiny to die here today.

Occasionally we had cause to fire our guns, but mostly we just breathed the dust from the ground as we remained prostrate and helpless there. Near midmorning, the fog finally began to lift and the battle lost its dream-like quality. Below us, as if we were witnessing a performance upon a grand stage, lined in rows, grouped in columns, were more men than could be counted. We were later to learn it was sixty-five thousand men, an impressive display of might. No sooner did we have a clear view of them, than the white puffs of smoke in the distance appeared and the sounds of rifle and cannon fire began in earnest. The noise was deafening. You would hear the cannons fire and the sound of the ball flying through the air and then the explosion as it hit. It shook the ground and made the earth quake beneath us.

Like dogs, we lay on the ground cowering, completely helpless to do anything at all but attempt to preserve ourselves from the fire pouring over us like rains from heaven. If we got a fair chance at it, we returned fire, but mostly we remained at their mercy. They unquestionably had the upper hand, as they were positioned upon the higher ground just above us. I felt ill every time someone close-by fell. We were no better off than fish in a barrel.

Colonel Upton meant to encourage us as he rode back and forth on the front line now and again, making himself an easy target for enemy fire. I thought he was crazy for exposing himself that way. The fear I had for him made me sweat, made me want to cry out for him to stop, but I also thought he was heroic for not being afraid like I was.

"You've got guns, just as they!" he yelled to us. "Don't be afraid to use them!" I would have liked to have used my rifle as he recommended, but I dared not lift my head for fear of having it taken off. Each time he rode past, I kept my eyes fastened upon him, gritted my teeth, and prayed he wouldn't be hit. Some of the men grew restless from lying there with nothing to do but wait, and they brazenly jumped up to shoot, putting themselves in harm's way in the process.

From our miserable vantage point we saw the men who looked as though they had come dressed for a parade charging up the hill, trying to make Marye's Heights where the enemy was safely entrenched behind a stone wall, only to be repelled in wave after wave. There were fourteen charges in all and not a one of all of those men came even close to the stone wall running along the top of the hill which our enemy sat quite comfortably behind. Only a few made it to within fifty yards. Worse than the sounds of gunfire and cannon were the wretched cries of the wounded and dying upon the fields before us. At one point, there was an informal cease-fire from both sides as one of the Rebels, risking life and limb, left the safety of the wall and went about with canteens in hand to administer aid to the men who lay in agony begging for relief. I suppose we might have joined him if we hadn't been suspicious as to his intentions.

"Do you think we ought to go help?" I asked.

"I don't know what he's up to…" Sam said with suspicion in his voice.

"What if he's trying to lure us out so that the others may dispense with us?" Big Frank suggested.

"Seems as though he's just giving out water to the suffering," Reed Haney added. "Maybe we *should* help him."

"You'd be plum fool crazy to leave cover and put yourself out there in the open," Marcus said. His scorn gave me second thoughts. There was a little voice in my head telling me I ought to go minister to the dying, I ought to go help that young man, but there was also a nagging doubt, persistent and loud in my head, giving me pause. And so I stayed where I was in the ditch and didn't go to help.

I noticed Vern Stapleton had a bead on the boy. I wondered how many others were ready to shoot him down. How many others had him marked? I was more than a little concerned for him.

"Vern, don't even think of it!" I managed to grow bold enough to say.

Vern smiled, inched his finger closer to the trigger, as though he would do it anyway. I thought for sure the Good Samaritan was as good as dead and I clenched my jaw waiting for the report of the rifle, but Vern was just toying with me. He didn't kill the boy after all.

Later I was sorry I hadn't had the courage to venture out, and help him give the wounded a drink. When he'd finished his task, he launched himself back over the wall. The cease-fire was ended and the noise and fighting began again.

This was how it played out all day long, until nightfall came and the Rebs yelled down to us to "Stop firing now, Yank!" A group of a dozen or more men from our infantry were brave enough, under the guise of darkness, to elude enemy fire as they crossed an open stretch of field, then back over the pontoons, to get supplies. They brought us back food enough to hold off the hunger awhile. We ate a bit of hardtack. We sipped from our canteens, doing our best to leave enough provisions for the next day. Filled with apprehension, we managed to sleep where we were, lying upon our riffles.

"How much longer do you suppose we'll be stuck here?" I murmured to Sam.

"Don't know. We can't keep it up much longer. We're barely hanging in as it is. Never seen such a slaughter."

"Every time there's a failed charge, I thought well, that's it. But then they send another up the hill," I lamented.

"Got a feeling they'll be sending us in soon."

"You think?" I felt the immediate effects of fear and the prickle of the hairs on the back of my neck. I knew if we charged up the hill it would be with the same results. We would be dead like all the others.

"I don't know. I only know it can't go on for much longer. Look, it's a hard thing," Sam whispered, "but we must try to rest. Who knows what tomorrow will bring."

It reminded me of the talk we had just yesterday. As much as I appreciated Sam looking out for me, it wore on my nerves. I didn't want to be told what to do or what was good for me right then. My patience was gone after the long hours of being in peril.

"All right," I replied. I got as comfortable as I could and closed my eyes. But the day's events played out in my head in the darkness behind my eyelids. I couldn't sleep. I kept checking Caleb's watch, holding it up close to my face, squinting in the moonlight to see what time it was. After several torturous hours in that manner, I finally drifted off into a troubled sleep.

The next morning General Burnside attempted again to overtake General Lee in his fortress. Again he was repelled far too easily. Our numbers were greatly depleted after another full day, and it became obvious this had not been a battle but a slaughter. With nothing left to do for it, the General admitted defeat. As we lay in the ditch to the side of the road, ducking the bullets, he decided it was time to get while the getting was good. Sometime after midnight we were ordered to retreat.

Back over the river across those accursed pontoons, through the field where we had camped earlier, and on we went. Burnside cleared us all out before the light of a new day could greet us. When the Rebs woke, they found the place completely deserted. Later, under

the flag of truce, we worked alongside the very men we were shooting at just the day before in order to bury the dead. Now that I had
grown accustomed to decaying bodies, I worked quickly and skill-
fully at it. While we worked, it was not hard to see our dead were far
more numerous than that of the men dressed in gray. We had been
overwhelmingly defeated. And somehow the 121st had managed to
avoid combat yet again.

We departed Fredericksburg relieved to be alive. We marched with
our tails between our legs, eager to find a place to rest and recuperate,
to lick our wounds and try to become strong again. As we marched,
I thought we were headed back to Belle Plain. We never made it
that far. Instead we came upon the White Oak Church, and that is
where we stayed. The uppers decided to use it as a hospital for the
wounded. The building itself was not a very impressive structure. It
was shaped like nothing more than a large box. The soldiers stripped
the wood siding away from its bottom half to use in constructing
huts, making the church look rather pitiful. The army in its entirety
set up for winter camp all around it.

Once we had made camp, I wrote to my father and told him I
was working at the church. I told him how lovely it was, and how it
gave me great comfort to be in a house of worship. Yes, I lied to him,
but some of what I wrote to him was true, about the men we lost
and how they died. I couldn't seem to stop myself from remembering
them and sharing some of my sadness.

Camp life was a tedious life, mostly boring and filled with predictable
and loathsome routine. Some evenings the camp was full of the music
of drums, fife, and horns as the band played for us. Also, Big Frank
had a fiddle he played impressively. There were times when I felt close
to tears when he chose to play a hauntingly sad tune I didn't know
the name of. He also played lively tunes we all endeavored to sing
along with, tunes like "We Will Hang Jeff Davis from a Sour Apple
Tree" and "John Brown's Body" and "The Star Spangled Banner."

Most every night you could find men gambling with cards, or
playing a game to amuse themselves. There were evenings when Sam
and I went foraging for food, or explored our surroundings to see what
we could see. We were exceptionally good at foraging and got sent
out often. There were also times when we wrote letters home. Some
of the others wrote in a journal, which I was too fearful to undertake.

It got easier for me. The men who were suspicious of me began to treat me fairly civil. All but Vern Stapleton tolerated me. Vern, however, did all he could to make me miserable. It was little things, nothing too obvious because he knew Sam wouldn't tolerate it. Flicking me with his fingers, knocking me in the head, bumping into me to try to intimidate me, things that a school yard bully would do.

Sam told me, "I don't like Vern, not a bit. I know he's making it hard on you. Now, I want you to know I'll say something to him on your behalf if you'd like me to. Don't know what good it'll do, but I will."

I smiled half-heartedly because I thought it was a kind gesture, but I knew Sam shouldn't do what he was offering. "That would only serve to provoke Vern further," I told him.

"Vern is rotten to the center. He only harasses you to make himself feel like a big shot."

"Well, I suppose he is doing a good job of it. I keep thinking he'll tire of it, and one day just give it up and move on to something else. But his determination is beginning to make me wonder."

"Vern Stapleton is silly and childish. Never you worry, Frank. We all know who would win in a pissing contest. Don't let him get to you." I couldn't tell him I would most certainly lose such a contest.

One day Vern was taunting me about my bathing habits, when he knew it was safe and there was no one around who would intercede on my behalf. None of them knew I waited until everyone was asleep and then I went in the dark of night to bathe. I suppose they thought I didn't wash at all. It was winter so mostly we all just washed ourselves from a bucket or basin or whatever we could get our hands on, anyhow. It was too cold to head for the river, so I didn't see how he should have such a problem with me not bathing in the first place. The mocking continued and Sam wasn't around, so Vern grew confident. It escalated until he grabbed hold of me and hauled me off to the river.

I did my best to resist. I pulled away every chance I got, but he just kept hold of me and towed me along. I was yelling and pleading for him to let me go. I set my boot-heels to the ground and struggled to keep him from dragging me any further, but Vern managed to get me close enough to the river to toss me into the frigid water. I coughed and sputtered, and then he waded in, grabbed me by the pants, and held me fast as I urgently worked to get away from him.

Chapter Twenty-One

"You know, Frank, I never seen you wash. I mean to say not *once* in all this time," he said, ever so casually. His tone was matter-of-fact, as if it took him no effort at all to hold on to me while I resisted him with all of my strength.

"Let me go!" I was begging. I thought he might drown me. Did he know I couldn't swim? My struggle began in earnest. I was twisting and striking out, doing my best to break free, my arms making a big splash as I battled to escape him. But he was as calm as a summer's breeze. The more I fought against him, the more he seemed to enjoy it. I can't say how long this went on, but it seemed a lifetime to me. I knew his intent was to hurt me and this was only the beginning. He was toying with me, like a cat does a mouse or bird just before he ends its life.

"Vern, let him go." In my state of alarm, the words hardly registered. But I recognized the voice at once. It was Sam.

Vern didn't seem to waver. He held fast to me. "I had nothing but his best interest at heart," he told Sam, who was standing on the bank of the river looking down upon us.

"You haven't got a heart!" I screamed, still flailing frantically. "Sam! Sam! Please help me!"

"He stinks. I thought I ought to tutor him on how to bathe."

"Let him go," Sam said again firmly.

At this point Vern relaxed his hold on me just enough. I was frightened beyond all reasoning. I don't know just how I did it, but

I managed to wrap myself around his body and hoist myself up on his shoulders as though I were climbing a rope. I accidentally ended up dunking him.

"He aims to drown me!" I was yelling to no one in particular.

"Put your feet down, Frank. It isn't that deep," Sam advised me. I did as he said, and sure enough it was only about shoulder deep. Feeling foolish, I hauled myself to the bank of the river, shivering and shaking from the cold.

Vern stayed where he was. I suppose he thought he was safe there because Sam wouldn't come in after him. Sam stood with his arms crossed, looking very angry, waiting.

"You ought to lay off of him," Sam said, ignoring me as I coughed and gagged and trembled just next to him.

"I was only trying to help him out," Vern maintained.

"Bull," Sam said. "That's bull and you know it." Sam turned to me and said, "Go on back to camp, Frank. Get yourself together. Vern and I are going to have words."

I walked away, grateful to still be alive and eager to put some distance between myself and Vern. Oh, how I hated the fellow. The bitterness welled inside of me. I hurried back to our little cabin and quickly changed into my spare uniform before Sam could return. I sat close to the fire to try to warm my hands and feet and dry my hair. After a while Sam came back all ruffled and filthy.

"He shouldn't bother you no more," Sam informed me.

I knew something had gone on, but I didn't say anything and he didn't say anything. I caught sight of Vern Stapleton over supper. His face was battered and bruised. His expression told me straight-away his feelings for me had not changed, but he didn't say a thing and would hardly glance my way. I was hopeful Sam interceding for me would put an end to his tormenting. Yet another reason to be grateful to Sam.

Shortly before Christmas, a wealthy Northern man came through distributing handkerchiefs to the troops in camp. He was an older frail looking gentleman. Big Frank had gotten the lowdown on him. He told Sam and me all about it. It amused me some that at times Big Frank reminded me of the women back home who were busybodies. The same women who had to be in the know on all of the goings on and made sure to share with everyone what information they had. I noted that passing things on gave him a particular joy that I thought uncharacteristic of most men.

"He's a wealthy textile mill owner from Massachusetts, or was it Maine? Anyhow, he wanted to show his patriotic fervor by giving as many enlisted men as he could a handkerchief."

"That's useless," I complained. Both Sam and Big Frank seemed mildly surprised by my outburst. "Well, what do we need a handkerchief for when we've got no beef, no warm clothing, no woman within miles to even offer a handkerchief to anyhow?"

They both chuckled at me, as though they found my complaint infinitely amusing. Regardless of its practicality, we all dutifully lined up when the older man came through distributing his wares. He went down the line giving his thanks to us. Saying things like, "I can't tell you how deeply my gratitude runs," or, "If not for you our country would be in ruins," and other such patriotic sentiments.

He handed a piece of fine, white linen cloth to me. I accepted it and respectfully said, "Thank you, sir."

He looked on me with a sufficiently concerned expression on his face. "No more than a boy in the bloom of youth. What a brave lad…" To my horror he patted me on the head. I saw Vern and Rueben snickering and I grew angry, but there wasn't much I could do so I bit my tongue and bore it.

He made his way down the line and came to Vern. "Thank you, sir. Awful good of you," Vern said, shaking the man's hand enthusiastically.

"It's a small token for the gratitude I feel for your service to our great country. I wish it were within my ability to join up myself. Get some of those gray-backed, gobble-talking cowards myself if I could." His words were filled with such contempt, such hatred it surprised me. He certainly didn't seem the type to talk in such a manner.

Vern's face spread in a great big grin. "I hear you," he said with gleeful satisfaction. "I got my fair share, that's for certain."

"Well, bless you. Next time you get a few for me, won't you?" the man said.

"Oh, I will. You can count on it."

Then the man went on down the line, handing out his handkerchiefs. I looked at Sam with an exasperated roll of my eyes. "What a liar," I whispered. Sam smiled broadly and winked at me.

When the man was out of ear shot and was engaged in talking with someone else, Sam said to Vern, "Hey, Vern, I'm just curious… What's a *fair share?*"

"What are you going on about?" Vern shot back defensively. But he knew that Sam was having some fun at his expense. None of us had killed any Confederates yet, and his bragging was nothing more than a lot of hot air.

"You just told that man you got your *fair share*. I'm just wondering, number-wise, what would you say a fair share was?"

Vern grew indignant. "Why don't you shut your mouth, Barlow?"

"Now, Vern, no need to get defensive. I was just, you know, for future reference, trying to put a number on *fair share*."

Vern didn't say anything more. He scowled at Sam and then stomped off, most angry that he had been made a fool of in front of the others. Sam and I laughed at him loud enough that he could hear us enjoying his displeasure as he fled.

"He can dish it out but he can't take it," Sam said with a shake of his head.

"You just made my day," I told him. "Did you see his face?"

"Frank, be civil," he said as though he were scolding me. I took the handkerchief I had been given, fluttered it in the air ceremoniously and then bowed stiffly to him.

I saw a colored man for the first time in the camp there. Some of the escaped Negros came through on occasion, now that we had set roots and stayed in one place. We were a safe stopping place for them on their way north. He was a big man, noticeably so, with a frame he only could have built through hard labor. I thought his skin looked like a good rye bread, smooth and rich dark brown. I did my best not to stare, but it was difficult to keep from being curious after everything that had been said about them and all of the to-do over should they or shouldn't they be freed.

He had a deep sorrow in his eyes which reminded me of my father. I didn't know his history, but I felt empathy for him still. You don't appear so worn, so knowing, without earning it the hard way. He must have seen some hard things.

"What are you staring at?" Sam wondered.

"I've never seen a colored man before," I whispered.

"Two arms, two legs, two eyes, two ears, a nose and a mouth, just like us. Nothing to look at," Sam said pointedly. He was trying to tell me to stop staring.

"I know. I'm sorry," I replied, forcing my eyes away from the man. "I didn't mean to be rude."

We lived the simplest of lives there in camp, with nothing much to call our own. Not like our superiors. The officers had spacious and comfortable tents with cots. They were allowed a trunk of personal possessions which we hauled about on the mule wagons wherever we went. They had some furnishings, such as tables and chairs too. I heard, but didn't know if it is true, the general had his own hen for laying eggs, and he had them fresh for his breakfast each morning. They lived a more easy existence than the rest of us. I would have liked very much to have a meal at a table, instead of squatting around the fire with nothing good to eat anyhow.

We tried to make the place as livable as possible, so we were as comfortable as could be. Sam and I built a structure made from hewn logs, about six feet by six feet, long enough for a man to lie down stretched out, wide enough for two men to sleep side by side, but not much bigger. The bottom half was stacked like a log cabin, while the roof was just our shelter tent tethered around the logs to keep the elements out. You had to duck down to get through the door. When you entered into the cabin itself, you could stand straight at the middle point, otherwise you had to crouch to walk about. We lined the dirt floor with wooden planks, so we didn't have to sleep directly on the cold ground. At the rear of our little home we made a fireplace from rocks, the chimney an old wood barrel.

When the wind howled and the cold was nearly unbearable, it was a refuge. It was not as warm as I would have liked but better than just sleeping in our tent. To have a fire was nice. I grew very fond of our little shelter. I felt safe there.

The camp was surrounded by a forest of giant oaks, so the woodpile was stocked and the fuel plentiful. Between drilling we went out and cut wood for the pile. I strung up a rope so I had a line to hang the laundry from. I knew it was wrong of me, but I thought of it as me and Sam's homestead. When the weather grew terribly cold we huddled before our small fireplace and were content. We hunted occasionally and ate pheasant or rabbit or squirrel which we cooked at our hearth, otherwise we existed on the meager rations the army provided. Little food and no supplies were given to us.

One day I told Sam my last pair of stockings had worn through. When you have only one pair and you wear them day in and day out, they wear out quickly.

"Do you suppose the sutler might have a pair for sale?" I asked him.

Sam looked doubtful. "Oh, I suppose he'd have a pair, but as to the price, I don't know that you could afford them."

"Well, I must try. I've got nothing to warm my feet, and my shoes are rubbing me raw," I complained.

The next day I went to the sutler's wagon, where he had displayed all sorts of wares. Many of the soldiers tried very hard not to have to use his services. They resented being taken advantage of and having a man who made a profit off of their misfortunes. But there was no place else for me to get a pair of stockings, so I considered it a necessity. I glanced over his offerings with a desire for them all, a kettle, some mugs, proper silverware, boots, and pants, and herbs and ointments. Doing without for so long made all of these things seem like riches to me.

"What can I do for you, son?" he asked.

"Why, you're Mr. Davies the town tinker!" I said in surprise. I knew this man; in fact I had seen him many times before back home. It was difficult for me to reconcile myself to the fact it was Mr. Davies. After all no one liked a sutler. They took advantage of the men fighting for our country and benefitted from their misery. It was common knowledge a sutler would rob you blind if he should get the chance to. I was a little unsettled to recognize this sutler was from back home. I knew him, even if it wasn't very well.

"That's me, Davies," he said. "What can I do for you?" He gave me what was meant to be a friendly smile, but it was a smile I did not trust. I wasn't sure why. It seemed as though he had a devious glint to his eyes and a serpentine curl to his lips.

I browsed over his selection a second time and then offhandedly asked, "Do you happen to have a pair of stockings?"

His smile grew broader still. "Why, yes indeed, I do just happen to," he affirmed. "Nice thick wool pair, knitted by the delicate hand of a woman who knows her craft. They sure might come in handy for a march or two. And in this cold weather…Why, they'd keep your feet good and warm."

He didn't need to sell me on them. I was already desperate to have them. But I did my best to act only mildly interested. He probably saw right through me.

"Well, now, how much would you ask for such a thing?" I said, trying to keep the desperation from my voice.

"Pair of stockings…" He scratched his chin thoughtfully. "Oh I'd say five dollars."

I could have fallen over in shock. It was the worst case of robbery I'd ever heard of. "Five dollars?" I gasped. "Five dollars?"

"That's what I said."

"Who could afford it?" I wondered.

"Well, if you can't, someone will." He chuckled.

I huffed, and puffed, and opened my mouth as if I might say something more, but nothing came out. Then I thought, *I'll not let him have the satisfaction of a rebuttal.* So I turned on my heels and I stormed off. It certainly didn't serve to chasten him. I could hear him laughing at me as I walked away.

Chapter Twenty-Two

When I told Sam what had happened he laughed too. "No conscience whatsoever, the blackguard," he said.

"It isn't funny. It's robbery! How can he get away with it?" I fumed.

"Easy. He's the only one to sell to our regiment, he can charge whatever he likes," Sam informed me. "Don't feel bad, it isn't just you. He takes equal advantage of everyone. From what I hear, all them sutlers do. Not a man I've met has had anything good to say of 'em."

"But he always seemed such a nice sort back home," I complained.

"You didn't know him all that well," Sam said. "He was never the dependable kind. And I've seen him carrying on with a lady for whom you must pay to be in her company. I'm afraid our dear Mr. Davies is thriving in this environment."

"You don't say," I replied, thoroughly scandalized. I don't suppose Sam would have shared this bit of information with me if he had known I was a woman. It wasn't the sort of thing you discussed in polite society.

"Oh, yes. He is the bane of every soldier in the 121st. If he must rake you over the coals for a dollar's sake, well, then by gosh he'll do it. No one would be sorry to see him come under enemy fire. Or friendly fire for that matter."

"What will I do without stockings?" I wondered.

"Do as some of the other men have done. Tear some strips of cloth and wrap your feet in them. It's better than nothing," he asserted.

I did as he suggested. I took some cloth, ripped it in long broad strips and wrapped it around my feet and ankles. It didn't help much with blisters, but at least my feet were a little warmer. I vowed to get me a pair of stockings as soon as possible. Strange how the smallest of comforts can be taken for granted until you are forced to do without.

We were required to drill during the days, sometimes with only our Company H, sometimes with the regiment, and sometimes with all of the men, thousands and thousands of us upon the field, but our nights were free. Most nights Sam and I sat with the others and talked and visited, and sometimes we were alone in our cabin. Sam taught me to play at chess, although he said I should never think to gamble my hard earned money on the pastime. He told me a fool and his money are soon parted. And with how I played chess I knew he was right. I would never win unless I betted against myself.

Sometimes we went down to the river to help unload boats bringing supplies in to the army. They came through sporadically and we worked to unload them in exchange for provisions, which was how we acquired extra food and a very little money. We still had not been paid in all the time we had been in the army. Finding work helped take the edge off as we waited for our money to finally be distributed.

"If I ever get paid," Sam confided in me, "I may just have enough for a down payment for a farm of my own when this is all over."

"You think you'll be a farmer?"

"I don't know if I'll be dedicated to just farming. I thought once I might become a preacher, you know. Considered it seriously for a time."

"I didn't know that. What made you change your mind?" I wondered, surprised by his admission. Sam a preacher? I could maybe see it. He was a serious sort, not like some of the other men around here, and I knew that he thought of God and religion because sometimes he talked of it, but when I thought of the pious Reverend James back home I could not picture Sam doing his job.

"I couldn't decide for sure if that's what I wanted to do. I was conflicted. And then my father told me if I chose to devote myself to it he would certainly be proud, but there was no reason to become a preacher if I had any doubts about it. I could dedicate myself to God and live a worthy life as a farmer, miller, butcher, baker — anything I chose, just as easily."

"What a nice thought. So you changed your mind and decided on farming?"

"I plan on owning a nice farm, but I'll probably continue to work with my father too."

"What sort of a farm would it be?" I wanted to know. "Would you deal in beef, or dairy, or would you grow a crop?"

"I don't expect I'll focus on just one thing," he explained. "I'll have a milk cow, and cows for beef. I'd like to grow enough for feed and for my family too. I might have an orchard for apples and peaches. And a fine barn for my livestock. More like a gentleman's farm. There's a place back home I've got my eye on. It'll provide nicely for my family and then besides that I could still help run the mill."

"Yes, it all sounds good," I agreed. "I'm of the same mind."

He smiled, as though he were amused by me, as though he were humoring the naïve kid. But I didn't care really. It was a pleasure to hear him share his plans for the future. I so very much desired to be a part of them.

"You don't have any plans all your own?"

"I thought once to be a teacher," I admitted.

"An honorable profession. Although it don't pay much," he commented.

Moments like those made it seem worthy of me being there, of me lying about who I was. Being so close to him, having him confide in me, sharing his aspirations and dreams of the future with me, it was all I could have hoped for, except for the fact that he was sharing them with Frank and not Serena. I sorely wanted him, and being with him day in and day out, so close to him, made the wanting all the more desperate. But these were things I kept to myself, things I allowed to stew inside of me and oh, they burned with flames that at times felt as if they may very well consume me.

Some nights, with the glow of the waning fire to give off the faintest light, I would stay awake and watch him while he slept. He had a fine face that was uniquely his, with a strong square chin and perfectly formed brows the color of his dark hair. His nose was slightly lopsided from having been broken, which I thought gave his face character, and he had a small round birthmark upon his right jawline. When he shaved he had to take care not to cut it. His lips were neither thick nor thin, and seemed to me to be the perfect size and shape.

I ached to reach out and touch his birthmark, to run my fingertips across those lips of his and see if they were as soft as they looked.

In the morning I trained myself to get up before him so that I could get his breakfast. It was a small thing, but I reasoned it was one less thing he had to worry over. In the beginning he protested, but then he gave in, and simply said a polite thank you after he had eaten. Always he treated me as he would his little brother. It was something I learned to settle for, although at times I begrudged it sorely.

Just before Christmas, Sam got a package from his family. They sent him some foodstuff, and mittens and a scarf to keep him warm, and a jug of cider, some candles and a razor, all things he would have had to purchase from the sutler if he hadn't gotten them from home. I enjoyed watching him pull the gifts out of the crate, seeing the pleased look he wore.

They included a newspaper in his package and he read it aloud so I might know of the news from home. He read an article about the Copperheads, a group that was gaining more and more support up North. This group was bent on ending the war no matter the cost. They felt that we should make amends with the South, accommodate them, let them go their own way and allow them to decide for themselves the slavery issue. They wanted peace without regard for the Union or for the slaves.

"No wonder we've had no success," Sam said after reading it to me. "We haven't been sufficiently chastened. If we are to win the war, God will have us earn it first. And if we are to win, it will not be on account of these weak men who are nothing more than appeasers."

"After Antietam I have begun to see why they might think we should seek peace. The loss of life on both sides was so terrible. I don't believe God would want such suffering to go on," I replied.

"So rather than kill the dragon, you'd have us sacrifice a virgin every year?"

I balked at his response. "I certainly didn't mean it like that."

"If we don't stop this here and now, our very liberty is at stake, and we will forever after pay the price. The thing about an appeaser is that he will sacrifice the virgin till there are none left to give. And what then?" he asked.

"I don't know, Sam. It's a hard thing to see such destruction and not wonder what it's all for. I'm not saying that I agree with the Copperheads, but I do feel that war is an evil thing."

"We see eye to eye upon that," Sam agreed. "But I do believe that God would have us fight a righteous fight. He would have us fight to defend our homes, our freedoms, our liberties. It's not his will that we should bow down in submission because it's the easy thing to do. There are principles of great importance at stake here."

"But how will you change their minds? How will you get them to see their folly?" I asked. "Because they have a firm conviction that they're right just as much as we believe we're right."

"Let the fighting venture up North," he said. "That ought to bring them to an understanding of what this is all about. There's nothing like misery and suffering in your own backyard to rouse you to your senses and spur you to action, give you a good sense of indignation."

Indeed many of the other men had the same strong opinions. They said similar things, only with more name-calling, and less religion. I agreed with Sam on much of it, especially after hearing him word it as he did, but in my mind the mass slaughter of so many human beings was a hard thing for me to ignore, a terrible thing to try to justify.

Christmas came, but not in quite the usual fashion. There wasn't much to celebrate, what with our overwhelming defeat in Fredericksburg, but we managed to enjoy ourselves as much as possible. I grew melancholy thinking of Father. I knew my mother was not much company. He was essentially alone without me there. Perhaps he would celebrate with our neighbor, his dear friend, George Dobbs. George had a daughter he and Father had hoped would someday marry with Caleb. Yes, maybe George and his wife would have Father over, keep him company.

When Caleb was alive, Christmas was always a joyful affair. That was when we prospered, when Father had a son to help around the farm. Mother would read us the story of our Savior's birth from the Bible in Luke chapter two. She read it with such feeling that we might have thought we ourselves had been there with the wise men and the angels and the shepherds to see the babe. We would sing songs as Mother and I baked all morning long. And while our baked goods were still warm we would wrap them in cloth and climb into the sleigh Father had made ready. We had two horses then pulling the sleigh for us. Last year we had to sell off Billy and now just had old Gus. But back then the two pulled our sleigh as we made our rounds.

I loved riding in the sleigh. Father made us so warm and comfortable. He would load us with blankets and our feet rested on hot bricks that he had left on the hearth to heat. Off we went to visit friends and neighbors. We were served eggnog and wassail and we would pass out our baked goods while our bricks warmed on their hearth before we were off again.

When we returned home in the evening, we would exchange a gift. My favorite gift was a china doll. Mother said the doll was hers when she was but a girl, which only made her more precious to me. She had brown hair and blue eyes and a dress of pale blue satin and little black leather slippers upon her feet. But that was many years ago. I kept her in my hope chest with the intent to give her to my daughter someday. Those were far away times which only served to make the present more difficult to endure. I tried not to think about it so I wouldn't feel so sad.

There was no drilling on Christmas Day. We were permitted to pass the time as we wished, something I was pleased with. For the first time in a long while, I slept in. I must have gotten a good two hours of extra sleep. When I awoke Sam had a surprise for me.

"Merry Christmas," Sam said, offering me a tin mug.

"What is this?" I asked him, sitting up and looking into the mug.

"Just try it and see," he said.

I took a sip from the mug and felt as if I were in heaven. "Warm cider!" I exclaimed. I could feel the heat of it slide down my throat and spread through my chest. It tasted better than anything I ever tasted before, on such a bitter cold morning. While the snow fell and the chilly winds howled outside we drank cider that had been heated over the fire.

"You must not drink it all now," I told him. "Don't you want to save some for later?"

"It is Christmas and I will drink every last drop of it," he said with a smile. I supposed it wasn't such a bad thing. The rest of the army was enjoying a bit of whiskey in their morning coffees. This seemed a small indulgence in comparison. I let him fill my glass again.

"This is some treat," I told him. "Thank you for sharing in your good fortunes."

"That isn't all," he said. "I've saved my mother's sweet bread for our breakfast."

The bread was filled with dates and nuts and was a welcome change to our normal fare. I tried to eat it slowly, to savor each bite. There would be no sweet bread once it was gone. It would be back to those hard crackers they gave us for bread. So I lived in the moment and took the time to truly appreciate it. How had I never noticed what a gift good food was? How had I not noticed before what cheer a hearty bread or stew could be? Had I really taken so much for granted?

"Have you ever tasted something so good before?" I asked Sam.

"No, never," he said, his mouth full of bread.

"I cannot think the last time I've had sweet bread."

"Forever ago," he agreed.

"You'd think the army would try to feed us well, if they wish us to claim any victories for them," I complained. "You'd think they would feed us sweet bread every day, all day."

"We would not be near so grateful for it if we hadn't been deprived for so long. If we had it every day we would take it for granted, think it was nothing special."

"True. But I wouldn't mind taking it for granted."

He laughed. When we had finished another slice of sweet bread and the cider was gone, Sam said, "Now for a gift."

"What?" I asked. I wasn't sure what he meant.

"These are for you, Frank," he said pulling a pair of stockings from beneath his blanket. "May you wear them ever in good health."

I was surprised to say the least. I took them from his hands and ran my fingers over them with my mouth agape and my eyes wide.

"Stockings! But, Sam, where did you get them from?"

"I asked my mother to send them," he said.

"Well, but *you* must have them. I can't take your stockings."

"I asked her to especially send them for you. She knitted them herself," he boasted. "I warned her against red wool. I didn't want to get you killed on account of your stockings."

I laughed. "It is so generous, but I have nothing for you."

"I didn't expect anything in return," he informed me.

"Yes, but you're my good friend. You have made my Christmas first-rate, and I sincerely wish I could do the same for you," I told him.

He acted as if he were uncomfortable by my statement. Perhaps it was too sentimental. I tried to alleviate the unease by diverting the subject. I pulled my boots off and tugged my new stockings on.

"They fit right nice," I said, wiggling my toes in them. "Your mother has a fair hand for knitting."

"And baking," he said, stuffing another piece of sweet bread into his mouth.

"You must write to her and tell her thank you on my behalf," I said.

"I will."

It was a terrible cold day, but it didn't seem to hinder anyone's wanting to celebrate, despite being homesick and missing loved ones. The band played Christmas hymns all the day long, to keep our spirits high. Supper was good enough. Fresh ham for the first time in a very long time, a soup of beans with chunks of fresh meat, and coffee. It went a ways to bringing cheer to us all. After supper a group of us went about spreading our good will with song. Big Frank and his deep bass was something to hear. They went from tent to tent singing "Silent Night," "Oh Little Town of Bethlehem," "Hark the Herald Angels Sing," "God Rest Ye Merry Gentleman," and my favorite, "Oh, Holy Night."

As night fell we could spot the distant points of light dotting the horizon across the river. The Confederate army was doing their best to celebrate too, I suppose. We could hear their band playing and their voices in song as well, as faint as a memory. Just another reminder that they were human too, probably just as homesick and cold as we. Who knew when we should meet again on the battlefield, but just then we both gave thanks for a baby born a thousand and more years ago. We both felt gratitude for his birth and his life and rejoiced in it on that day.

We were given another day of leisure for New Year's. To ring in the New Year we were permitted to fire the cannons. I wasn't feeling well that day, so I didn't venture far from our little cabin. I could tell I was feverish and my body ached and I was sometimes very hot with the sweats, thrusting the blankets away from me, and sometimes very cold pulling my blanket back over me and shivering.

Sam was out and about with some of the other men from our company, enjoying himself. I wanted very much to go out with him, but I couldn't bring myself to get up from my pallet. I slept on and off, having the sense to put another log upon the fire in between my napping. Luckily my discomfort passed within a few days' time. My father always said I was of a good, healthy constitution. I began to take his words seriously, for although many of the men suffered through some very grievous illnesses, on the whole I came through without much trouble.

When Sam came home to our little cabin, home to me again, his spirits seemed high. And I was glad for it. I liked to see him happy, even if I was miserable. He told me about how he and Marcus Carvey and Gaston Shriver and Big Frank had snuck across the river, eluding the Reb picket line. He said they had waited until all was dark and quiet to place a few firecrackers in the midst of the camp before they lit them.

"You never saw so much cursing and clamor!" he said gleefully. "They thought they was under attack."

"You didn't!"

"Yes, sir. And in the confusion with men running about we run off too," he said.

"They could've killed you," I pointed out.

"If they had caught us. But they didn't. Took us most of the night, hiding out and trying to get past the picket line again to get back to camp. Oh, but it was worth all of the trouble."

"I wish I could've been there to see it," I told him.

"Well, now, it was a sight, seeing them all riled. But someone as young as you ought to avoid that kind of trouble."

"You aren't much older than me," I pointed out.

"I should be old enough to know better, anyhow. But it was worth it. Oh, it was worth it."

I didn't mind that I had missed it so much when he recounted his tale. He said that they had nearly been discovered. But somehow they had evaded capture. Yet it had taken much of the night to make it back to our friendly camp. He shared this all with me before the fire in our hut.

"I'll take you along on our next mission, Frank," he said before he fell off to sleep.

While I played house with Sam, General Burnside sought to redeem himself. He endeavored to come up with a plan to take Lee's army by surprise so he might defeat him and press on to Richmond.

For nearly a month we camped at White Oak Church when we were told it was time to march again. This was somewhat of a shock to us, because we had thought to hunker down there for the winter. No one in their right mind would have come up with such a plan. All of us thought it was crazy. But we did as we were told. That was our job.

Old Burnside didn't know what he had put us in for, nor that by the end of the month he would be out of a job, and Lincoln was to move on to yet another General. It was an unseasonably warm January, and Burnside thought that good fortune was on our side. But he was terribly wrong.

Chapter Twenty-Three

To begin with, it was doomed. Burnside was smarting from the defeat at Fredericksburg and eager to prove he could do better. I suppose that the knowledge of the Rebels, only miles away, occupying the town we had lost to them only one month previous, burned him as much as my awareness of Sam sleeping next to me but not being mine to have did for me. We thought to stay the winter in our tiny cabin, but the General forced us out so we would march for him again. His plan was to surprise the enemy and take back what we had surrendered at Fredericksburg, then press on to Richmond. General Burnside wanted to cross the Rappahannock River once again and slip in to attack Lee above the town of Fredericksburg where Lee was holed up all safe and sound like a lofty bird in an elevated nest atop the highest tree.

The day before we left, Reed Haney had received a sizable package from home, from his brother and his brother's wife, filled with food of all sorts. Cheeses, breads, pies, and smoked meats. It was close to seventy pounds of food in his gifted crate. When we got the orders to march, you better believe it vexed him sorely.

"I don't mean to leave it behind!" he said. "Not after going half-starved for five months now!" He would rather share it than see it go to ruin, so Reed passed out his food to just about anyone he crossed paths with.

"Eat up!" he encouraged everyone. "Have some more! Here, here's some more of that good cheese."

We all set to stuffing our haversacks with the goods he was handing out. What didn't fit we took to eating. We were all in high spirits, gorging ourselves gluttonously upon his bounty. We stood in a large circle, dipping our hands into the crate and then cramming what we had snatched up into our mouths. There was spontaneous laughter and foolish grins on every man's face as we ate our fill. If our hands ended up empty we would dip them down into the crate again, filling it with something more until there was nothing left. Christmas had come quietly, with no real celebration to speak of, just an intimate breakfast for me and Sam, but this was merriment to rival any Christmas before. With our bellies full, bursting to the seams, we left camp for our march.

Some of the soldiers were certain we would be victorious this time. They believed with such conviction that we would push on to Richmond and end the war that they foolishly burned the shelters they had built for themselves at winter camp. After such a shameful defeat at Fredericksburg, I didn't share the same view and neither did Sam. We saw to it that our little cabin was in good repair, clean and tidy, before we reluctantly left it.

Though the nights got downright chilly, the days were pleasant and only mildly cool. Under such conditions we began our march to Fredericksburg. But the Good Lord must have had different ideas for the Army of the Potomac because at that point the skies broke open and a torrential downpour fell from the heavens. If it wasn't for the promise given to Noah after God had cleansed the earth by flood, I may have thought he had set his mind to do it again in a like manner.

For the first several hours, we bore it, vainly continuing on, until the rain became so terrible that we were drenched all the way through and the ground had turned to mud. Let me not understate how desperately bad the mud was. Mud, mud, and more mud! I hope to never see such mud again. The wagons got the worst of it. Weighed down with ammunitions, supplies, and such, they mired quickly, as did the pontoons. The teams of mules they had hitched up to pull the wagons tried to dislodge the wheels, but their strength couldn't budge them. So we were told to bind ropes to the wagons and assist the mules in their task. Without any traction under our feet we did nothing more than slide around on the ground, completely caking our bodies in the mud.

I didn't see a single man not covered from head to toe. As night came, we were a disheartened lot that had tried vainly to press on all day, only making perhaps a half of a mile headway. To make matters worse, after so many months of eating little else but hardtack, dried beef, and coffee, the food Reed Haney had passed around, the food we had eaten until it was gone, ended up making us terribly sick. Our systems didn't have the fortitude to handle such rich fare, a thing I do not wish to elaborate upon, but only to say the lot of us got the quick step and were frequently forced to find a place to do our business in desperation.

Heaped upon our discomfort was the insult of having the Rebs, who were nice and warm around their fires just across the river, take up laughing at and mocking us with derision. So much for Burnside's intent to surprise. Fighting the elements and the mud wore us out completely. I would have done anything to sit and rest. The irony of it was that every time I felt I was growing comfortable with the physical demands put upon me, it somehow grew worse. It was as if I were being shown I was not up to the task so I might not grow proud in my abilities.

With no shelter, we did the best we could to try to find cover as the rain poured on. Sam and I, along with Big Frank and Ruben Morrell, ducked beneath a wagon that was half buried in the muddy mess upon the road.

"The pigs wouldn't even find *this* suitable," Sam tried to joke. But no one laughed. It was just too painful.

I wish I could say that the new day brought a stop to the driving rain, but it did not. No, the wind picked up and the downpour came fast and steady. Every inch of us was either wet through or covered in mud. That morning, we attempted to march again, still with the cursed rain falling down upon us. Heavy at heart we got our haversacks and took things out to prepare for breakfast, but Captain Kidder came by and told us to pack up, we would not be having breakfast.

Ruben was shoving things back into his pack with enough force to tear it to pieces. He was beyond angry, as were all of us. I could hear many of the men speaking out in open rebellion against our superiors. The general mood was contentious and quarrelsome.

"Do they think to starve us?" he fumed. "That would certainly be convenient, wouldn't it? Then they wouldn't have to dig a grave, they could just bury us in the mud!"

Hungry and tired and downhearted, we continued on. The road a ghastly mess, we passed cannons with only the barrel sticking out of the thick liquid, dead livestock, their bodies mired in the oozing black sludge, and there was no end in sight. At one point I became lodged in the muck and was stuck fast.

"Sam!" I hollered. The more I attempted to extricate myself, the more firmly I became planted. It was an odd feeling to be unable to move my feet from the spot they were rooted in. I twisted this way and that, trying to pull my knees up. No matter what I did, it didn't seem to make a difference. I panicked, thinking all sorts of outlandish thoughts. What if I was stuck here for good? What if, like quick sand, it ate me whole and I drowned in this sea of mud? Along the way we had seen all of those pathetic animals mired in their death. Would I become encased in this ground and be trampled over too? It was all silly, but in my state it seemed to make sense.

Sam and Big Frank took hold of each of my hands and pulled. When I didn't come out right away, they each got hold of my belt too, giving me a terrific heave. If I could have observed it from afar, I'm sure it would have been quite laughable. Between the two of them, both strong and capable men, it took a mighty effort to get me out of that spot. When I finally broke loose, my boots were sucked right off and remained in the pit that had held me fast.

"My boots!" I yelled. "They're the only ones I've got. I can't do without them!" Getting down on my belly and thrusting my hands into the mess, I dug for them, as did Sam and we managed between the two of us to find the pair. He tossed a boot which looked more like a giant clot of mud to me. I tried to catch it but it slipped out of my hands and landed with a thud to the ground.

"There you go, good as new," he said.

When I put them back on, the insides were squishy and it was terrible to walk in them. My feet made a sucking sound with every uncomfortable step I took. I felt as though I were walking with weights tied around my ankles. I wondered if it would be better to take them off and walk barefooted.

Another night came and we couldn't have been a more dejected bunch. We had no choice but to sleep in several inches of water, huddled and shivering. We witnessed the great General himself ride up on his horse, just as dirty and wet as the rest of us, the rain pouring down upon him, his hat drooping and the water running from it like a spout down his back. He addressed Colonel Upton and then asked after our welfare.

Colonel Upton tried to look up at the General, the rain pelting him in his face so he was squinting fiercely. He shifted from one leg to the other and then shrugged. I knew Colonel Upton to be a good upstanding man who could not tell a lie, and he didn't disappoint me.

"My men are miserable, General, sir. They have not eaten proper, they have not slept proper. This is a pitiful and desperate situation, and I don't believe they can go on in this manner," Upton said frankly. "Should we still undertake to cross the river, and should we manage to overtake Lee's troops, I doubt very much my men will be up to fighting a fair and decent fight. My feeling, General Burnside, is that it would be a colossal mistake to continue."

Burnside looked positively crestfallen as he gave a curt nod and rode away at a trot. He likewise consulted several other commanding officers, as though what the colonel had said to him was not spot on. They, too, all agreed it was time to stop this nonsense and cut our losses. Seeing it was no good, the general's orders changed. We were to head back to winter camp with all haste.

I was more than pleased with the decision. At the time I was not very concerned at all about Lee or his army or over the fact they had left the Union and it was our job to get them back. Politics be hanged. All I wanted was to be dry and to get a good night's sleep.

We tramped back to winter camp in a similar manner to the one we had left in: cold, wet, and miserable. There across the river were the Rebs having some fun at our expense. Big Frank couldn't read. Often times he had sought me out to read the letters he received from home because he couldn't decipher them on his own. That is how I had gotten to know him so well. When you read about the intimate details of a man's life, you grow to feel a kinship to him.

When he saw they had posted signs he asked us, "What does it say?"

"You don't wanna know," Sam told him.

"Just tell him," Ruben growled. "He'll find out sooner or later."

"It says *Burnside's Army Stuck in the Mud*," I read. I grew angry at the insult. "And that one there with the arrow says *This Way To Richmond*," I went on. "And that one says *If You Can't Place Your Pontoon, Yanks, We Will Send Help*," I finished in a huff.

"Just look at 'em over there all warm by their fires," Big Frank said in indignation. "I ought to go over there and make 'em eat those words."

"It'll do no good to get yourself all worked up, Big Frank. It only makes them laugh harder. Besides it wasn't them that got us into this mess," Sam pointed out. I could tell he was not happy either, but that was the extent of what he would say against the general and our superiors.

"Couldn't agree more," Ruben muttered. "It was Burnside. To hell with him. He's got nothing but bad luck. Fredericksburg and now this?" He was only saying what everyone else was thinking. We all had lost confidence in his ability to lead. We all were frustrated with him.

Burnside must have realized what a dreadful mistake he had made. One thing that let me know he was sorely repentant for the trouble he had put us through was the fact that he gave us an extra ration the next morning. I suppose he then thought to keep up the men's morale by issuing all of us liquor, which turned out to be another misjudgment on his part. I refused to drink my share and so did Sam. There were some, like us, that didn't partake in the revelry. But on the whole, a great majority of the men did. So, compounding the mud and the rain and the wretched state of affairs, the men became drunk and were unable to keep themselves in check as they might with a clear head and rational thinking.

My mother taught me liquor is the Devil's vice, that Satan lives in the bottle, and after seeing what fools it makes of men, I agreed with her. Grown men wobbled about like babies that had not learned to walk, yelling insults and shamefully carrying on. I might have found it funny if I wasn't so disturbed by it.

"This is a bad idea," Sam said as we observed a man stagger around and behave like he was out of his head. Tipsy turned to dead drunk and all manner of imprudence played out. I always thought Big Frank a good fellow. But when he got drunk he was a mean, nasty type. He got into it with Sam over rations.

"That's my food you aim to take from me," Big Frank accused Sam over nothing more than a piece of salted beef.

"It's mine, Big Frank. You already ate yours," Sam said firmly. He was not unkind about it, but he was not going to give up his meal. Something I admired very much in Sam was that he took care of himself and stood his ground, even in the face of overwhelming odds. Big Frank was no small man, and he was drunk and unreasonable to make it all the worse. But Sam wouldn't bow to him, even if it was over nothing more than salted beef.

"You calling me a liar?" he accused, his indignation rapidly accelerating. He fairly sneered at Sam, daring him to say more.

"No, sir. I'm just saying this here is my beef," Sam replied matter-of-factly. I suppose never having seen him in such a mood, Sam didn't know Big Frank might become violent. Or maybe he did and still was not willing to back down. It was hard to read him as he remained calmly resolute. I have seen that look before, when his jaw begins to twitch and his expression is determined. He was not going to give in.

Big Frank stood to his full height, like a cross old bear and got pushy. "That is my beef and I mean to have it!" he asserted.

As the two of them squared off, I thought I should intervene and do my part at being a peacemaker. Big Frank had always seemed to have a soft spot for me, and I thought I might smooth things over between them.

"Now, Big Frank," I said. "You're mistaken. And you ought to know Sam wouldn't cheat you out of your fair share." I was taken completely off guard by his reaction. He turned on me like a rabid dog on its master. I saw his face, contorted with rage, his nostrils flaring and his mouth clamped shut in a grim line, and I immediately grew still. All indications were I had overstepped my bounds and was now in jeopardy because of it. There was a moment of fear that engulfed me, as my stomach pitched and my senses were enlivened.

"Nobody asked you. You're always meddling in things that don't concern you." Big Frank motioned to Sam with a jerk of his head. "Always taking up sides with him, aren't you, *little boy?* What are you sweet on him or something?"

His snide accusation hung in the air like smoke, thick and unpleasant, threatening to choke the life out of me. I suppose Big Frank didn't know how close to truth his words were. Whether he really knew or not I couldn't be sure, but it produced in me an instant reaction. I straightaway became defensive, because I didn't want anyone to know how right he was. The fact that I overreacted was obvious, but I was seeking desperately to squelch any suspicions he might have aroused in the others. Is that really what he thought, what the other men thought, or was he simply a drunk mess, lashing out at me any way he could?

"Why, no I'm not sweet on him! Why would you say such a thing?" I roared.

Sam tried to soothe me. "He's not in his right mind, Frank. Pay it no heed. He only means to make you angry. Just walk away."

"Pay it no heed? Pay it no heed? What sort of friend would say such a thing? It's downright insulting!" I fumed. "You keep your tongue in check, you great big ox!" I yelled at Big Frank, shaking from head to toe, and feeling my heart race.

"What was that you called me?" he raged.

I knew then I had said too much, but it was too late to back down. In order to save face I had to stand behind my insult. I had to be a man and not a timid, simpering girl. A man doesn't back down.

"You heard me! Accusing Sam of taking your beef, and accusing me of worse. What sort of man are you? I'll tell you what, you're no man, you're a great lumbering ox! That's what you are!"

Quick as lightning and without any warning at all, he lunged out at me and popped me good right in the nose. I felt his impressively solid fist make contact with my face in stunned disbelief. I staggered backward and then fell on my rear end with a thump. The blood began to flow right off. My eyes teared up so badly I couldn't see straight, and my head immediately began to throb.

I just sat there like a dumb fool, trying to comprehend what had just happened. I was not the only one shocked by Big Frank's response. Sam's mouth fell open for the briefest moment, his eyes bulging in disbelief, and then he launched himself with his whole body, feet in the air and all, at Big Frank, knocking him flat in the mud. The two of them were wrestling around in the muck, throwing punches at one another with savage fury. Normally Big Frank could have walloped Sam hands down, but with the drink in him, his reflexes were slower, and his abilities dulled, so Sam got a few good punches in, but Big Frank certainly had the upper hand with his size.

As bewildered as I was I managed to collect myself enough to decide I couldn't let Sam be hurt by him. I got up, my head reeling, my sight still blurred. I attempted to pull them apart.

"Stop! Big Frank, please stop!" I yelled as I staggered toward them. They were rolling around in a frenzy of motion, making it difficult to keep up with. I got too close and they bowled me over. I got up again and continued to try to break it up the best I could.

Marcus Carvey saw the row and came to try to help me. He looked at me with astonishment, I'm sure thinking we all had gotten along so well before and wondering what might have provoked such a fight. I didn't have any time to explain. I was too busy trying to separate Big Frank and Sam.

"Big Frank! Stop! You're hurting him!" I screamed. "You're hurting him!"

Marcus and I finally somehow managed to break the two of them apart, Marcus being the one to grab hold of Big Frank, and myself managing Sam by nearly lying on top of him. I looked at Big Frank from my awkward position with an angry rage I couldn't hide, nor did I wish to for that matter. Everyone was heaving, trying to catch their breath and there was a moment of stunned silence.

"What's gotten in to you anyway?" I spat at him. He didn't answer. "Look what you've done! What have you got to say for yourself?"

Without a word he broke free of Marcus, got to his feet, and ran away.

Chapter Twenty-Four

"You all right?" Sam asked me. I thought it was a fine thing for him to do, because he seemed quite unconcerned with himself. There he was with a busted lip and a black eye and he wanted to know if I was all right.

"Me? What about you? Are you all right?" I asked.

He ran his tongue along his lip to feel the damage and lick the blood away. "Well, now," he said, "I suppose I been better."

"You're a brick!" I told him.

"Me? What's a boy like you, half Big Frank's size, poking at him for? You're lucky you still got your head on, Frank." He chuckled.

"You've got a shiner for sure."

"Let me have a look at your nose," he offered. "Surprised if it isn't broke." He put his fingers on the bridge of my nose and wiggled it back and forth. I winced in pain and cried out.

"Well, you're in the gravy, Frank. It isn't broken. That's good news. Although if you had a crooked nose it might have added character to that cupid face of yours," he teased. "But you're already starting to color up. Yes, it will be black and blue for a while and you'll have to grow accustomed to the ladies looking you over for once."

I gave him a sour expression. "You don't look so good yourself," I shot back. But I wasn't really mad. I was too depressed to be mad. I couldn't have been mad at Sam anyway. Even with his insults I was unable to feel anything more than relieved. And how could I be displeased with him after he had risked so much to come to my aid when Big Frank had attacked me?

Much later, when some semblance of order began to return, Big Frank came around. He looked dejected and completely miserable as he approached us with his head bowed and his face filled with remorse. It was strange to see such a giant of a man resemble something like a child who was about to be scolded. Part of me didn't want to hear him say he was sorry. I was so ashamed for him that it made me feel just as uncomfortable as he probably felt.

He took one look at my bruised nose, the color seeping down under my eyes where it looked yellowish, and Sam's lip that was so big it looked as if it might burst, with a black eye to boot, and I thought Big Frank might cry.

"Did I do that?" Big Frank wanted to know.

Sam didn't say anything, he just gave a little nod. I couldn't meet Big Frank's eyes. It is a very hard thing to see someone for whom you care, a man who has always seemed so strong in character, have to do penance and admit he is weak. I suppose we all have something in our natures to make us fragile so we might rely upon the Lord more fully, and maybe that was why I forgave him right away, because I myself was doing my best to try to be a better person. But I couldn't be cross with Big Frank because I felt sorry for him. I also knew that Big Frank never would have raised a finger against me if he had been able to reason with himself. Why, if he'd known he belted a girl in the face, he'd probably be mortified.

"I don't know why I would've done such a lowdown thing," he said. "I just sort of snapped. But with you two…some of my good friends…"

"It was the liquor, Big Frank," I told him. Indeed I had never seen him exhibit any violence toward anyone until then. He never seemed to have a propensity for anger until he had been drinking.

"That's no excuse," he replied. "None of it is, but, well, after all that's happened, and the letters from home…I just can't take it anymore," he groaned. I knew what he was referring to. I had read the letters from home to him, or at least a great many of them, and I knew he worried for his wife who would soon give birth to their first child. I knew how I felt about Sam and how I had followed him here because I couldn't bear the thought of being away from him when he was not even a sweetheart, and I wondered what agony it must be for Big Frank to be away from his wife, knowing she needed him, knowing he wouldn't be there to see his child born. He must have worried over her welfare, must have wondered if he would ever see her again.

"My Nell's going to have the baby soon, and she has had a hard time of it," he explained. "I just want to go home. And well, what I'm trying to say is I'm sorry for what I done. I should never have turned to drink in the first place. I just sought to comfort myself."

Sam extended his hand to Big Frank and shook with him, his hand almost swallowed up in Big Frank's.

"It's over, Big Frank. I accept your apology. We're friends and I don't mean to hold a grudge over it."

Big Frank was not content with the hand shake. He embraced Sam in his oversized arms and wept like a baby on his shoulder. Sam was giving me a look to let me know he wasn't exactly comfortable with this, but he patted Big Frank on the back and let him cry it out. He sat with us at our fire that night and ate a meal with us. Before long he went off to his own hut, wishing us a good night when he left. He looked so haggard; I thought he would probably benefit from a good night's sleep.

I wouldn't be sleeping much of the night myself. I had been assigned picket duty. I hated picket duty. For one thing, I felt the burden heavy upon me to stay alert and to be on the ready in case something should happen. If I shirked my responsibility it could mean the welfare of many men, or severe punishment for me. For another, the nights were so cold, and I wanted nothing more than to be in my little cabin with a fire to warm me and Sam close-by.

When Sam had picket duty it was far worse on me. I grew lonesome and felt guilty that I was sleeping and he wasn't. I knew he probably didn't share the sentiment. He was likely sleeping just fine without me. I was nothing more than a child to Sam, a boy far from home who needed someone to look out for him. He probably welcomed the moments when he didn't have to be responsible for me, when he could be alone and have some peace.

It began snowing and the temperatures dropped dramatically. I wore my winter issued underwear, my regular coat and my overcoat, and some mittens but still felt the cold. My face began to feel numb as the flakes descended in loose fluffy flurries that melted as soon as they touched my skin. Just before morning, in the silence of the predawn, I saw him. He was as stealthy as he could be, with his great size so obviously an inconvenience to his sneaking. I didn't know it was him right off, only that someone was leaving camp…or trying to get in.

I was frightened. Should I sound the alarm, wake the others? I readied my gun, on the fear it might be an enemy soldier poking about, spying, or up to some other mischief. But then I came face to face with him, and I knew he wasn't attempting treason. At least not the spying kind of treason.

"Big Frank?" I whispered, more as a question than a statement. I couldn't understand what he was doing out here so late at night. He knew he had been caught, and he stopped in his tracks.

"Shhh! Keep quiet."

"What are you up to?" I asked him.

"I'm leaving," he told me. I right away knew this was a bad idea. Since Fredericksburg and now our ill-fated march, there had been men leaving right and left, jumping ship like rats on a sinking boat. There were severe penalties for deserters, and the men who hated the army but stayed anyhow resented it terribly, that they were there still fighting and others had ducked out and left them high and dry… Well, it was an insult to them.

"What? You can't leave," I said in outrage.

"I'm going home. I'm going to be there for my Nelly when our child is born," he told me.

"If you should get caught, they'll shoot you for it!" I warned him. "And if I let you go, I'll be in trouble too."

"Nobody knows you saw me," he reasoned. "Just don't say nothing about it. Or tell them I made you let me go. I don't care. But either way, I'm headed home today." His voice was firm and insistent.

I looked at him long and hard. All I had to do was raise my voice, call out for help. But how could I turn him in? He was my good friend, and he was in danger of getting himself into some serious trouble. We regarded one another for a long time, both of us wondering what the other might be capable of, I suppose. Finally, without a word, I turned my back on him and went about my duties, as if I had never seen him, and he took the opportunity and left, on his way back to New York, back to home. I wasn't sorry I did it. He only wanted to see his wife, to see his babe. How could I have denied him that? But I did feel a dread growing within me, because I knew I had broken the rules, and I knew I would have to pay for it.

At roll call in the morning, running on no sleep and a lack of decent food, I felt drained. The threat of discovery and worrying over it can certainly take its toll upon a body. They called out each man's name and when Frank Garner was called there was no one there to answer. I noted Sam's curious gaze as they marked him gone and went on down the list. Sam knew me better than I would have liked. He knew I had something to hide. The more I tried to act like I was innocent in the matter, the more he seemed to suspect me.

We went out onto the open field and did our drills as usual. And when we parted for midday meal, Sam was upon me before I could even think of a reason to avoid him.

"What do you know of it?" he asked, as soon as we were apart from anyone who might be able to hear.

"What do you mean?" I asked.

I thought if I played innocent, he would not question me further. But he gave me a shrewd smile and said, "You know what I mean, Frank. Don't play dumb. What happened with Big Frank?"

"Why do you think I know something about it?"

"Because you do. Come on now, out with it."

"He left this morning," I said. "Before it got light out." Just like that he got it out of me. If it was someone else, I might have been able to be more deceptive, and I might have held out longer. But I couldn't lie to Sam. I felt the irony of the painful realization that was exactly what I was doing. I was a liar. I lied to him every day!

"You let him go?" Sam pressed.

"I tried to tell him he shouldn't leave, but he wouldn't listen. He was set on it. He wanted to see Nelly and the baby."

"Ah, Frank. You know what they do to deserters?" Sam groaned.

"I tried to tell him that too," I said defensively. "He wouldn't hear me out. I could've shot him myself I suppose or I could've turned him in and he would have been in trouble a-plenty. And maybe that's what I should've done, but I couldn't. I just couldn't. I don't blame him for wanting to leave. What would *you* have done, Sam? If you were me what would *you* have done?"

"I wouldn't have let the bonehead run off! That's for certain."

"Well, they'll have to catch him first, right?"

"Someone as conspicuous as Big Frank, I'm sure it's only a matter of time. First off he's not exactly forgettable and second off he isn't the smartest fellow. He probably didn't even have the sense to change his coat. They see his uniform and they'll know a mile off what he's up to," Sam informed me. "And now you could get into trouble too."

"I know it. I'll just have to accept the consequences if it comes to that," I said, trying to be brave.

"Well, now, don't go telling anyone else about any of this. You keep it between you and me? You understand?"

"Yes, Sam," I replied.

"And if you get called in and they start asking questions, you don't admit to anything. You didn't see anything, all right? Don't say a word to anyone."

"Yes, Sam," I agreed.

"Not a word."

"Yes, Sam. I won't."

But when I was called in for questioning by my superiors, I dutifully followed after the private they sent to fetch me. Sam wore a sympathetic look on his face as I left to answer to them. I'm sure he suspected what I was in for. That's how it was with Sam, he knew me all too well. I looked back once, to see him standing near the door of our little cabin with his hands deep in his pockets, his head tilted to the side and his mouth turned down into a frown. I was sick to my stomach as I let the private lead me on to Colonel Upton's tent, but I did my best to keep my posture straight and my head high. After all, if you must take punishment, you may as well take it like a man.

Chapter Twenty-Five

When I came back to our cabin, Sam was waiting for me. He thought I might speak of my own accord, I suppose, but I was trying not to cry and so I didn't say a thing. I lay down upon my blanket with my face to the wall and tried to talk myself out of being hysterical. I needed to be a man about it. But you must understand that with me being a perfectly ordinary girl, I was never singled out. Neither for praise, nor for discipline. And being one who managed to stay out of trouble, it was hard on me to now be called to atone for what I had done. To have everyone's eyes upon me…to have my superior's disapproval squarely on my shoulders, it was a keen humiliation.

"Frank?"

"Huh?" I still could not look at him.

"What happened?" he asked. "Did you tell them?" His voice was quiet, concerned. I don't know why he was asking, because I knew he already knew.

"Yes," I said simply. There was silence for a moment.

"And what did they say?" he prodded.

I didn't want to talk. I didn't want to admit I was to be disciplined. I knew Sam would most certainly have pity for me, but I didn't want to be pitied, to be an object of sympathy. I did not want to feel the shame that made my chest hurt and my face feel hot. He knew. It was not something I could keep a secret, the way I had kept other secrets from him.

"Colonel Upton has assigned me thirty days picket duty so I might learn the duty well and do it right," I answered.

"That's not so bad," he tried to console. But even he did not have it in him to sound convincing. It was bad. It was very bad.

"Yes," I said again. I agreed with him because what else could I do? To state the obvious was not really necessary. We both recognized it was a severe penalty, and I deserved it too. I had willingly and knowingly let Big Frank go. It was my own fault.

After I told him, he left me alone. I suppose he understood I was not in the mood to talk. And really what more was there to say? I messed up and now I was living with the consequences. And although thirty days of picket duty seemed a horrible punishment to me, I would've done it again to help Big Frank. Because I know he would have done the same for me.

I was not the only one to be chastened for my sins. General Burnside was brought to penance as well. He was stripped of his command shortly after our mud march. Lincoln just couldn't allow the demoralization of his army to go on any longer. Burnside served a little over one month as head general of the Potomac Army before he was relieved of his post and the president replaced him with General Joe Hooker, one of Burnside's least favorite people. General Hooker was exceedingly critical of Burnside and the two had a rocky relationship. Boy, I bet that added insult to injury.

I don't know if Burnside was exactly sad to leave. He had been offered, and had declined, the position of General twice before he reluctantly agreed to it the third time. He tried to tell them he was not qualified for such a position. He knew his limits, but they did not. I couldn't feel all that angry with him like some of the others did. Old Ambrose Burnside did not want command of the Army of the Potomac, but neither did he want to be let go in disgrace.

Right off General Joe Hooker implemented changes. He reorganized us from our larger divisions into corps. We then became a part of the sixth corps. In addition, Hooker wanted to keep us distinguished from other corps, so that keeping track of us would be more manageable. We were given a cap with a red cross upon it to wear. I didn't exactly like the cap, thinking it was hazardous to my health.

"It looks like a target," I complained to Sam. "Those Rebs will find an easy aim with this on our heads." Sam thought that was tremendously funny.

Something I would say for General Hooker was he found a way to boost the men's morale. Finally, after six months of service, he saw to it we received our pay. And he promised each month at the first of that month, we should continue to receive pay. Why, you never saw a happier bunch when we each got a stack of cash, six months' worth of back pay all at once. Now this was a fine thing, but not to overshadow another improvement — the food.

Tired to death of salted beef that left you with an unquenchable thirst, and the hardtack, dry and brittle as a bone and sometimes rife with maggots, it was a great day when soft bread and an assortment of vegetables were served us. Still not as much as we would have liked, because at times we were still hungry when the food didn't come through to us in a timely manner, but it beat hardtack any day. We were all given supper duty, taking turns making supper for a group of men in rotations so everyone had the responsibility on a regular basis. I was comfortable in the fact that I must only prepare supper every two weeks or so. There were a few of the fellows who made us shudder to eat supper after they made it. They didn't cook well. But on the whole, it was a good thing.

Colonel Upton also did his part in trying to make us more contented. He petitioned the ladies from home to send us straw pallets and bedding to keep us warm and aid in our comfort. It was certainly a step up from sleeping on the dirt with nothing more than a blanket to protect you from the elements.

Didn't benefit me much. I spent the entire month of February sleep deprived and wanting nothing more than to have one night of uninterrupted slumber. During the day I drilled, but in the afternoon and again in the evening I crawled upon my straw mattress and slept like a rock, until again I suffered through guard duty all the night long. I was not able to spend time with Sam near as much, because all of my spare time was spent in sleeping. In the beginning of March, his father and two brothers came to visit.

"Frank!" he called to me one afternoon as I slept. "Frank! You must get up and see who's come to call on us!"

I was fairly groggy when I came from our hut. Had I known who it was, I might have feigned a deeper sleep. I was at once on my guard. *I must watch what I say*, I thought. I was hoping the dirt and the uniform would go a ways to making me look more like a boy. It was a good thing on my part the men here in camp were half-starved and looked thin and hollow. I didn't seem so out of place on that account, what with my puny size. When I came out, there was John Barlow and his sons Jacob and Hyrum. Stanley must have not been considered old enough to make the trip.

"This is Matthew Stark's nephew, the one I have written you about," Sam introduced. "Frank, this is my father, John Barlow."

"Good to meet you, sir," I said, accepting his hand and giving it a firm shake. I was trying desperately to seem as masculine as possible. Was it my imagination or did he look me over carefully, even curiously? Did he suspect?

"These are my brothers, Jacob and Hyrum," Sam continued. "Jacob is only slightly older than you," Sam informed me.

"It is good to meet you," I repeated, giving them a shake as well.

"Frank here has been my tent mate since the beginning," Sam told his brothers. "We take care of one another, don't we, Frank?"

"I would be sorely lost without him," I admitted. And it was the truth, but it sounded odd coming from my mouth like that.

"I'm surprised Matthew hasn't mentioned you before," John Barlow said with a great and welcoming smile. "He did send a letter and some monies along with me to deliver to his daughter though."

Sam took notice of this. "Caleb's sister?"

"Yes, the one and only," John said. "Seems he's had the devil of a time getting any letters through to her. So I suppose he thought if he sent it with me directly, I would personally put it in her hands."

"Where is she that you'd have cause to deliver a letter?" Sam asked.

"Matthew said she is serving as a nurse," his father replied. "Here with the Army of the Potomac."

Boy I could feel the heat. Was I thus to be discovered? Here they were discussing me right there in front of me. Sam looked quizzically in my direction.

"Did you know of this, Frank?"

"Yes. I do believe I've seen her a few times here and there," I replied.

"Well, why haven't you pointed her out to me?" Sam wanted to know. "I would like to say hello to her. As a matter of fact, I might have sought her out before, had I known she was so close."

"If you'd like, sir," I said to Sam's father, "I can deliver the letter for you, and then you won't need to be concerned over it any longer."

"That would be good of you," John said, pulling the letter from his breast pocket and handing it over.

"I should leave you to visit," I offered.

"Nonsense," John scoffed. "Sam's mother has sent a heap of food, and you'll dine with us this evening."

"I wouldn't want to be a bother," I protested.

"Any friend of Sam's is a friend of ours."

I could see he was adamant, and rather than argue the point I nodded my agreement and didn't say any more. Sam went to show them around camp and introduce them to others and I went back into our hut alone. Once I was sure they were nowhere around, I opened the letter from my father. He had enclosed a whole dollar within the folded pages. I knew he would have been hard pressed to come up with such money. As low as I was now, it brought tears to my eyes and I allowed myself a good cry.

Father said that he missed me. He said Mother was doing a little better, and she asked after me the other evening. He was concerned for my welfare and wondered if I might be able to visit soon. Was I well? Was I treated kindly? His tender words made me more homesick than I could've imagined. The punishment I was enduring and the lack of sleep and the cold of winter left me feeling empty and feeling fragile. Now my father's words added another weight. How much longer would I be able to keep up with my deception?

I couldn't keep the letter my father sent me. I read it and then promptly burned it, tossing it reluctantly into our fireplace for fear someone might come across it and discover my terrible lie. I watched the pages curl, and turn black, then disintegrate and float in bits of ash into the air and up out of the chimney. There was nothing left of Serena on paper or with me. She was disappearing completely. For once I seriously considered leaving like Big Frank had.

It would be so easy. Everyone would be looking for Frank Stark. I would be Serena Stark again, and they couldn't put me in prison for desertion. They couldn't put me up in front of a firing squad and shoot me. I could go home to Father and Mother and pretend this whole thing had never happened. After all, the only reason I had done such a foolish and dangerous thing was so I could be close to Sam. It was a blessing and a curse all wrapped up in one. Day after day I was with him. But not really. Not the way I had always wanted to be. Not the way a woman longs to be with the man she loves.

In some respects it was worse to know Sam the way I knew him, with his guard down in a brutally honest manner, and not have him know the real me too. Certainly I would do anything for him. And I loved him all the more for the fine man I knew him to be, faults and all. But being reminded day in and day out that my true goal was unattainable was breaking my heart. There was no way around it, Sam would never be mine. Perhaps it was time to give in to the tug of war inside of myself. Perhaps it was time to go home.

Chapter Twenty-Six

I made up my mind I would go. It was now only a question of when. There were so many men deserting that they came up with various ways of trying to stop the flow of soldiers leaving. I figured this turn of events would make it difficult for me to get away. I decided if I could just get past the guards on duty I would be home free. After all, I could easily acquire a dress and avoid suspicion entirely once I was away from here.

The resolution made me feel lighter, made me feel a lift in spirits. I had three nights of picket duty left, and I devised a plan in which I would leave on the third night. What better time than that to sneak away? I would then not have to worry about getting past the picket line, because I was part of the picket. Now that we were paid, I would have a little money in my pocket and could cover food and lodging until I got home. The farther away I got from Virginia, the easier it would be. I might even be able to take the train much of the way.

It was as if I were in a trance. I spoke when spoken to, I carried on as I ought to with my duties and my responsibilities, but in my mind I was planning. Sam was distracted with his father and brothers visiting. It did him good and it made me happy to see him so contented. I watched him with Jacob and Hyrum, and saw he treated them with the same spirit of mentoring he did me. I thought, with a sense of longing and regret, how he would make some lady a good and fine husband, and he would be a good father to some lucky child someday.

The third night of picket, I made sure I put everything I would need in my haversack. Most nights I did picket duty I didn't bring it with me. Perhaps Sam noted this. Perhaps he was just showing me a kindness as usual, I couldn't be sure. But for whatever reason it was, he took me aside at supper time.

"I have something for you," he informed me.

"Oh?" I said.

"I saved it aside. A meat pie all the way from Richfield, New York," he boasted. And he held this pie out to me, the crust all browned and beautiful.

"Your mother made this pie special for you," I said. "You should keep it for yourself."

"It's yours. And I know my mother would be glad for it," he said with a smile.

"Thank you, Sam, but you must at least have a portion of it," I tried to insist.

"No. It's for you. I've seen what a hard thing it's been for you to carry on with picket, and I know it's been difficult to do a man's work, you being so young and inexperienced in the world, but you've done it without complaint and you've done it well, Frank. You've stuck it out and I'm real proud of you. And tonight, you finish with it and things will be back to the way they should be. It will be easier now."

I wondered how much he suspected, and if this pie was a bribe to keep me from doing something foolish. The pie was in his outstretched hands, waiting for me to take it. Would I take it? But how could I not? Right then my heart sank. I knew I couldn't leave, not after all he had said to me. I gave in and accepted the pie from him. Wouldn't you know it, I ate the pie and it gave me terrible indigestion.

So I was to stay. And in a way Sam had been right. Once I wasn't so sleep deprived and the weather started to warm up, I began to feel a little better. All of us had been held up for the winter in our cramped shelters, with nothing to do but fight off the cold. Spring was finally beginning to arrive and we were grateful for the diversion. At times the wind could pick up and cause an awful stir, but for the most part we were seeing the weather improve.

One afternoon the men took up a game of baseball. This was one of the few sports I approved of. Some of the soldiers took up gambling and sadly lost all of their hard earned pay to it. At least baseball could not be the downfall of a man, unless of course, you cared to make a wager on which side would win.

It seemed some of the men took the opportunity to put away cards to observe the game and make a wager on it. Whether it was cock fighting, wrestling, horse racing or a baseball game they could turn it into a game of vice if given the chance. I refrained from such indulgences. I thought it was a bad habit, although I could understand why they took up such activities. The monotony of our daily lives had driven them to find a thrill where they could. Living among others who did not have religion, and without a good mother to guide them, they had fallen into ungodly ways.

I was merely an observer, although several of my comrades goaded me on and tried to persuade me to play. I didn't want anyone suspecting me of being a girl, and I figured if I played there would no doubt be some suspicions after my inability to hit the ball.

I watched Sam with his lean frame, naturally inclined toward athletics, hit the leather ball Vern Stapleton pitched him far out beyond the men in the outfield. Vern took off his hat and slapped it against his thigh in agitation as Sam jogged around the makeshift bases with a large smile spread across his face. His teammates pounded his back, whooping and hollering. I cheered for him too. I remembered a time when he and Caleb were the dread of anyone on the opposing team.

As I sat there observing, someone came up next to me and sat down heavy, and then bumped into me roughly with his shoulder. It took me by surprise. At first I thought to scold the fellow because I was not sure what his intentions were. I was used to Vern and his crew tormenting and harassing me. I turned with my mouth open, the words ready to spill out, but then I stopped. A smile spread across my face.

"Big Frank!"

Big Frank was grinning too. It amused him greatly to see my reaction. He looked well fed and tanned and his eyes had a merry gleam to them again. He put his arm around my shoulder and clapped his hand on my other shoulder.

"Good to see you friend," he said.

"Big Frank, what are you doing here?"

He shrugged. "I knew you all missed me so much, I figured I ought to come on back and make you all cheerful again," he teased.

As excited as I was to see him, I was experiencing a moment of panic. I was concerned for what might become of him once the superior officers got wind he was back.

"Big Frank, you've got to get out of here before they catch you," I said earnestly.

"All is well, Frank. All is well."

"What do you mean?" I asked. I was perplexed by his flippant attitude. After all, if he were caught after desertion the penalty could be death.

"Our good president wanted to encourage the men who left the army to return of their own accord. He made it so any deserter could come back without being punished," Big Frank explained.

"Really?"

"Yes, sir. I will lose my pay whilst I was away, but that's about the worst of it."

"Well, how do you like that! Come on now. We must tell Sam!" I got up and pulled him along with me. "Sam!" I was shouting. "Sam!"

Sam dropped his bat and began walking toward me, perhaps worried by my yelling and carrying on. He looked confused, until he saw Big Frank. When Sam saw him he jogged over to us, clasped hands with him and then leaned in to pat him on the back.

"Big Frank, it's good to see you again," Sam said.

"Big Frank says the president is giving a pardon to deserters if they return of their own free will," I explained.

"That's good news," Sam said. "Good, good news."

I wasn't sure what to make of Sam's reaction. He seemed glad Big Frank was back, but I thought I may have sensed some reservations in his voice. Or maybe the smile on his face was not as broad as I expected it to be. It confused me, but I let it go. If Sam wanted to say something, he would have.

We headed back to our little cabin, built up a fire and celebrated with rabbit meat and beans. Sam and I seemed to be the only two who wanted to speak to Big Frank. Everyone else steered clear of him. I noted a few even frowned when they saw him. I didn't see why they would be unhappy by his return. They all liked him before he left.

"You know when you left, I thought I'd never see you again," I confessed to Big Frank.

"Oh, now, I always planned on coming back," he said. But I remembered the night when I let him go, and I don't think he was being perfectly honest about it. I saw Sam change ever so slightly, drop his head so he wasn't looking Big Frank in the eyes and fiddle with his knife. He was acting very reserved, which worried me a little. It wasn't like Sam.

"I only wanted to see my Nell and be there when the baby came," Big Frank explained.

"And were you? Did you make it in time?" I wanted to know.

"Yes, just."

"And…" I prodded.

"And I have a fine big baby back home," he said with a very pleased expression. "You'll be glad to know there is another Little Frank in this world now," he told me.

"A boy!" I said enthusiastically.

"A boy," he confirmed.

"A Frank Junior."

"And Nell is well, but sorry to see me go," he said.

"How are things back home?" Sam wondered. "Did you have cause to go to Richfield at all?"

"No, not to Richfield. I'm lucky I was able to stay as long as I did," he confessed. "Sheriff Mather got wind I was home. He come out to my place and was intent upon arresting me."

"Sheriff Mather?" Sam said.

"Yes, sir. But I sat him down and had a talk with him and convinced him not to arrest me until the baby came. I gave him my word as a gentleman I didn't aim on running again."

"And he let you go?" Sam asked with the slightest hint of suspicion in his voice.

"That he did," Big Frank confirmed. "Many of the folks back home are sympathetic to those who leave the army. They don't want their boys to suffer, you know. They hear of the conditions we must live with and fear for our safety, and they feel compassion. Sheriff Mather blames the townsfolk more than he blames them that desert because it's the town's people that are encouraging deserters and are harboring 'em.

"Anyhow, Nell had the baby and I stayed with her for a few weeks, taking care of her needs and getting the farm in order. Well, by the time Sheriff Mather come round again, he told me about this amnesty the president offers and said if I was to come back I would be free and clear. I thought it was a fair deal, so I took it. I said good-bye to the wife and babe and high tailed it back here. And now here I am before you."

"You're a father?" Sam said with a grin, his mood changing for the better.

"I am!" Big Frank agreed.

"Congratulations," I offered.

"Thank you, Frank. It's a feeling like nothing else. You ought to see my boy, round as he is tall with a strong set of lungs. Should hear him carry on when he gets upset."

"And Nell is fine and well too?"

"Now my Nell, she is a strong woman. There's no keeping her down," he said with pride. "Looky here," he said, digging into his pocket and procuring a likeness on tin. "She sent it with me as a remembrance."

Nelly Garner was not the most beautiful woman I'd ever seen but there was something very becoming about her as she held her newborn in her arm at an angle so he could be seen clearly. He was sleeping peacefully within the cradle of her arms. Boy he was a fat thing.

"That's a fine baby, Big Frank," Sam commented. "And Nell is a handsome woman."

"Isn't she though? She wanted me to thank you most especially, Frank," he revealed.

"Me? Whatever for?" I asked.

"For what you done for me," Big Frank replied.

"He done a lot more than you even know," Sam said to Big Frank. "Frank here got picket duty for thirty days after you left as a punishment for letting you go."

Big Frank seemed sorry. "I aim to make it up to you," he promised.

I didn't care for the attention upon me, the two of them both staring. It made me squirm to have both of them looking at me. I'm sure I was red faced, and I couldn't think of a thing to say. I shrugged and tried to act like it was nothing. And really it was worth all the trouble to see Big Frank so happy. It was a whole other pleasure to hear Sam bragging on me. What an odd feeling to be the object of his praise. I fleetingly wondered if he might feel the same about me if he knew I was a girl. It was so difficult to keep it to myself, the biggest part of me I was keeping from him.

It ate me up I couldn't share it with him. But Sam was a good man. Maybe if I told him the truth, maybe he would understand… And maybe not. Maybe he would be angry with me. Maybe he would expose me to Colonel Upton. There was the very probable chance.

That night, as we lay upon the floor of our little cabin, on our straw pallets, I thought I might tell him. What could it hurt if I did? And finally there would be some resolution. It could easily end here and now. I debated back and forth, until finally I whispered to him in the dark.

"Sam?"

"Yeah, Frank?" he responded. But I sensed he was on the verge of sleep, his voice deep and sluggish, his words slightly slurred. I could tell he was just moments away from it, as if it took determination for him to speak in reply.

"There's something I need to tell you," I said softly. And then I waited for him to respond.

Chapter Twenty-Seven

S am lethargically rolled to his side, as if his arms and legs took a great effort to move. He was now facing me with his eyes still shut.

"What is it?" he asked in a half asleep voice. The silence was too much for me. My nerve completely failed me. It was as though my courage had quit me all at once, and I nearly got up and ran for the door. I knew I couldn't tell him. I was too afraid of what the consequences of my revelation might be. Maybe he would be kind about it. Maybe he would understand. But maybe he would not…

"You don't know me, Sam," I said hastily. "Not the real me anyway."

"I know you, Frank," he scoffed. The way he said it was as if he thought I was a silly fool for even suggesting he didn't.

"No you don't," I insisted. I rushed on before he could silence me. "I don't know that you would like me very well if you were to know the real me."

He let out a sigh. I suppose he wanted to sleep and I was keeping him from it.

"Frank, I like you very much. We're good friends, you and I. And there's nothing you could tell me now that would change it," he said.

Here was the part when I was supposed to blurt it out. I was supposed to come clean and tell him the truth. But it wouldn't come out. It stayed stuck in my mouth. I cleared my throat a few times and then gave up. I couldn't do it. I just couldn't.

"What's bothering you?" Sam wanted to know.

"Nothing," I murmured. "Nothing."

"Something," he said.

How was I to get out of it? I had aroused his suspicions now. He was not going to let it go because I had gotten his interest in what I was trying to say. I woke the man from his sleep to say nothing? What an idiot!

"Nothing!" I insisted. "I'm just not as good as you say I am." I paused, trying to come up with some excuse for my behavior. "You went on and on about me with Big Frank. And, well…I didn't deserve it."

"Yes you did, Frank. You let him go on home, even though it was you who had to suffer for it. Big Frank isn't in trouble at all. He got off free and clear, but you did picket duty for a whole month for it," Sam said. His voice was edged with disapproval. I remembered the impression I had of Sam being vaguely off. Is that why he seemed so strange that afternoon with Big Frank? He didn't think it was fair Big Frank hadn't gotten punished?

"I did something wrong. I suppose I got what was coming to me," I said.

"That says something for your integrity."

"I have no integrity," I insisted. "I was going to leave too." Sam did not say anything so I continued. "Like Big Frank. I was going to leave the day you gave me the meat pie. Did you know? Is that why you gave me the pie? What do you think of me now?" Not only did it feel good to say it, but it also led the conversation in a different direction. A safer direction.

"I've been lying to you. I've been lying to everyone," I went on. No more honest words had ever been spoken.

"Wanting to leave and actually doing it are two very different things," Sam finally said. "The fact that you didn't desert just shows you've got character. You are a good boy. You wouldn't leave your pals to fight while you're living high off the hog at home."

"Oh, Sam, you just don't want to see it," I continued.

"See what?"

"I am no good. I'm not worthy of your praise."

"Frank, what is it in you that won't let you see the good in yourself?" he asked. I didn't answer.

"Look," he said, "I'm not going to stay up all night and argue on behalf of you. It's too late and I'm too weary. All I will say is you've proven yourself worthy in my eyes." His statement carried a tone of finality to it, and I knew he was unwilling to discuss it any further. He rolled over with his back to me again and all was still.

It couldn't have gone more badly. Not only had I annoyed him, but I hadn't managed to get the part out about me being a girl. I had passed up my opportunity and felt like nothing but a miserable coward. There couldn't have been a better chance and I ruined it. I came so close, so very close to telling him. Why did I lose my resolve? But I knew why. I knew it was because I couldn't stand the thought of having Sam hate me. I knew I didn't want him to be cross with me or lose his friendship.

I felt tears burning my eyes, but I refused to cry. Eventually I heard Sam's even breathing and knew he was asleep. I rolled my back to him and concentrated my efforts into relaxing, doing my best to forget the struggle raging within me. I shut my eyes and forced myself to sleep. After a time my limbs grew heavy and my brain became fuzzy.

Then I was floating. It was all too familiar. The grass blew, the trees whispered. There was the faint sound of the fife music. I bobbed along upon the breeze like the seed of a dandelion, slow and tranquil, without any control over which way I went. I saw it again just in the distance. The cornfield. Every stalk cut down, every piece of corn gone on account of the battle that had taken place there.

I wanted to move away, but I had no will of my own. I was at the mercy of the wind, and the wind was moving me in this direction. I saw the men. They were murmuring in low, tragic tones. A few of them moved away and began to dig a grave off near the tree line. A handful remained. One of them was Sam. He was shaking his head with a disheartened look on his face, his eyes full of the misery of witnessing something so horrific. The men parted, and I knew what I would see. I knew with the same instinct an animal has when a predator is near. There was the body laid out upon the ground; there was the woman for whom they had dug a grave. It was me. It was me dead among the broken down cornstalks.

I fought desperately to steer myself in the other direction, to keep floating and floating until I became a small speck on the horizon and then just disappeared completely. But for some reason I was anchored to her, the girl on the ground.

I struggled against her, trying to turn back, fighting to break free. I didn't want to see her. I didn't want to feel this anguish as it welled up within my breast. I didn't want to be filled with such overwhelming fear. I was face to face with her, the pallid skin, the slack muscles, her eyes closed. I couldn't understand why I must endure such torture. And then the body spoke to me.

Her eyes fluttered open suddenly and her gaze was focused right on me, and then she said, in a dry and cracked whisper, *Serena*…She said my name all stretched out and lingering as if she were calling out to me, as if she were searching for me and could not find me. I opened my own mouth to scream, but nothing came out. There was no sound although I tried and tried to cry out. The next thing I was aware of was Sam nudging me hard.

"Frank?" he said. "Wake up."

My feet were flopping and tangled up in my blanket. I was moaning loudly, as I came out of my sleep. I looked around disoriented and frightened, breathing hard, my head pounding, my body damp with sweat. It took a brief moment for the terror to subside, for my heart to stop beating so, and then I realized I was in my little cabin. I was with Sam, and for the moment I was safe. It was a dream. Only a dream. I sat up, trying to gain control of myself. I looked over at Sam and he was watching me with his perfect eyebrows drawn together, a look of concern on his face.

"Are you all right?" he asked.

"Yes," I whispered, gulping air frantically. "I'm all right."

"You must have been having a right good one. You woke me up with your clamor."

"I'm sorry," I said, wiping my forehead with the sleeve of my coat.

"What was it, Frank?"

I sighed deeply, throwing my arm over my eyes. The impression of the dream still lingered in the darkness. So I opened my eyes and blinked rapidly to make sure this was the reality and not the other. He was still watching me, waiting.

"Antietam," I replied. I didn't need to elaborate. He was acquainted himself with the horrors of that battle. He had been there with me, digging grave after grave. Sam nodded knowingly.

"You must forget that place," he said sympathetically. And then he lay down and tried to go back to sleep. But I could not. In the stillness which followed I could hear the dead woman calling to me. The lengthy and tormented *Serena* pouring from her dead lips.

Chapter Twenty-Eight

General Hooker couldn't wait any longer. He had been patient during the long winter, and now he was ready for action. Many of the men felt the same. I suppose facing death seemed attractive enough compared to the cold and the boredom they endured during winter camp. They talked of how they wished they could have another go at it, of how they would show the Rebels by giving them a good whipping, and then send them packing back to the South.

It was spring and we couldn't continue indefinitely at camp. The war was still on and many men, win or lose, wanted a definitive outcome so they could get on with their lives, go back home to a wife and family, or go back home to find a wife so they could have a family. To be at the mercy of the army, to have no say in your life or future is a cruel and helpless feeling. One way or the other, win or lose, at least we wouldn't be in limbo any longer.

When General Hooker's plan was made known, I wondered why must every strategy involve those cursed pontoons? Back to Fredericksburg, back to the place of our humiliation of last December. Should I, an amateur at best in soldiering, point out the folly of such a plan? Wasn't it obvious when we failed so miserably and lost so many men in the Battle of Fredericksburg just how impossible and unreasonable it was to assume we could win a victory there? So why go back?

I grew weary of the fact that a few men who possessed unlimited power could hold the destiny or fate of so many who were nothing more than pawns in a chess match to them. But I was only a lowly foot soldier, and so I did as I was told, as I had done before and would continue to do. I packed up my things and moved along with the rest of them toward Fredericksburg for what I was hoping would be the last battle we must fight.

Along the way it was hard to forget our doomed march in January and the wretched mud we were forced to trample through. Then I thought of how things could be worse. In fact, the remembrances of that miserable winter boosted my spirits. We were at least on dry ground and the weather was fine for the end of April. No rain or even a hint of it. Perhaps God was on our side this time around. Once we reached the river, we could clearly see the tents and encampment of the Confederates on the other side.

Here was Hooker's plan: we should show a big presence below Fredericksburg so Lee's army would be deceived into believing we were the main body that came to fight. Yes, we were the diversion. In the meantime, Hooker would move another larger group to the northwest, trying to sneak in behind General Lee near a town called Chancellorsville. We were instructed to draw the Confederate army's attention so Hooker could then try to outmaneuver them with the second group and take them by surprise.

Many of the men were relieved to be doing something, anything, other than sitting around and waiting. They looked upon the coming battle as an opportunity. Every one of us resented being the losers and looked forward to rectifying the situation. All along the march they seemed optimistic and confident, believing the outcome would be a positive one. But then seeing the enemy encamped just a stone's throw away brought on a nervous tension difficult to describe. You know it is either them or you, live or die, and you are mentally preparing yourself to take their lives.

We made camp and slept very little. The next morning brought no peace. We knew we were just around the corner from a fight. Coffee seemed to make the uncertainty worse. My nerves were positively addled.

Colonel Upton assembled our regiment, and we headed out to be positioned behind Falmouth Heights, where we were told we would be crossing the river. In order to do this they brought in the pontoons. They waited by the river's edge, great hulking wooden structures on wheels, until the time would come when they were needed and they would be placed in the water.

It grew dark. Nearly a whole day of moving here and there and still we made no real progress. I wondered why they didn't just get it over with.

"They'll be making their move soon," Sam whispered to me. Odd how so many men could remain so hauntingly quiet. It made me feel as though I shouldn't speak. I nodded my head to let him know I understood what he said. I could feel it too. I knew he was right. Through the night we moved the pontoons into place in the water. In the dark, we began crossing over the river in boats. Why did the dark frighten me so? Because I couldn't see what was coming around the bend.

It was a short crossing in theory, but in reality, it seemed to last forever. The fog was thick, wet upon my skin, and it was impossible to see anything ahead of us. The sound of the oars dipping rhythmically into the water was the only noise we made. It was far too quiet. At home, when I was alone and the silence bore heavily upon me, and I felt discomfort in it, I would sing. What a powerful comfort a hymn could be. But I couldn't sing there. I dare not utter a word. I knew if I made a noise, something far worse than the silence might await me.

Out of the eerie hush we heard someone call out.

"Fire!"

If we hadn't been low to the ground in our boats the bullets would have sliced through us like a hot knife through butter. We could not only hear them sail over our heads, we could feel them whizzing through the air above us. The Rebs were standing on the banks of the river, and we were down in the water, as of yet still unseen. I suppose they knew something was amiss, but the fog had disguised us well. No one said a word, no one made a peep. We continued on across the river and hit shore.

A great rush of us pressed forward upon the shore and made for the Rebs who had been shooting. In the confusion, I didn't really know what was going on, just that I was following, because I was in a state of uncertainty and I couldn't see anything clearly. More shots were fired and in quick work, we had run out a few of the Rebel picket lines who were vainly trying to hold their positions.

By midmorning, the fog had lifted enough for me to see where we were being led. It was the very place we had camped before. Waiting below the town of Fredericksburg the men were like ants coming to and from their ant hill. We ducked down behind our entrenchments, and waited for further command. From our spot we could see the town clearly, the great wheel of the mill churning in the water, the grand houses our men had looted before, and the burned out shells of the ones that suffered the most during our last conflict. If I had the chance, I might have called upon the old house where Sam and I had dined upon peaches, to see if the woman who lived there was in good health, if she was cared for. I certainly hoped she might return to her home someday, to see better times there.

As we waited, a truly terrible thing happened. In one of the houses near the edge of town, within view of our men, a woman stood and completely disrobed right before the window for all to see, her pale breasts like sirens calling to sailors.

"Take a look at that!" one fellow shouted out.

It certainly didn't take much to draw a man's attention to a woman in this group. If a girl should walk through camp the boys all stared and salivated after her. Some of the wives came to visit their husbands during the winter, and you'd think they were single with the way the menfolk carried on over them. They had no sense of decency when it came to women. They were starved for female companionship.

"She hasn't got a stitch of clothing on!"

You better believe she got attention. All along the lines men began to pop their heads up, eager to see the show. I was horrified to find a lady would behave that way, equally horrified by the men who had no shame in the fact that they were looking upon her with such excitement and pleasure. I wondered why she would do such a thing.

Up and down the lines the men hooted and hollered, angling to get a better view of her. Sam acted as if he might take a look too. He craned his neck, his muscles tensed as if he might get up from his squatting position in the trenches, but then he didn't. Maybe he was still trying to decide whether he should or not. I felt sick inside. I didn't want Sam to see. I couldn't explain it, but the thought of him laying eyes upon another woman made me more jealous than I could stand.

"You wouldn't!" I said in horror.

His expression was like a fox caught in the henhouse. He lowered his face and shrugged.

"I only wanted to see what all of the fuss was about," he said defensively. He was peeved, I could tell. Either he was mad he hadn't gotten any fun out of it, or he was feeling guilty for having considered looking. I thought it was probably the former and not the latter.

All around us men were giving in to their natural curiosities and standing up to see the temptress, the Jezebel in all of her naked splendor. Then without warning, we heard the crack of the rifles and a handful of the men who were standing to watch fell over dead on the spot. The Confederate snipers held up in the town above had fired upon us. The woman had lured those men to their deaths. You can imagine the rage running through everyone when they realized they had been tricked so grievously.

Now instead of exclamations and wonder and the excited catcalls up and down the lines, they were planning retribution for the harlot who had exposed her body to bring about the downfall of their friends.

"If you see her face again, shoot her!" the men were saying.

Sure enough, the woman materialized before the window again. She paraded herself before the men, hoping to get a few more. Before she had a chance to blink an eye, several of the men took aim and shot her dead on the spot. I wondered if she had anticipated getting caught in her own trap. I should have felt sorry for her, but I didn't. I was angry.

Not long after, we heard gun and cannon fire in the far distance rumbling like a thousand horse hooves from the direction of Chancellorsville. There was fighting close-by and we were on guard. The day wore on in a tedious fashion. We ate a quick meal, filled our canteens, and when the night came we slept upon the ground. We did not sleep long. Sometime in the night we were aroused and told it was time.

Up the Bowling Green Road to Fredericksburg we marched. Our commanding officer, Major General John Sedgwick, informed us Hooker had got himself in a spot of trouble and we must make haste to come to his aid. It grew light in the east, a beautiful clear sunrise that lit the sky on fire. Upon the road we began to receive artillery fire. They knew we were coming.

The further we got, the worse it grew. Somewhere hidden above, a Confederate battery unloaded grapeshot and canisters upon us. Right away men started dropping like flies. How do you make yourself go on when everything inside of you is warning you to run? I saw the dead fall in front, beside, behind me, and I continued on, although my brain was fighting me and telling me to go back.

I'm not sure if it was God looking out for us or if it was merely another stroke of luck, but the 121st was again held in reserve. We fell back and waited as Sedgwick moved past us with his group into the town. From their higher vantage point, those Rebs managed to hold us off at first. But then a second wave of soldiers pushed on to the town and overwhelmed the Rebels, driving them back.

We saw a bit of the conflict ourselves, although it was not serious. We exchanged fire, but never felt the heat of it. A small group of Confederates were trying their best to be a nuisance to us by keeping us engaged. They fired, without much result, and then we fired back. Eventually they left us alone. It was nearly noon when the rifles became silent.

The 121st was still waiting below the town, eager to see which way the conflict would go, when we saw the stars and stripes hoisted up and waving cheerfully upon the breeze above Fredericksburg. The excitement spread through us like wildfire through brush. We knew then we were the victors and we all spontaneously broke out in a cheer as we threw our fists up into the air.

"Now that is something to see!" Sam said with a whoop. Then he pounded my back jovially.

The Colonel brought us up the road, through the center of town, on our way to catch up with the rest. The place was a pitiful sight, with its damaged buildings and the corpses of freshly claimed victims strewn about the streets. There were many more deceased waiting for us upon the hill as we headed for Marye's Heights. We joined the main body of troops once again upon the hill.

After resting briefly, sipping from our canteens and sitting in the shade, we were told we would be pushing onward to Chancellorsville to assist Hooker's men there. We were told by our superiors the Rebs were on the run. We had them licked. It was upon the Plank Road, about two and a half miles from the Heights, that we encountered trouble.

Chapter Twenty-Nine

Our corps came under fire only a short ways into our march. They had been waiting for us there all along. It was not what I'd call chaos, but there was a general astonishment surging through all of us because we were not expecting it. We thought it must be only the retreating lines of the Confederate forces who had only just been beaten in Marye's Heights.

When the bullets began to fly, James Roberts's hat flew right from his head. He bent down and picked it up, dusting it off as he inspected it closely. He stuck his finger in the hole the ball had entered and chuckled to himself, showing everyone in amusement.

"That one almost had my name on it!" he said. And no sooner had he got the words out of his mouth than he was shot right in the head and fell over dead.

Upon the road we were sitting ducks. We scattered, doing our best to find cover. Their rifles fired upon us from just off in the distance. We saw a scattered crew of Rebels who were aiming our way, and we began returning fire. They must have seen they were outnumbered and took off at a run into the thick woods just off to the side of the main road. We left the road too, pursuing them to the boundary of the woods.

Once we reached the woods, though, we didn't know what we should do. I looked over to Sam to see what he was going to do. He shrugged and his expression was as if he were trying to say, *I don't know what to do. What are you looking at me for?* No one else seemed to know either.

"Take chase, Boys," Colonel Upton yelled.

That was all the direction we needed. We breeched the woods, climbing over a fence, and did our best to keep up with the retreating Rebs as they dodged between limbs and trunks of trees and thick brush-wood that made it difficult to follow. It was all I could do to try to keep my footing as I sprinted through several hundred yards of timber and underbrush, scrambling through bushes sharp with thistle and thorn, jumping over fallen logs. My heart was pumping so fast I didn't even notice how those thorns had torn into my flesh and left me bleeding.

I was running through those woods, feeling a sense of confusion over which direction I was headed. It was reminiscent of the game of hide and seek we played as children. I had my rifle clutched tight in my hands, so tight my knuckles were white. We managed to make it only a short distance when they opened fire on us. Thinking all the while we were taking chase on a few stragglers, they had led us right into a clever ambush.

Now as I rushed carelessly through those woods, it was clear to me that I was reckless. I was irresponsible. I should surely have thought it out more carefully. I should be at home, making supper for my father. I should be finishing my schooling so that I might become a school teacher. I should not be here with these men who were thirsty for blood. I was never meant to be in the army.

What with the gunfire and loud noises all about me, the confusion of thousands and more in the act of running and yelling and crying out in pain, I couldn't figure what possessed me. I didn't know how I had gotten here. I felt as if I were in a daze. Sam was running in front of me and I saw him dispense of a fellow whose intent it was to run me through with his bayonet.

"Frank!" he screamed. "Move it before you get your throat ripped out!"

The dead man fell at my feet and snapped me out of my spell. I followed behind Sam with all the need of a pup depending upon its mother for survival. He was the one thing that kept me anchored. But as he laid waste to the men coming at us, I grew all the more frightened. I had seen him gentle. I had seen him kind. I had never seen him fight with such ferocity and it nearly terrified me to watch it. I wondered if I really knew him at all.

Above the noise Upton called to his men. I trained my ear to listen. I knew he knew what he was doing. All of those many years at West Point had given him the knowledge required to lead us. I trained my ear to listen, and I could hear his clear, commanding voice despite the din and the chaos about me.

"Fix bayonets!" he was yelling frantically. Without hesitation we followed his command.

Sam and I dropped down behind the shelter of a tree to put our bayonets on the ends of our rifles. While we were in the process of doing so, we were defenseless. A Confederate came from behind Sam. I saw him, but did not have time to even form words to warn him. I instinctively pulled my gun to my shoulder and shot. The man fell dead over Sam's shoulder.

Sam was in shock. He pushed the body away, looked from the dead man to me, and said, "Good shot."

Then we were up and running again. We had run those rascals all the way through the woods. We got to the other side and came out into an open field in hot pursuit. Again we thought we had defeated them, and they were retreating, but like the water of the dew evaporates in the sun, our apparent victory was short lived.

We pressed forward out of the woods and into a clearing and right into a Rebel line lying in wait for us. We ran straight into it. Everyone panicked at once. In a full run, we hastily tried to stop ourselves. Some of the men looked from the Rebel line to the woods in desperate calculation. They were trying to figure if it was possible to make it back before they were shot down.

By some stroke of luck the waiting men, low upon the ground on their bellies, overestimated their mark and the shots rang out in deafening unison and sailed right over our heads. Only a little lower and I have no doubt we all would have been among the slain that day. It grew unnaturally quiet. In disbelief we checked ourselves to make sure we hadn't somehow missed being hit by a ball. It only took a brief second to realize they had missed us.

Someone yelled, "Get them!" and the screaming and yelling picked up again in earnest.

As they frantically reloaded, we now had the advantage. We fired upon them, killing a good number. But a second row of men rose up from behind the first and fired again. This time their shots rang true. I watched Ruben Morrell, in a full run, take a mini ball to the chest. He didn't even have the time to utter a sound; his legs immediately went limp and his body tumbled and sprawled in a flurry of loose limbs. It was a disturbing display of how quickly a spirit can leave a body. It was as if a puppeteer had dropped the strings to his doll in the midst of a performance, and the doll became a heap of jumbled body parts. All around me they fell, and there was nothing to do for it but keep moving forward because I didn't want to be next.

The Rebels were situated in a ditch, which they began to abandon once we made some headway. They fell back to the reinforcements directly behind them. They were well positioned above us in yet another trench. Directly behind that trench lay a picturesque church and a small schoolhouse. From the church sharpshooters were taking aim at us and picking us off with no trouble at all. Oh, they had planned it well.

At one point we saw Colonel Upton upon his horse. The horse had been hit with a bullet and was madly running about, panicked beyond Upton's ability to control him. The horse, called Manassas, trampled over several of our soldiers and was making for enemy lines. The Colonel was forced to abandon his saddle, jumping as best he could away from the animal. From there on out he fought on foot, leading some of the men in a brazen charge. His fighting certainly invoked the respect of me and many of the others, for he fought like a wild man. Sam and I followed close behind, scattering the Reb defenses as we went.

Miracle of miracles, we somehow managed to force them out of the second trench and had them falling back further. We rushed forward in a great burst, managing to make it to the church. The men used the shelter of the church building itself to avoid being fired upon, pressing themselves against the walls so the snipers inside could not get a clear shot at them. Ironically it was the Sabbath. And it was a chapel that stood between us and slaughter. Those who made it to the shelter of the church were then able to overtake it and overcome its occupants inside.

Now despite the sinister ambush plotted against us, we momentarily had the upper hand. We pressed hard against their lines of defense and broke through. If we had only been followed by men of a like valor. But it was the 96th Pennsylvania covering our backsides. I remembered how difficult they made it for us in the beginning when we had first joined up with them. How they had taunted us and called us names and criticized our being green. When it came down to it though, they were the cowards, leaving us high and dry in our time of need. We could at least hold our heads high, knowing we had done our best.

Once we had pressed past the enemy lines, the 96th should have followed just behind, backing us, but they became disorganized and lost their nerve in the confusion, and we were left on our own, surrounded by enemy troops. They turned on us from all directions and began firing. Such fighting I had never seen and never did see again. Upton was calling out above the fray, pleading with us and nearly emotional in the disarray, trying desperately to rally us.

"In the name of your country, gentleman, stand by the flag! Avenge your fallen comrades this day!" It was him and his words that kept me focused, kept me fighting, because had it not been for him, in all the smoke and noise and fear, I don't know what I would have been capable of.

When the fighting got so bad we hardly knew where the gunfire was coming from or which direction we should return it, Upton was yelling. "Don't flinch, men! Stand by me! I am not afraid of the devil!"

Sam and I were nearly back to back doing our best to cover one another as they fired volley upon volley. All around us the destruction was apparent. Men were falling like flies upon the ground. They literally cut us to pieces.

I don't know whether it was just that we were determined not to lose, or simply too stupid to run in the confusion of the moment, but we managed to hold our ground for a time. Then we heard someone call out, telling us we should run or be captured. The closest cover and the only way out was back through the woods we had just come through. Sam stayed close to me as we made for the tree line in a desperate attempt at saving ourselves. Neither of us was aware of anyone or anything else, only those trees and that they meant safety. It was kill or be killed, and we didn't plan on being killed right then.

He stopped once and squatted in the grass, in an attempt at reloading his rifle. I stood next to him, wheeling about wildly, looking for the source of our next threat. Up came a Rebel at full run with the intent to shoot Sam before he had the chance to finish his task of restocking his ammunition. I yelled out to warn him, but couldn't do much more.

It was so swift it seemed to happen in the blink of an eye. Sam had only a breath to react but even still he recognized his life was on the line. In a fervent attempt at self-preservation, he took the barrel of the other fellow's rifle in one hand and wrenched it from the soldier's grasp, then taking his own rifle which he still clutched in his other hand, he turned his bayonet upon the Reb and ran him clean through. That Reb fell to the ground with a groan as he clutched at his wound.

Another descended upon us with a wild shriek that froze me in my tracks. Without even a pause Sam leapt up to his feet on the defense. He had the Reb's rifle still clutched by the long barrel. He dropped his own rifle to the ground, grasped the barrel with both hands, and wielding it like a club he swung, connecting with the other man's head, felling him proper. He busted the man's head and splintered the stock all at once. Sam didn't pause for a second; tossing his foe's rifle aside and picking up his own, he kept up his run, dashing toward the woods. I only had the wherewithal to follow him.

We were just a few feet from the shelter of trees, almost there, nearly safe, when I heard the roar of a cannon ball as it exploded, and felt the impact upon the ground close-by. We were knocked from our feet with the force of the terrible blast. I could feel my body suspended in midair for the briefest of moments, and time seemed to slow as I was lifted up and then tossed down like a rag doll. Dirt rained down upon us, showering my face, choking me as I inhaled it. I lay dazed, my ears ringing, my head pounding. It hardly registered that Sam was crying out in agony, that he too was on the ground lying next to me.

"Get up!" Sam was screaming at me.

My hearing was somewhat muted. I reached my hand up to touch my ear and came away with my fingers wet with blood. I couldn't be sure if I was hit or if it was only minor damage. I got to my feet and shook my head, trying to restore some semblance of clarity, then became dizzy and stumbled to the ground again.

"Get up!" Sam was yelling again. "Get up!"

I got up again with some effort, staggering and a little unsure on my feet. Sam was pulling me on, making me keep pace with him. I didn't notice right off he was hurt. It wasn't until we reached the trees when I saw his arm. It had been ripped through by shrapnel from the cannon ball just below his shoulder. It was impossible to ascertain the damage, but his coat was soaked through with his own blood.

Once we made it to the safety of the woods, the Rebels held back, not too eager to follow. They seemed content with the fact that they had whipped us, and came after us at their leisure. We ran headlong through the trees, desperate to get away from there. Those woods were so tangled and overgrown it was close to impossible to find your way through. Tripping over brushwood and scrub and decaying timbers scattered in our path, the way was difficult and painful. The branches tore at our clothing, at our flesh. Briars snagged and ripped the legs of our pants, tangled about our ankles. I found it nearly impossible to keep my balance. I would hit the ground, pick myself up and take off running, only to fall again.

Still the sounds of rifles filled the air and the smell of gun powder permeated our nostrils. Fear, like a separate being, hovered over us, casting a stark shadow as though it had substance and existed in the real and physical world we too occupied. Sam held fast to my arm, worried, I suppose, that he might misplace me in the confusion. From the look on his face, he seemed in shock. We crouched down among the trees to catch our breath and try to restore some of our strength. I could see he was in terrible pain. The blood had run down his arm and was dripping from his fingertips which were trembling ever so slightly. We made ready to run again, when we heard someone calling to us.

"Sam! Frank! Sam…" It was Big Frank. I knew his voice right off. Sam and I looked around to try to discover where his cries came from. He lay on his back in thick underbrush that nearly hid him completely, his coat front soaked through with blood. I knelt next to him with a terrible foreboding.

"Big Frank!" I said. "You must get up! We are on the run!"

"I can't move," he told us. "I been gut shot and shall die here."

"What should we do, Sam?" I asked in desperation.

Sam was standing just above us. His face was tormented as he looked over Big Frank. He didn't say anything and I knew what it must mean. We were in real trouble. Frank was in bad shape, and Sam could see no way out of it.

After a short pause he said to me, "Get on your feet, Frank. You gotta keep moving. I will stay with him. But you must go."

I gave him a look I was sure was withering. "I won't leave him!" I screamed. "I won't leave you, and I won't leave him!"

Big Frank was coughing and moaning. He took my hand and said, "You must go, Frank. You must go."

"I won't leave this spot!" I was shouting. "Not without him! Not without you!" I was afraid, more than I'd been my whole life. But I couldn't leave my good friend to die here alone on the forest floor in some strange place, forlorn and without help. And I would not leave the man I loved to be captured and left to rot in a prison somewhere. I would not desert them. I could not.

Sam was indecisive. I knew he wanted to help but felt powerless to do so. His only solution was to send me away and stay by Big Frank's side. But then just waiting around was a dangerous game to play. If we were to do something, we had to do it right then. He slung his rifle across his torso and bent over Big Frank. With his good arm he grasped Big Frank by his hand.

"Grab his other arm," he barked at me, the stress of the situation beginning to take its toll on him.

I did what he told me to and we managed to haul Big Frank a few yards, the heels of his boots dragging along the ground. I saw the futility of it right off. He was just too heavy and even between the two of us, we could not manage it. Still I refused to give up. I stooped down and began dragging him again. Sam wouldn't say a word, but he likewise did the same. Somehow we managed to make it through the woods and to the road after a mighty struggle. But then there was the fence. I knew just as well as he did there was no way the two of us were going to get him over the fence.

"What is to be done?" I murmured to myself. "What is to be done?" In my head I was praying, begging God to somehow intercede on our behalf. For surely it would take a miracle to get Big Frank from this place. I hunched down and took a drink from my canteen and then gave some to Big Frank.

"Don't argue with me this time around, Frank," Sam said with determination in his voice. He made it clear he wouldn't take no for an answer. "You go and try to get help," he told me. "I'll stay with him and wait for you to come back. There's nothing else to be done for it."

I let the reality of his words sink in. He expected me to leave him here, alone and defenseless. The Rebs had not come after us yet, but most surely they would at some point. And he was telling me to leave them. He was telling me to go on without them. I felt so desperate I nearly cried.

Chapter Thirty

"I told you, I cannot leave you!" I yelled. "If something should happen to you—" I stopped myself from saying more because then he would discover the true nature of my feelings for him.

"It is the only thing to do," he reasoned.

"Then *you* go and *I'll* stay with him."

"Frank, between the two of us, you'll be the faster. With my arm like this…" He didn't finish. "You go on down the road, and you'll come upon someone who can help. I know you don't want to leave, but Big Frank won't make it, and I can't go on like this much more."

I gave him a look that was purely tortured. I didn't want to leave him, but I didn't see how I had any other option.

"Keep my canteen," I said, taking the strap off of my shoulder and handing it over to him. "Keep down next to this fence, and I swear to you I'll be back."

He nodded and took the canteen from me. I suspect he might have declined the offer, but he was afraid it would delay me further if I stopped to quarrel over it. I took off at a run, vaulted over the fence and dashed down the road as Sam had told me to do. I soon overtook the men who were retreating in a disorganized mass.

"Where can I find an ambulance?" I asked the first man I came upon. "My friend, he's hurt."

He didn't even acknowledge me. His eyes were wild, and it was as if he were in a trance of some sort. He just continued on as if I weren't there. I ran on.

I stopped another man and asked him.

"I couldn't say," the fellow said.

On I went. Everywhere I turned there were beaten men, haunted, injured, and disorganized. No one seemed to have any idea where I could find help. It was surreal, as if I were an outside observer, detached from everything going on around me. All I could feel was the panic that drove me on, that made me refuse to quit. I overcame Marcus Carvey, who was limping heavily, trying to use his rifle as a crutch.

"Marcus, please you must help me! Big Frank and Sam, they are both back by the fence and I must get help!" I begged him.

Marcus seemed sympathetic. "They are doing their best to get the wounded out first," he said. "You will find someone near the front lines, I suppose."

I ran on past him, trying to get in front of the crowd in their mass exodus. Once I had made it to the town of Fredericksburg I came upon a nurse tending to some of the wounded. She was covered in blood and grime, but seemed unshaken by everything happening around her.

"I must have an ambulance!" I cried. "My friends, they are waiting for me!"

The man she was inspecting thrashed about in the throes of agony with a most piteous wail.

He was crying, "Mary, oh Mary! I am not long for this earth! My Mary!" From the looks of him, he was right.

The nurse looked up at me as calm as a summer's breeze or at least it felt that way with the state I was in. Did she not sense my urgency? Did she not care for my predicament? How could she remain so indifferent?

"Many of the ambulances are down near the river," she informed me. "They are making preparations to remove the injured. But it'll be difficult to find an empty one."

I didn't wait to converse with her further. I ran toward the river. They were working furiously to get troops, artillery guns, and animals across the pontoons in a desperate withdraw. I noted a doctor instructing a group of soldiers as he tried to ascertain who needed immediate assistance, who might wait, and who might be a lost cause not to be bothered with. I jogged over to him getting into his pathway to get his attention.

"I need an ambulance!" I burst out. "Please, can you help me?"

He was not diverted from his task for a moment, his hands remained busy. He just side stepped around me and went on with his work, stalking about among the men who lay on nothing but the ground.

"We are very busy here," he scolded me.

"Yes, but my friends…I need an ambulance, sir. I need one now!"

"We are using the ambulances at present, son. If you can't see it for yourself, we are moving these men across the river."

"I can see that!" I yelled. "But I must have one. My friend, he is back on the Plank Road, and if I don't return soon I don't know what will happen! They'll most certainly capture him!" He could sense my desperation, but didn't seem to be rattled by it at all. Smooth under pressure, he was.

"Please! I need help! Won't anyone help me?" I shouted. Not just to him, but to anyone who would listen.

He stopped for the briefest of moments. "I cannot afford to spare a man to help, but if you're so intent upon it, you may take one yourself," he told me.

I didn't wait for him to change his mind. I took one of the small two-wheeled handcarts used for transporting the wounded and I ran off with it. The farther I went, the less I saw of any living man or beast. It filled me with dread. In the dim light of the late and fading evening the smell of acrid smoke and the flames of a fire began to fill the air. I was on the road, dead tired, but still managing to trot when I saw it. The very woods we had crossed over twice that day with its decaying leaves and dry underbrush had caught fire somehow, most likely from the discharge of the rifles we fired. The smoke was nauseating as I drew closer.

"Sam!" I murmured under my breath to myself. This spurred me on anew. I thought of the many men who now lay in those woods, wounded and unable to help themselves. It brought tears to my eyes. The despondency I felt as I was alone on that road seemed so overwhelming that I had to talk myself into not sitting down in the road and giving up. I finally came to the place where I had left Sam at the fence. In the increasing darkness of the late evening it was difficult to make him out all hunched over and hiding. He had not moved from the spot.

"Sam!" I called out. "Sam, I've got an ambulance!"

"Hurry, Frank! The forest is on fire!" I ran across the ditch and positioned myself on the opposite side of the fence. Using my feet as leverage against one of the posts, I reached through the bottom half of the fence, grabbed Big Frank by the arms, and pulled with all my might. I managed to get the top half of him under the fence, but couldn't seem to do more.

"Here," Sam offered. "Let me have a go at it." He tried, too. He was groaning in pain, trembling at the effort of it. Big Frank inched a little farther out.

"You take one arm, I'll take the other," he said. We each pushed a foot against the fence as we pulled Big Frank again. This time he moved even farther. Using the momentum, we dragged him up the ditch and to the road. How we managed it is still a mystery to me. Perhaps the rush of fear and emotion gave us more strength than we actually had.

Now how were we to put him on the ambulance? I was completely empty of energy and Sam was hurt bad. Between the two of us, I didn't know if it was at all possible. I bent down over Big Frank.

"Big Frank, are you able at all to crawl up on the cart?" He tried to rouse himself but was unable to pick himself up.

"I can't manage it," he moaned. "I shall die here. Please, Frank. See to it my Nell gets my things." He nearly didn't have the ability to say these words he was so bad off.

Sam motioned for me to take his arms, and he wedged Big Frank's feet beneath his arm pits and with a great struggle we managed between the two of us to slide him onto the cart. Sam sat down for a moment. He took his belt off and threaded it over his neck and then put his arm into it like a sling. He drank long and hard from the canteen, then offered it to me. I drank too. When I gave it back to him, he wetted Big Frank's mouth with it.

"We must get away from here, before the smoke consumes us, or the Rebels overtake us," he told me.

I took hold of the poles and moved the cart down the road with Sam stumbling next to me. He had lost an awful lot of blood. I was concerned for him. I knew he was a strong man, but even strong men can be brought low to their graves. There was no such thing as an immortal man. We all must die sometime.

"You all right, Sam?" I asked him as we traveled down the road with our path lit by the flames of the terrible fire.

"I only just got a nick. It'll take more than them Rebs have got to finish me," he joked. I did not like his humor. It wasn't funny at all.

"Sam, you are bad off whether you want to admit it or not. Why must you always be so—" I stopped myself before I said more. It was full on night by the time we made it to the edge of town. Fredericksburg was dark and cold in the gloomy night, the smell of fire hanging in the atmosphere. There didn't seem to be a living soul left behind, only the dead or nearly dead.

"I need to sit for a while," Sam told me.

"We can't. They're crossing the river as we speak, and I don't wish to hang about and be captured. We must press on," I said with resolve. "As soon as we are across, then you can rest."

"Yes," he said. "We'll cross, and then I will rest."

We traversed down the deserted street in silence, as I recalled that morning when we had come filled with optimism at our early success. Here we were leaving it in shame and despair for a second time, beaten again. I hated this place. I hoped I would never come back.

"I never wish to see this place again," I admitted to Sam.

"We agree upon that."

We reached the river going at a snail's pace for I was completely worn out, and Sam hardly had the strength to put one foot in front of the other. There weren't nearly as many wounded as there had been earlier. Scores of them had managed to cross back over the river in ambulance wagons. The main body of the army was still camped right on the opposite bank. I left Sam sitting beneath a tree and Big Frank on the cart next to him so I might go in search of help. I discovered a commanding officer and inquired of him where I might find a doctor.

"They have taken a great deal of the wounded over the river already," he said. "Headed toward the Potomac Creek Hospital with the ones they could save."

"I have two badly injured here. They require medical attention," I informed him.

Perhaps he could sense the desperation in my voice. He was patient enough with me to quit what he was doing and come to see for himself if he might give assistance. He went first to Sam.

"How badly are you hurt, soldier?" he asked Sam.

"Not bad," Sam lied.

"Might you cross the river on your own without assistance, Private?" he asked.

"I believe I can manage it, sir," Sam said.

I was angry at him for trying to be brave. Why didn't he just admit he needed help? I bit my tongue to keep from speaking out. Who was I to tell Sam what to do? He was a grown man, and I had no right to compel him to get assistance. I was neither his mother nor his sweetheart. I had no claim to him at all.

The officer moved on to Big Frank. He unbuttoned his coat and examined him closely, then shook his head sadly. He turned to me with his mouth set in a grim line.

"This man can't be helped," he said to me. "He's dead."

Chapter Thirty-One

I couldn't believe him. Big Frank was a giant of a man, a fit man. He had a wife and a son. He was young and had every reason to live. It would take more than a mini ball to bring him down. I knew this, knew it without a doubt. I pushed the officer aside and put my ear to his chest, trying desperately to hear his heart beating. But there was nothing…nothing. It was so very quiet.

The officer said to me, "You must work to get your other friend here over the river and to the hospital. Do you understand?"

I nodded absently. There was nothing more I could do for Big Frank. I must now care for Sam. Sam needed me. He needed my help whether he wanted it or not.

"Yes, sir," I finally managed to say.

Before we left, I slipped Big Frank's wedding band from his finger. It was not easy because his body had already begun to stiffen. I took the tintype of Nell and his baby boy from his pocket. I stored them in my pocket so I might return them to his beloved Nelly, as he had requested. Then Sam and I left him there beneath the tree. There was nothing more I could do for him now.

Once we had crossed the river, I took up with Sam's slow stride and we headed back toward camp. Neither of us spoke. I wondered what Sam might be thinking, but I was too much of a coward to ask. I was too afraid to hear what he might say. Men don't talk much, and I had found sometimes that was best.

"I must get you to the hospital," I said to him after a while.

"I'm not going to the hospital," Sam replied.

"Well, of course you are, Sam. They must work on your arm," I said in an incredulous huff. Why would he say such a thing? He was hurt very badly. Of course he would go to the hospital.

"I won't go there. With all those men heaped up there right now, I doubt they'd even look at it. They'd just take it off without a thought or care," he told me. "The bone is not broken, but that wouldn't stop them."

"You've lost a great deal of blood. You're tired. You aren't thinking clearly," I said.

"I am thinking very clearly. I don't want to lose my arm. I'll care for it myself and see if it doesn't get better."

I kept my mouth shut then. It seemed no matter what I said he wouldn't hear it. And maybe he was right. Maybe they would saw his arm off without trying to heal it properly first. I remembered the last battle at Fredericksburg we had lost so overwhelmingly. Outside the hospital tents there were severed limbs piled high from where they had amputated the wounded soldier's arms and legs. It was a gruesome sight and will forever be impressed upon my memory. I didn't blame Sam for fearing.

We didn't make it far, before Sam said, "I can't go on. I must sleep. I must sleep." I steered him to a wooded area where we found shelter among the trees.

"Can you manage to take off your coat?" I asked Sam. "Let me have a look at it?"

He shook his head. "Not now. If I can only rest for a while." I pulled his blanket from his haversack and covered him with it. We slept on the ground with only our blankets for comfort.

The next morning I had a difficult time waking Sam up. He was terribly pale, and I knew it must be from the loss of blood. He scarce had the strength to sit up. I gave him a cracker to chew on, which he took gratefully. Neither of us had eaten in more than a day.

"Do you think you might make it back to camp?" I asked him.

"Yes, I think so," he told me.

"Then let's have a go at it," I proposed.

Our progress was painfully slow. I kept pace with him. I could see he was having a difficult time lifting his feet. He was forced to sit down and rest frequently. Once, while we sat beneath the shade of a great oak, he dozed off, and I let him sleep for a while. It was past dark when we made it to our little log cabin back at White Oak Church. He crawled in and sank down on his straw mat and slept again.

All through the night I watched him, unable to sleep for fear I might wake up and find him dead. If I thought he seemed not to be breathing, I reached out and put my hand to his chest to reassure myself he was. He developed a fever before the night was out, and his sleep became troubled. In the morning I suggested to him again we go to the hospital. Again, he refused.

I was determined to get him help, with or without his approval. I knew where to get what I needed. Loath to do it, I nonetheless headed for Mr. Davies and his wagon of high priced supplies. He seemed pleased to see someone who wanted to do business. Many of the troops were still over by the river, and unbeknownst to me at the time, in serious peril, surrounded by the Confederates on all sides but one, and that was because their backs were to the Rappahannock River.

"Mr. Davies," I addressed him. "I must have some bandaging and silver nitrate if you have them."

"Someone hurt?" he inquired.

"Yes, sir."

"I see," he said, with a shrewd look upon his face. I could see him calculating sums in his head. What would a desperate man pay?

"Do you have them or don't you?" I pressed impatiently.

"I might. I might not. I'll have to look and see," he said with a half-smile upon his lips.

"Please do so then," I prodded, annoyed by his offhand manner. I was sure he had grown quite proficient in shady dealings and his intent was for me to be another of his hapless victims. He rooted around in his wagon for a while and came back with the items I had required tucked under his arm. I could see right off he would not part with them easily. I eyed them hungrily. I needed them. There was no choice but for me to get them at any cost.

"Looks like you're in luck today," he said gleefully. "I got all those things."

"How much?" I asked. I was not in the mood to take part in his games. Neither was I going to linger and play to his sympathies or grovel and beg for his mercies, for that matter.

"Oh, I don't know," he said. "These items is in demand, ya know. And I could get a fair price for them from just about anybody in camp. Specially after the fighting you all saw over there." He rubbed his hand vigorously over the back of his neck then shrugged. "Say fifty?"

"Fifty?" I said incredulously. "Why, Mr. Davies that's four months' worth of pay! Surely you can't be serious!"

He smiled at me and chuckled a little. "Now that was my best price. I was giving you a deal," he told me.

"You must be one of the most unpatriotic sorts I've ever had the misfortune of meeting. A man's life hangs in the balance, a man who has given up home and comforts in order to defend your liberties, and that you would behave in such a way is insulting to say the least!" I fumed.

My indignant ranting did not affect him at all. The smile didn't leave his face. I'm sure he was quite used to being addressed in such a manner. He had probably been called worse, the scoundrel.

"For you," he said. "I'll give you the whole lot for sixty."

Well, I had certainly shot myself in the foot. My mouth dropped open and I looked at him with a mixture of shock and hatred. Wool socks were one thing, but much needed medical supplies a whole different matter.

"I can't pay it," I said. "I haven't got that kind of money." He turned as if he might go to put the nitrate and bandaging away.

"Wait, please!" I begged him.

"Do you got it, or don't ya?" he barked.

"Perhaps we can come to some sort of an arrangement," I coaxed. "I could work for you to make up the rest."

"Cash monies only," he said adamantly. "'Sides, what happens to me if you get yourself killed before you work off the debt?"

How cold hearted and calculating he was! I was angry and helpless all at once. And then I recalled what Sam had told me of his dealings with the women who follow the army about, who offer their company in exchange for money. I cleared my throat.

"I remember you well, Mr. Davies. You may not remember me, but I remember you. From Richfield?" My eyes narrowed onto him and I felt a smug satisfaction.

"And so what?" he asked.

"You and Mrs. Davies you have five children. And to think of the poor lady back home caring for them on her own," I said. "What should she think if I was to send her a letter, Mr. Davies?"

"Tell her whatever you like. She knows I must earn a living," he said indifferently. "I take risks too, you know. It's a dangerous thing I do to bring you all these goods."

"I wasn't referring to your indecent prices and how you would rob the men blind, sir. I was referring to your dalliances with certain women who do a bit of bartering and sales of their own," I sneered. "How much have you withheld from your wife to pay for those services? I'm sure it doesn't come cheap. Money that could have gone to feeding those five children. What would she say about it, Mr. Davies, the town tinker?"

He froze. I do believe he was summing me up, seeing whether I was serious about what I had said. It seems to be a man's code of conduct to never betray the wrong doings of another man, no matter how despicable. They may know how downright rotten another fellow is, but they simply remain silent over it. Mr. Davies just didn't know I was not a man. I sincerely would have followed through with my threat if he chose to push it. Besides his poor wife had a right to know what a villain she was hitched to. I gazed right back at him, intent and resolute in my mission, unflinching, unblinking. I wouldn't leave without those bandages and nitrate. I would not fail in my errand.

"You wouldn't."

"You don't know me at all. Go ahead and force my hand and see what I'm capable of, you snake." Again he seemed to be thinking it over. I grew impatient. "So what will it be, Mr. Davies?"

He threw the items at my feet. "Get out of here 'fore I shoot you for thieving!" he growled.

I scrambled to pick them up and then got away from there as fast as I could. I had no doubt he *would* shoot me if he got the chance. I went straight back to Sam. I put the items out in front of him. I could tell he was surprised. I suppose he thought I couldn't take care of myself at all. I suppose he thought I was helpless in every regard. He looked from the nitrate and bandages to me and then he grew troubled.

"You went to the hospital," he accused.

"No, I didn't."

"Then how did you get these?"

"I had to deal with the devil," I said, "But they are mine free and clear. Now what do you need of me?"

"Go and boil some water for me," he said.

I scrambled to do as he had asked. I filled my small pot from my mess kit with water and put it over the fire. Sam sat with his head resting against the wall, his eyes closed. He was nursing his arm in his lap. When the water in the pot came to a rolling boil I took it back to him.

"Do you need any help?" I wondered.

"I can manage it," he said, shrugging his jacket off. The arm of his shirt was thoroughly saturated with his blood. I could see he had lost a great deal, and I feared it would be a long, slow recovery for him. He unbuttoned his shirt and peeled it away, wincing at the pain it brought on. When he pulled the fabric away from his skin it began to bleed anew. The hole in the fatty part of his upper arm was evidence of where the shrapnel had gone in on one side, and it was jagged and rough where it had passed through the other. It had torn through muscle and skin on its way through. The exit wound was shredded flesh and a flap of skin had been blown away and was dangling loose from his arm. He was lucky it hadn't passed through the bone, because then there would have been nothing for him but sawing it off. But I could see this gash was very serious even if it hadn't broken the bone.

He used his good hand to clean his arm with the boiled water, washing away the grime and dirt until it looked clean. He had to dig fragments of metal and pieces of his coat fabric from it in the process as he pursed his lips shut tight and sweated it out, his fingers shaking as he did so. He then took the silver nitrate and anointed it with that. The pain must have been horrible for him. His face was contorted, but he stayed silent, only now and again sucking air through his gritted teeth. Once he was satisfied it was good and clean he took a moment to recuperate, breathing deep and shutting his eyes as he leaned back against the wall again.

"Are you all right, Sam?" I asked, hurting for him as I watched. The silence plagued me. I couldn't stand how there were no words, how there was no comfort in the quiet. I felt compelled to speak but then didn't know what to say. The helplessness of seeing someone you care about suffer and not be able to do anything to help is torment.

"Yes, Frank," he said low and shaky. "Now fetch me my knife."

"What for?" I wanted to know.

"Just get my knife for me, will you?" he said. I was trying his patience. I could almost hear his thoughts: *Why doesn't he just do as I say? Why must he be so insufferably slow?*

I followed his direction, searching through his haversack until I procured the knife for him, determined to test him no more. He took it from me and then held it carefully over the fire. I watched him with no real understanding of what he was doing. The sweat was pouring from his face, carrying away the black powder from yesterday's fight, leaving him looking like he was striped. I had never seen him so vulnerable and it frightened me. It left me feeling completely helpless.

"What are you doing?" I asked him.

"I don't think I can manage holding it," he admitted.

"I will do it for you," I said. I took the knife from him and put it over the flames, just as he had done.

After a few moments he said to me, "That should be good." I nodded and handed it back to him.

Sam took a deep breath as if he were plunging into a bottomless lake and may not come up for air for a long time, and then he put the hot knife to the back of his arm, closing and fusing the mangled flesh by searing it shut. He was shaking from the pain and screaming, such unbearable screaming. He dropped the knife and began to pound the ground with his good hand, while his other arm was limp to his side. I was in shock. It never occurred to me he would do such a thing.

"Sam…" I began in horror. But for once in my life, I had nothing I could think to say.

After a while he roused himself. "Put the knife back over the fire," he told me through his pressed lips.

I was overcome with fear. "No!" I shouted. "What have you done?"

He looked at me with a strange mix of pleading and rage. He took the knife and tossed it near where I was sitting. "Put the knife over the fire!" he demanded. "Do you hear?"

"It'll kill you, Sam," I reasoned.

"I won't let them slice me up. I won't let them take my arm. I didn't make it through only to have them butcher me. That is what they are, butchers of men! Hack into a human just as thoughtlessly as a cow is separated into cuts. Not me! No, sir, not me. Now do as I say and put the knife over the fire!"

I finally gave in and did as he said. I could feel the tears coming on. I knew I was losing control, and I struggled to keep myself in check. I didn't want him to see me cry. This was not the time to burden him with my emotions. He gestured with his hand, flapping his fingers frantically, to let me know it was time and he needed the knife. I gave it to him reluctantly, slowly extending my arm to hand it to him. He urgently snatched it away, and I suppose, not wishing to prolong the inevitable, he straightaway pressed it over the wound on the front of his arm.

He shrieked again, dropping the knife from his trembling hand. I thought for a moment he might pass out. But he managed to keep his wits about him. He didn't speak, he just pointed at the silver nitrate, and I handed it to him. He put it on the back and front of his arm, sucking in his breath sharply and closing his eyes in an agonizing grimace.

"Oh, Lord," he whispered. "Oh, Lord deliver me." He was motionless for a time and then he murmured, "Here, help me with the bandaging. Is the water cooled yet?"

I touched the water in the pot to test it. "Yes," I answered.

"Soak the bandages in the water, get it good and wet, and then we'll put it on." His voice was nothing more than a whisper. He didn't even have the energy to speak.

I took the bandage in my hands and dipped it in the cooled water. I pulled an edge of it out and began wrapping it around his arm, unrolling it out from the water as I went. At the end of the roll, I split the ends in two with Sam's knife and tied it loosely. "That good?" I asked.

"It'll do," he said with a nod. "I must rest now." Not bothering with his shirt, he scarce had the strength left in him to lie down upon his pallet. I pulled his blanket over him. Thinking to leave him in peace, I took his shirt and jacket and went to wash them and hang them out to dry. His shirt was stained beyond repair, with a tear where the shrapnel had gone through. I stitched it with my sewing kit, but there wasn't much I could do for the stain. At least it would be clean for him.

Later that day the army began to filter back into camp. A more beaten and dejected crew you've never seen. It was shocking and sad to see so many empty tents and the drastic dip in numbers. I noted with sorrow Big Frank and Ruben Morrell were not the only men to fall in battle. I was sad to find Marcus Carvey's leg was lame. He was being shipped back to Washington to recover there, but they had little hope it would ever function as it should again. One thing was certain, his days in the army were over. He would never fight in another battle. I pictured him hobbling along the road, dragging his foot and doing his best to keep up with the others on a leg that was beyond repair. The fastest man with his rifle, and it availed him nothing after all.

Our group of five hundred or so men in the 121st had suffered roughly two hundred dead or wounded. Our numbers were so depleted by the battle in Fredericksburg it seemed there was nothing but empty cabins and deserted tents everywhere. We were fairly slaughtered at Salem Church. The fighting was so fierce it was a wonder any of us had made it out alive. If I hadn't been there myself, I wouldn't have believed it. I still found it hard to grasp.

I waited until it was late into the night, when most of the fires had gone out, and there was a general stillness that settled over the camp. I took my half used bar of lye soap and went down to the river, taking myself a ways away from the encampment of men. I always bathed with my shirt and short drawers still on, just in case someone should come upon me. The water was cool, and woke up my senses as I lathered up, using my fingers to rub the soap through my hair, and then washing under my arms. I used the soap to clean my clothing as well.

Once I had finished, I sat on the bank, shivering in the chill of the night. I looked up to the yellow moon hanging bright and clear in the black sky and I felt so small, so insignificant. For the first time in my life, I questioned who I was, what I was doing here. Was there a plan? A grand design? Was it God's will that Big Frank's son should be left without a father? Was it his will I had somehow survived, and come out of it unscathed? And Sam's suffering…was God aware of that?

I felt so alone, so completely and utterly abandoned. I drew my knees up, put my face into my hands, and I cried. I felt the tears run through my fingers, felt them wet my cheeks, and I didn't try to stop them. I let them come. I let them come until they had run out, and still I sat there, unable to bring myself to move. It was as if my insides had been scooped out and I was hollow, as if there were no heart beating within my breast, and the thing that kept me human and alive was gone. How many men had I killed at Salem Church? How many men had I spilled the blood of upon Virginia soil?

I began to pray as I rocked back and forth with my face between my hands. I began to pray for comfort, for relief, and the tears came again. And I wept and I pleaded until I must have fallen asleep there. I woke just as dawn was breaking, finding myself curled in a ball in the grass. I shrugged on my pants and coat and pulled my hat on, then slipped my worn boots onto my bare feet.

Chapter Thirty-Two

I trod wearily back to camp, feeling as if I hadn't slept at all. I thought I must get breakfast for Sam. He hadn't eaten. The important thing for him would be to keep his strength up. But when I checked in on him, he hadn't moved from his pallet and he was still sleeping. I didn't wish to wake him. Perhaps in his slumber he might find at least a measure of comfort.

The following day was one of quiet, disheartened anguish. Sam mostly slept, waking only long enough to eat or take care of his personal needs. I tried to stay out of his way unless he specifically said he needed my assistance. I didn't want to be a bother to him. But my concern for him was never far from my mind.

I'm sure it would've been against his wishes, but I went to the hospital anyhow. I hung about trying to figure how I might procure more supplies for Sam without anyone noticing it, when one of the female nurses addressed me from across the room. She was sitting next to the bed of a man who was wrapped up in bandaging from the crown of his head to the top of his collarbone, ears and all. And she called out to me.

"Might I help you with something?" I hesitated before I walked over to her, so no one else should hear the specifics of our conversation.

"Yes, Ma'am," I said in hushed tones. "I'm in need of a bit of muslin for a sling perhaps," I told her. "And do you have any salve?"

She couldn't have been any older than twenty, her dark hair pulled back in a tight bun. She wore a black dress, the garb of a widow. Many of the female nurses did this. I guessed they wanted to seem sufficiently sober for their gruesome tasks. She was not a bad woman to look at, but for some reason I avoided her eyes. She cocked her head and studied me closely, openly curious. I felt immediately uncomfortable, and thought I should leave.

"What for?"

"Well, you see, a friend of mine was hurt badly and I thought I might get a sling for him and some ointment if you have it," I said.

"Bring him in and we will have a look at him," she offered.

"I would like that very much, but he refuses to be seen. He fears they will try to amputate."

"That is something to fear," she admitted. "What is the nature of his wound?"

I hesitated. I was sure Sam would be angry with me if he knew what I was doing. If I gave out too much information, perhaps they would find him and bring him in against his will. I had made promises to him.

"He was hit with shrapnel," I said simply. I thought honest and directness the best course to take.

"Was it clean through, or does the wound still need to have metal removed?" she asked.

"Mostly clean through."

"Did he doctor it himself?" I nodded my head. "Does he appear to be recovering?"

"I don't know. It's too soon to tell. He cured it with silver nitrate."

"That will help," she said.

"But then he burned it shut with a hot knife. Now it is the burn I am concerned for and not just the wound itself."

"Is there any color spreading down his arm? Lines of red?"

"No," I replied. "Not that I have noted."

"Then he may be all right," she told me. "But you must watch for it, because if he should get a strange color to him or it starts to stink it means he has an infection in his arm and it is spreading. You let it go too long and he will die from it. Will you see to it he comes in if this happens?"

"I will," I assured her. But I was promising something I knew I might not be able to deliver. If Sam wouldn't let me, then I would have nothing to say for it.

"Just see to it that it's kept clean. Put a fresh bandage on it. Boil the old ones before you reuse them. A wheat flour paste is also known to help with burns, but make sure you use good cold water in the making, and make sure you don't let it dry completely."

"Yes, ma'am," I said. She nodded and then got up and walked to a supply cabinet against the wall. The cabinet was close to being completely empty.

"We're out of nearly everything," she confided. "Tried to care for as many as we might before they could be shipped out to other hospitals. Some went as far away as Washington. Looks as though I do have some bandaging and I can spare a bit of muslin for a sling." She opened the cupboard and began to rummage through it, taking out what she had promised to me.

"You're welcome to that much anyway. I wish I had more to give."

"I'm very grateful," I said. There were others in the room, but they were all either sleeping, or disregarding us, preoccupied with other things, and she was speaking to me in low tones so she might not disturb them. Still the overall feel of the place made me uncomfortable. I felt like I wanted to bolt for the door, I was so nervous from the sickness and smells. I found a bit of mirth in it, for I was at this very moment supposed to be working in the hospital as a nurse. That was what I had told my father.

"Where are you from?" she asked as she turned toward me and stacked the items in my hands.

"New York," I said. "And you?"

"Massachusetts," she replied. "I always ask everyone I meet, so I might discover how many places I can document. I keep a record of it in my journal, you see."

"That's a clever thing."

"Yes," she agreed. "It's a silly hobby. But it whiles away the time, and it keeps me occupied."

"I'm sure it does," I said awkwardly.

"Not that I don't have plenty to do, but that's just for me you see?"

"You've probably had little rest since Sunday," I commented.

"It seems there haven't been enough hours in the day," she agreed. "I very much wanted to help when I signed on for hospital duty. I thought I knew what I was getting into. My father was a doctor, and he taught me a great deal about healing. I believed I had something to offer, and I might make a difference. Now I've seen more die than live. It's been hard to come to the realization I can't save the world."

"Maybe not the world. But you've probably done much to help a few of the wounded feel comfort and peace in their time of need," I reasoned. "And in this way you've saved their world." I didn't know this girl, she was a perfect stranger, and yet she spoke to me as if we were well acquainted. I felt a loss for words. I didn't know what to say to her and feared my feeble attempt at comforting her was a waste of breath, weak and inane.

"That was a kind thing to say," she told me with a genuine smile. She must have understood I was trying comfort her. "What's your name?"

"Frank, ma'am."

"I am Evelyn Rogers." She paused before she continued on, "May I ask you something else?" I grew restless. I was ready to leave now, but I couldn't be rude.

"Yes," I told her reluctantly.

"Do your mother and father know where you are? That you've joined up with the army?"

I felt the blood drain from my face. What did she mean asking me such a question? Perhaps she was referring to the fact that I appeared so young. But I couldn't be sure.

"My mother and father are dead in the grave," I said, using the same line I had cowed Sam into submission with. But she seemed completely unruffled by it.

"Is that why you've dressed like a boy and enlisted?" Just like we were discussing the weather. I was speechless. I stared at her with what I am sure was panic in my eyes, my mouth dumbly open.

"What are you talking about?" I said. But in my own ears I could hear the weakness in my voice.

"I knew it the moment I saw you," she confessed.

"You are mistaken," I maintained. "I'm no girl."

"It wasn't difficult to tell," she went on. "The men, I suppose they don't know it because they think a lady would never be so inclined to live a life of such hardship. Or perhaps it is so out of their element to see a girl with short hair and in trousers that it throws them off. I don't know. But I can tell a girl when I see one."

"This is nonsense," I replied indignantly. I thought perhaps if I became outraged she would stop harassing me. "It's insulting to say the least!"

"Oh, come now," she coaxed. "Out with it. You are no more a boy than I."

It was obvious my rhetoric had not swayed her one bit. She was certain, and no matter what I was to say, she wouldn't hear it. I hemmed and hawed, tried to avoid looking at her; it made no difference. The girl was resolute.

"Admit it," she prodded.

"Please…" I began haltingly.

"You need not worry," she reassured me with a small smile. "I won't tell anyone." When she had promised, I sighed in relief.

"You are the first to guess it," I told her. "I'd rather die than be discovered."

"How long have you gone on like this?" she wondered.

I shrugged. Although she had said she wouldn't tell anyone, I was unenthusiastic about divulging anything more than I had to. She seemed like a perfectly nice girl, but I didn't know her well enough to feel as if I could trust her.

"Since September last."

"For a long time then," she said. "Have you seen much fighting?"

"Some."

"Are your mother and father really dead?"

I waited a long while before I confessed. "No."

"Why did you say it then?" she asked.

"So you would stop asking questions."

"Oh," she said. "How have you managed to keep it a secret?"

"I don't know…"

"What about your monthlies?" She had already been whispering, but when she asked this her voice became nothing more than a hiss.

I could feel my face growing hot. Perhaps it was nothing to her, she being a nurse and used to dealing with embarrassing things, but I was horrified by her question. It was not something you talked about—ever. When my mother told me of it she said as little as possible and turned every shade of red in the process.

"I haven't had one in a very long time," I admitted sheepishly.

"Oh," she said again. "Does it worry you?" Her questions were all in a monotone voice. It seemed as if it were strictly fact gathering for her, while it was very personal to me.

I shrugged. "Really I should be going."

"Well, it was good to talk with you. I think you must be very brave to do what you have done. If you should need help again you may come to me," she offered. "Or you could come and visit with me if you'd like, if you ever need someone to talk to."

"I appreciate the offer," I told her. "I may call on you again if my friend grows worse."

I left the hospital feeling my stomach churn with apprehension. I hastily hurried away from the place knowing she had guessed my secret, and although she said she would keep my confidence, I was at her mercy. I didn't know her well enough to know for certain whether she really would keep her mouth shut. I desperately hoped she wouldn't tell anyone. But she knew my name was Frank. She knew that I was from New York. That information alone was enough for her to have me found out. Why hadn't I just left when I had gotten the feeling I should? I resolved to never go back again. I should never have gone in the first place.

When I folded the muslin in a triangle and gave it to Sam for a sling, he wasn't at all happy with me. I felt his quiet disapproval, though he still thanked me. He got good use out of the sling, but I don't think he was happy I had gone to the hospital. He, like me, was afraid of being found out.

One day for recovery was sufficient in the superior officer's eyes. Duties resumed nearly immediately. Those who were able picked up the slack for those who were not. Despite their expectations of us, the men were in a terrible state. Not one of us was untouched by the aftermath of the battle. All of us had lost a friend or more in Fredericksburg. We had given up so much to try to pull off a victory. Colonel Upton called those of us together that were of able body to congregate upon the field we drilled on. He seemed tired and strained. I'm sure he felt the loss as heavily as we did.

"I'm proud of you," he said. "You did your best for me, and that is all I could have asked. I wouldn't have wanted to go into such a fight with anyone but you. You've all proven your worth to me."

The Colonel paused thoughtfully. "I feel a great loss and a deep sorrow over the slaughter of so many good men, men like you and me who wanted to preserve our great nation, who wanted the same privilege of freedom for all and not just some. It is up to us now, the survivors, to make their sacrifice worth it in the battles to come. The defeat here will soon pass and be nothing more than a memory. But we will go on, and we will be gloriously victorious in the future, because we are part of a cause that is right and just."

Some of the men were so overcome by his words they began to weep openly. This surprised me. For as rousing a speech as it was, it seemed an odd thing for a man to cry over. Perhaps it was just that up to this point they had held all of their emotions in check, tried to be strong and not feel the bitter disappointment of what had just happened to us, and his words had broken down the walls they had built to hold back those feelings. I didn't understand men. Even after living among them for so long, and seeing them in such a candid way, I found them curious.

I already had my good cry, and I don't believe there was a tear left in me to shed. I was dried up. I waited until we were dismissed and then headed back to my cabin. I went in and helped Sam remove the bandages from his arm. I took the bandages and boiled them in some water to clean them and then let them set and get cool before I took them out and wrapped his arm again. He had explained to me how the cool bandages took the burn from his arm, and it soothed him some. I would do whatever I could to make him comfortable.

"Does it look any better?" I asked, hopeful, as I wrapped his arm.

"I don't see any change," he said. "It will take some time."

"Yes," I agreed, "It will take some time." I finished with the bandage and backed away from him. "I still have some of that salve you got with the mountain daisy."

"I don't know if mountain daisy is good for a burn, but I suppose it couldn't hurt."

"It doesn't show any color spreading. No infection," I said. "That is a good sign."

"Yes," he agreed. But he seemed completely despondent. I suppose he just simply didn't feel well.

"Is there anything I might do to help, Sam?"

He looked so tired, despite his constant sleeping over the past two days. I would have done anything if I thought it would ease his suffering. It is a terrible thing to see one you cherish dearly go through such agony and be able to do nothing but stand by and watch helplessly. My heart hurt for him. But Sam was not one who liked to accept help, and I knew that my offer would be politely declined.

"By and by it will grow better. Any news?"

"General Hooker has resigned. Heard it from Mr. Haney."

"First Fredericksburg, now this. I guess I shouldn't be surprised. We go through generals, don't we?"

I didn't care about General Hooker. What did it matter really? I was bitter angry over what had happened at Chancellorsville, as I was sure others were too. Someone had to be responsible. May as well be Hooker. Let him go. What concerned me was Sam. Let the rest of it go to rot. It made no difference.

"Who will replace him? Have they said?"

"No word yet." I set about cleaning up, emptying the water in the pot. There was something on my mind, something I wanted to discuss with Sam, but lacking the ability to know how to address him, I fumbled for words. Finally I grew bold and undertook to speak to him. "Sam?"

"Yes, Frank?"

I paused, considering whether I should talk to him about it after all. Finally I said, "You knew didn't you?"

I remembered back to the day of the battle, the look on his face when he had seen Big Frank lying there in the grove of trees. I felt it all over again, the way Sam had just seemed to fold and give up right then and there when he laid eyes on Big Frank's wound. I could feel my throat constricting and the tears gathering in the corners of my eyes.

"Knew what?" he asked.

"You knew Big Frank was going to die," I replied, and the acknowledgment of it made my voice high, thin, emotional. He didn't respond. But I could tell from his expression I was right. "You knew there was no help for him didn't you?"

"Yes," he said softly.

"You still stayed. Why? If it was a lost cause, why?"

Sam seemed troubled. I expect the question made him uncomfortable. In general, men are not good at sharing their feelings. They aren't like women, who seem to have words forever falling from their mouths and find it difficult to stay quiet, even when it is most prudent. I believe men think emotions make them weak.

"It's not what you think," he finally replied. "It's not because I'm heroic or anything like it."

I looked at him with what I was sure was a good measure of confusion and bewilderment. What did he mean by that? I wanted to say it certainly *was* heroic. I wanted to assure him he was a man of character, and I thought he was nothing short of perfection.

Instead I said, "I don't understand."

"I done it because it was the opposite of what I wanted to do. I wanted to run, Frank. I wanted to hightail it out of there and never look back. Everything in me was saying to get, to go as fast as my feet would carry me." He shrugged his shoulder. "The honest to God truth is, I'm nothing but a coward."

"You're no coward," I defended. "You told me once your actions are what count. You told me once that it was what you do and not what you were thinking of doing that mattered. That's what you said. And you stayed. You stayed!"

"Not because I wanted to. But then I couldn't leave Big Frank like that, to die in those woods alone," he replied. After a short pause, he added, "And I couldn't let you down."

His answer stunned me. What did I have to do with it?

"Let me down?" I asked.

"It did no good," he said, ignoring me. I could see he was working through something in his head, trying to figure it all out. "He died anyhow." His voice was hollow, emotionless. It was as if the feeling were gone from him.

"I thought that too," I confessed. "It doesn't make sense, how some are spared and some are not. I wish for his sake it could have been me instead." My mind was working furiously as I tried to work out what I should say to him. After all he had done, he considered himself a coward? I just couldn't let him go on thinking that, carrying such a weight.

"It doesn't matter what you wanted to do," I insisted. "What matters is what you did do. That's what you told me. Those were the very words you spoke to me. Don't you remember?" He didn't answer. "Big Frank may have died, but he didn't die alone. He died in the hands of friends who cared for him. He died knowing his Nell would get his things because he knew we would do that for him. He had some comfort in the end, didn't he?"

"Small comfort to a man who now lies in a cold grave beneath the ground."

"Small comforts are all we have."

He nodded with a half-smile. "I will be all right, Frank. By and by it will grow better," he repeated. "Don't worry over me anymore."

He really didn't have to explain himself to me. I understood better than anyone could. I was altered too, although I couldn't quite say how. I was the same girl, in the same skin. But everything felt different. I was changed and there was no going back to the person I was, only trying to reconcile my new self with the old one.

I wondered if it was possible to ever laugh or feel joy again. Some days the heaviness of it seemed so squarely upon me. I knew he must feel the same as I did. Happier times had gone, and they might never return. But for his sake, I attempted to be optimistic. I tried to be encouraging, so he would feel better. Yet, I could hardly make myself smile. I could barely pull myself out of bed in the morning. I was struggling to get over everything that had happened and the only thing compelling me to do these things was the thought that Sam needed me.

Chapter Thirty-Three

Sam was right. By and by it did grow better. Slowly he began to come around. Over the next few weeks he grew stronger and was able to move his arm more. It pained him, but he kept using it because he knew if he didn't it would never get better. And as his arm began to heal, his spirits began to rise a little too. It was the strangest thing; as he began to grow better I noticed a lift in my own gloomy disposition.

I was relieved to see him gradually become something like his old self again. I was tired of standing by and doing nothing while he seemed to sink into his sorrow and retreat from everyone and everything. Each day I looked for signs to tell me he was on the mend. It began with him coming out of our little cabin to have supper with the others. He was able to resume drills, although still incapable of using his gun properly on account of his shoulder. It was when he made a joke that I knew the old Sam was returning to me.

For a man who seemed to have something humorous to say, even during the worst of times, it was disheartening when he didn't seem to have a funny quip at the ready. So when he made a jest when it was Reed Haney's turn to cook, I laughed more out of relief and not so much over the joke itself.

Reed gave us each our serving and then sat down to help himself to some. Sam picked the charred chunk of meat up with his fork and inspected it with an alarmed expression upon his face.

"Reed Haney, I must say it!" He paused for effect. "This is a most shameful mishandling of beef."

Mr. Haney was surprised; his mouth was formed in such a way that it looked as though he were going to ask *what?* The rest of us remained silent, in shock I think, and waited to see what Reed would do. Mr. Haney opened his mouth as if he might speak, but didn't seem to know exactly what to say. Out of nowhere I burst out laughing. No one knew what to do. When Mr. Haney reluctantly joined in with my laughter, everyone else took it as permission to do the same. After they all got a chuckle out of it, I continued to laugh, unable to stop myself.

Sam seemed amused by my obvious overreaction. It was as though he couldn't help himself, a genuine smile spread across his face.

"You're making too much of it," he pointed out.

"Yes, I know it," I acknowledged. "But it was so good to have you be witty again."

"I certainly hope you're not suggesting I haven't been witty of late," he replied.

"I would never," I countered. But the laughter hadn't left my voice. He continued to smile and gave a derisive shake of his head as though he thought me hopeless. He was pleased, and I was glad to be the source of his satisfaction.

"I shall endeavor to eat it anyhow," he said, and bit into it with enthusiasm.

One evening he came to me, as he used to before, with a look of mischief. He whispered to me conspiratorially, saying we ought to go find something to eat. Everyone in our corps knew we were the most gifted at scrounging up a good meal or two. We had a talent for it, unrivaled by any other. Perhaps I should've felt shame for it. Because really it was just that we had grown expert at hunting and stealing. But the fact was, Sam and I were co-conspirators in the thing, and that it drew us together, made it pleasing to me. There were always the pangs of a guilty conscience, but my satisfaction in being with Sam and having such a commonality between us outweighed the remorse I felt for it.

In the shadows of the evening the two of us set out together on a mission to find food. The army was nothing if not predictable with their rations, something we had learned over the many months we had spent in service. But it was more than that to us. Our "missions" were diversions. They tended to break up the monotony of camp life as well as provide us with something to eat.

Sam took the lead, staying close to the main road, but keeping off of it, so we were jogging among the trees undercover. I was content to let him show the way. I knew where he was headed; we had seen it on many a jaunt. We'd waited for a long time now for ripe cherries. Only a few miles from where we were camped lay an orchard of trees, impressively green and at last heavy with ripened cherries, just waiting to be picked. Some poor farmer wouldn't benefit from them this year because of the constant fighting near and about Fredericksburg. Whoever it was had cleared out and left the farmhouse empty and the trees unpicked. I felt sorry for his loss, and yet it benefitted us when he was forced to leave. We now had free rein to help ourselves to as many as we liked.

Only enough. Just enough. We always said. *Only enough to fill us. Just enough to take away the hunger.* The truth was Sam and I felt bad for our thievery, but without it we might well have starved to death. Hunger can make a man do desperate things. It occurred to me that before we had grown so desperate, we were the ones casting judgment upon the group of men who stole melons, near the beginning of our journey together, in a field just outside the depot. But it couldn't be helped, could it? Those cherries would go a ways to filling our bellies for several days. If we didn't eat them they would go to waste, wouldn't they? How could we let the opportunity pass?

Sam was just a short ways ahead when he dropped down low, nearly out of sight, and lay flat on the ground. I straightaway did the same. He must've seen or heard something my ears had not picked up on. The night was quiet, the heat of the day gone, and in its place a soft and delicate breeze shook the trees in a combined rustles of limbs and leaves. I lay in the grass on my belly, waiting. Shortly two men walked by, conversing in low tones, their boots coming within a few feet of where Sam had slumped out of sight.

Their conversation didn't seem of any importance, just two men talking as they passed the time. Perhaps they were out on a similar errand. Who knew? Suffice to say it didn't matter what they were up to, only that they were hindering our escape. It was too dark to make out their features. But it wasn't hard to see they were not wearing blue. As it had been before on previous outings, the line between North and South was drawn up close. Their camp wasn't very far from our own. As they drew near to Sam, they stopped, in deep discussion, and lingered there. It was agony to watch it.

I struggled to keep my breath even and quiet. Sam was so dangerously close to being discovered it was difficult to keep myself still. In the dimness, I thought I could see him watching me, his eyes trained on mine. My mind raced as the panic began to set in. What if they found him? What, then, would become of him? His arm was still not healed properly, and he would have no way of even defending himself against them.

I looked toward the trees, seeing they were dense and would make a good cover. In one desperate moment of reckless decisiveness I jumped up and bolted headlong into its cloak of leaves, crashing through underbrush and dodging the large rough trunks of trees, hoping to act as a decoy.

I wanted to draw them away from Sam. They would follow after me, I was sure of it. It would give him a fair chance at getting away. Just as I planned, the two men were after me. I could hear them taking chase just behind me, cursing and clumsy in the darkness. I was certain I couldn't outrun them, and with the disadvantage of not knowing my surroundings I was looking about wildly to try to find a hideaway that might provide a safe haven. I could wait them out if I could just find a hiding place.

In my haste I nearly fell head-over-heels into a narrow ravine, which I thought might have been just the thing I had hoped for. The ditch was not much deeper than my chest and not much wider than me if I were lying down across it. Perhaps it was used as an irrigation ditch when the rains came. I lowered myself into it and belly crawled in a switchback the way I had come.

I heard the two men out of breath, talking again. "Which way?" one asked the other.

"You take that way, I'll take this one," the other replied. Better for me to have them split up, I thought. Should one encounter me, I at least had a chance against him. The odds would be more in my favor. I continued belly crawling at a snail's pace until the ditch began to grow broader and more shallow. Still on all fours, I cautiously found my way to a tree and was able to stand upright behind the shadow of the massive trunk.

I was close enough to the road now to think I may have gotten away from them. But then as I stumbled away from the tree line, like two startled rabbits, the both of us came face-to-face.

Chapter Thirty-Four

He was young. Probably close to my own age. I would estimate not more than seventeen or eighteen. He was all skin and bones, his homespun uniform hanging loose and ample on his thin frame. Before he could make a peep I had my knife up to his throat.

"Don't make a sound!" I hissed. "Not a sound."

His eyes were wide, and I could see he was terrified. I knew that fear. I could imagine what he must be thinking. He was probably very concerned this might be his last earthly experience. He was probably frightened he had drawn the last breath into his lungs, that as fast as his heart beat now, within moments it would beat no more. Indeed if I were smart I would have taken his life there where the consequences would've been less profound. But he was regarding me, and I him. Looking him over face-to-face, eye-to-eye, my hand trembling, the knife quivering at his throat, I couldn't muster the strength to take his life. After all, he was me, and I was him. I was just a hair away from being in his shoes a moment ago. It was not like combat, when you desperately strike out at anyone or anything that seems to be working against you in blind desperation. I was looking into his face. There was time to think about it, to try to get the courage up to do it.

The silence stretched on, and although it could have been but a moment it hung between us endlessly. He was frozen, and I was trembling and indecisive. Several times I endeavored to put my knife into him only to fail to bring myself to do it. Was God watching the two of us now? And if so, what would he say to my taking the life of another, somewhere outside the heat of battle, when I wasn't compelled by superiors and the threat of death to do so? If I should kill this boy, I would have no one but myself to blame for it. I finally gave in to my weakness and said as menacingly as I could in a barely audible whisper, "Git!"

He stood still. I'm not sure if he believed me. Perhaps he thought it was some sort of a trick, but his neck was still beneath my knife and he was watching me, measuring my sincerity. I knew he was probably frozen in fear, unable to make himself move. He wanted to leave, he wanted to take himself out of the situation, but his feet would not obey him. I pulled the knife back and told him more forcefully, but still quiet, so his friend did not hear me.

"Go on! Git!"

This time he didn't hesitate. He turned on his heel and took off at a run, whichever direction was opposite mine, off into the woods. I didn't waste time cutting out of there, either. I came to the road, scanning my surroundings, trying to get my bearings. Without Sam I was lost. He was the one who knew the way to the orchard. He was the one who knew the way back to camp. How far had I wandered from my point of entry into the woods?

I hastily turned toward the road I thought we came from, with the hope I was heading back to camp. As I tramped along, miserable for all my doubts about my ability to find my way, I nearly jumped out of my skin when Sam called to me.

"Psst…Frank."

"Sam!" I called. He pushed his hands downward, telling me to lower my voice.

"Keep quiet," he warned. He waited until he was closer to say, "What did you think you were doing back there?" He was trying to sound like he might give me a lecture, but I could tell he wasn't.

"Looked like you could use some help," I replied. It was hard to keep from sounding pathetic. It dawned on me that out of the two of us, Sam would be the one to hold his own in a fight. I had probably put him out more than I had helped him. Worrying over me would be the death of him, not two Rebs idle and looking for something to do in the dead of night.

"Next time you get such a notion, you get rid of it straightaway. I don't want to be responsible for you putting yourself in harm's way."

"You're a sight for sore eyes." And then I admitted to him, "I didn't know if I could find my way back to camp."

"I can tell you now, Frank. You never would have. You're headed due south now and camp is northwest."

He was chuckling at his own joke and I couldn't help but join in. It's much easier to laugh at yourself when you see no malice is intended in the other person's words.

"Well, I would've eventually ended up at *some* camp," I told him.

"Verdict's out on which one."

"Let's get out of here," I suggested. Truth is, after everything that had happened, I was spooked. I'd had enough excitement for one night, and I didn't want anything more to go wrong. I wanted only to be safe in our cabin, surrounded by a sea of blue.

"I'm still hungry," Sam complained. I let his words sink in and looked at him incredulously.

"You still intend on going to the orchard?" I was more than a little surprised. "After all that?" Sam didn't say anything. He just smiled. It was so terribly hard to resist his grin.

"I'm not about to let it ruin my evening."

"I don't know, Sam…" I began.

"Don't tell me you don't want it. A whole orchard of juicy cherries just waiting out there for us? Think about how good they'll taste." His persuasion was beginning to wear down my resolve. I couldn't tell him no and he knew it. I was sure he thought I was some idolizing kid who looked at him with wide eyes and the adoration of youth. Which was fine with me, because I didn't want him guessing what it really was. Because it was really the adoration of a woman for a man.

"Well, all right then," I grudgingly consented. And I tagged along in his quest for cherries.

It was a sight to behold, all bathed in moonlight, when we finally came upon it. Sam was like a boy, eager and excited as we plunged through the rows of trees ripe with their bounty. We were so hungry we might have eaten them all right there, if we hadn't had some restraint. We popped a few in our mouths here and there, but not wanting to get caught, we hastened to pick as many as we might carry away with us. Sam was loading the cherries into his pockets with his good arm until they were full to bursting, when he struck upon an idea. He realized that if he put his belt around his waist on the outside of his coat it would facilitate the perfect place to store more, and began to put some of the cherries inside his coat, using it like a sack. We were laughing like children, thrilled with the prospect we would soon be eating well.

Our folly was in letting our guard down. We were so completely and entirely engrossed in our task we didn't have any warning. It was too late when I called for Sam to look out. He wore an expression of surprise and wonder as I pushed him over with a hefty shove. His body hit the trunk of a tree, shaking the branches violently and raining down cherries upon us as he tumbled over and fell to the ground. There was a loud report from a rifle, and I felt a pain so intense that I too fell onto the packed earth partially on top of him with a groan.

Sam was quick to the draw. He shrugged me off of him and pulled out his pistol, shooting with such speed I scarce knew what was happening. I was only vaguely aware it was the same boy I had spared no more than an hour ago, in the woods just a short ways down the road. With his death face he looked not so different than when I'd last seen him frightened and pale under my blade. He must have followed me all this way from the woods, waiting for the perfect moment to spring upon us, or perhaps talking himself into it. I suppose I'll never know what he was really thinking. Sam had good aim. He had got him right in the chest. I should think he died nearly instantly.

At the time I was not so concerned for his suffering, but my own. I felt such affliction that it was impossible to keep quiet, to hold still. I writhed about on the ground my side hurting so badly I found it difficult to draw a breath. Sam's face wore an expression of horror, his eyes were searching mine. He knelt next to me and pushed his hand over my mouth to quiet me. I wasn't aware I was groaning until he did that. I realized then just how thunderous my howling had become. I was in such pain, so scared, I couldn't think of anything.

"I been shot!" I cried with a sick realization.

"Shhh," he cautioned. "Keep quiet, Frank. Someone's bound to hear it. We must get while we can."

He raised me up, and wrapping my arm around his neck, he wedged me beneath his good arm, using his hand to pull me along by my belt. I couldn't help but cry out. My feet stumbled and he dragged me through the orchard, dodging trunks and limbs, weaving in and out of the rows of cherry trees. It had become a nightmarish maze, impossible to judge where we were or which way we were headed. He was running as fast as he could with me as baggage, weighing him down, holding him back. Once we came to the edge of the orchard he hesitated, torn as to what he should do next. Should he stay under cover of the trees in the orchard, or should he run and try to get away?

Figuring it was better to risk exposure rather than be trapped where we were, Sam hauled me across an open field, through a ditch and into the trees on the other side. We staggered hastily along, doing our best to put some distance between us and the dead boy in the orchard. Once he felt we had some measure of defense, holed up behind a generously sized rock, he laid me out upon the forest floor. The effort of it brought fat tears that squeezed from the corners of my eyes and ran down into my ears and hairline. I tried to keep quiet as he warned me to, but I was still moaning and fretful.

"Where does it hurt?" He spoke in a hushed and desperate tone.

I couldn't say anything. I tried to put my hand to it but the pressure made it hurt all the more. I gasped and grunted, rolling to and fro. The fleeting memory of my dream, the cornfield at Antietam, and me dead as Sam looked on, flashed through my brain. Was I dying? Was this to be my end? Should my epitaph read that I was shot in a cherry orchard and discovered to be a woman?

Sam crouched down next to me and began to fumble to unbutton my wool jacket, to try to see how badly injured I was, to try to give me some sort of aid. But even through the pain, I knew I could not let him. There was still a shred of my brain able to warn me against it. I was able to somehow manage to reach past the pain and have some semblance of sensibility. I had kept my secret for so long that the fear of being revealed won out over my pain. I tried to push his hands away from me, to wriggle free of his grasp.

"No!" I told him. "Don't touch me!"

"Frank, hold still. I'm trying to help you," he hissed. "It's me. It's your old friend, Sam." I suppose he thought I was delirious, unaware of who he was or where I was at. Even so, I fought him still with the desperation of one who did not want to be exposed.

"All is well," I insisted. "I am well." I could hear my words, his words, with a shrill ringing in my ears which made my skull feel as if it might crack open. My vision grew dark and gray around the edges, and a flash of brilliant stars fired white and bright before my eyes. I knew I was in a swoon, and yet I managed to fight on, my hands battling against his as he strove to undo my jacket and then my shirt.

The moment his eyes were on me, I knew. And in the shame of my nakedness, I attempted to cover myself with my arms. He grew motionless, and I too, with nothing left to fight for, became silent. All this time he thought me a boy, a fellow soldier. It must have come as quite a shock to him when he discovered I was not—worse to find out in such an unexpected and astonishing way. I lay there trying my best to protect my modesty as he fell back on his haunches and stared at me with his mouth open and his eyes wide.

"Good Lord Almighty!" he said, panting. "What in the name of…"

He didn't finish his sentence. But then it occurred to him to let me in on the secret too. "Frank, you're a woman!"

And that is how I came to be discovered.

Teaser for the Upcoming Sequel

…Although I felt the heat spread through my body and I experienced the strangest sort of joy rushing through me all at once, I just stood there like a fool, frozen where I was. I must have worn a look of astonishment. He pulled away and seemed ashamed.

"I'm sorry," he murmured.

"Why?"

Sam cleared his throat. "For a moment I forgot myself."

"I liked it very much," I admitted, unable to bring my eyes to his. "I wish that you would forget yourself more often."

It seemed that that was all he needed to hear. He moved in purposefully toward me, tilting his head at an angle, then paused and studied my lips, as if they were the most fascinating thing he had ever seen. Then he put his mouth to mine again. This time it was not so chaste. It was more like being in water and desperately coming up for air before plunging back into the water again, as it was when I thought I was drowning in the Rappahannock. A kiss, a breath, a kiss. I felt a certain sense of desperation for it, aching to not have to breathe at all.

I let the pleasure of it run over me in flushed exhilaration. Sensations and emotions I had never experienced played over my body, through my brain, as I touched his face with my fingertips, and he held me fast with the pressure of his palm on my lower back and his other hand cradling the back of my neck…

Acknowledgments

As always I thank my friends and family for their generous support. I am very blessed to have such a wonderfully strong and stable support system. In undertaking such a huge project, it was they who encouraged me, believed in me, and at times even pushed me along. Without them, I have no illusions that I might have pulled it off on my own. A special acknowledgement to my husband, children, and parents Doug and Sharon Beaty. My brother Adam Beaty who served our country in Afghanistan and gave me some much needed feedback about his experiences there. Thank you!

For my friends who read the manuscript and gave me their feedback as well as sharing their editing skills, I can't tell you how much it helped me. A very big thank you to Michelle Glad and my editor, who shares the same passion for history, C.J. Creel.

I would also like to acknowledge the genius of those I took inspiration from. I was most grateful for my resource information that helped me to craft my story. *Upton's Regulars* by Salvatore G. Cilella Jr. gave me all of the great historical details I needed to make Serena's 121st experiences authentic. He has a rare quality for making non-fiction beautiful and exciting.

I also had the good fortune of reading *They Fought Like Demons* authored by DeAnne Blanton and Lauren M. Cook. It is obvious through their exhaustive research and fascinating stories that they are passionate about the subject of women who served during the Civil War. It was a real treat to discover through their writing the great adventures, hardships, and heartbreaks these women, and sometimes girls, lived through or died from. Certainly without the knowledge gleaned from these two books I would not have been able to complete my work.

I am also grateful to my own personal historian, Michael Nivens, who was willing to share his passion for the Civil War with me. When I told him of my intentions of writing this novel, he immediately pulled out all of his resource materials along with his vast knowledge of the Civil War history and had them at my disposal.

About the Author

Tracy Winegar enjoys cooking and gardening in her free time. She loves all things vintage and considers several family heirlooms to be her prized possessions. She's also always on the lookout to score pieces to add to her growing Jadeite collection.

Tracy lives with her husband and four beautiful children in Northern Utah. Although she doesn't mind living in a desert, she still misses the green of the Midwest where she was born and raised.

New Adult Romance

Three Daves by Nicki Elson
Streamline by Jennifer Lane
The Shades series: *Shades of Atlantis* & *Shades of Avalon* by Carol Oates
The Heart series: *Beside Your Heart, Disclosure of the Heart* & *Forever Your Heart* by Mary Whitney
Romancing the Bookworm by Kate Evangelista
Flirting with Chaos by Kenya Wright
The Vice, Virtue & Video series: *Revealed, Captured, Desired* & *Devoted* by Bianca Giovanni
Granton University series: *Loving Lies* by Linda Kage
Missing Pieces by Meredith Tate

Paranormal & Fantasy Romance

The Light series: *Seers of Light, Whisper of Light* & *Circle of Light* by Jennifer DeLucy
The Hanaford Park series: *Eve of Samhain* & *Pleasures Untold* by Lisa Sanchez
Immortal Awakening by KC Randall
The Seraphim series: *Crushed Seraphim* & *Bittersweet Seraphim* by Debra Anastasia
The Guardian's Wild Child by Feather Stone
Grave Refrain by Sarah M. Glover
The Divinity series: *Divinity* & *Entity* by Patricia Leever
The Blood Vine series: *Blood Vine, Blood Entangled* & *Blood Reunited*
by Amber Belldene
Divine Temptation by Nicki Elson
The Dead Rapture series: *Love in the Time of the Dead, Love at the End of Days* &
Love Starts with Z by Tera Shanley
The Hidden Races series: *Incandescent* (book 1) by M.V. Freeman
Something Wicked by Carol Oates
Chronicles of Midvalen: *Command the Tides* (book 1) by Wren Handman

Romantic Suspense

Whirlwind by Robin DeJarnett
The CONduct series: *With Good Behavior, Bad Behavior* & *On Best Behavior*
by Jennifer Lane
Indivisible by Jessica McQuinn
Between the Lies by Alison Oburia
Blind Man's Bargain by Tracy Winegar

Erotic Romance

The Keyhole series: *Becoming sage* (book 1) by Kasi Alexander
The Keyhole series: *Saving sunni* (book 2) by Kasi & Reggie Alexander
The Winemaker's Dinner: *Appetizers* & *Entrée* by Dr. Ivan Rusilko & Everly Drummond
The Winemaker's Dinner: *Dessert* by Dr. Ivan Rusilko
Client N° 5 by Joy Fulcher
The Enclave series: *Closer and Closer* (book 1) by Jenna Barton

New Flame by BJ Thornton
Shackled by Debra Anastasia
Swim Recruit by Jennifer Lane
Sway by Nicki Elson
Full Speed Ahead by Susan Kaye Quinn
The Second Sunrise by Hannah Downing
The Summer Prince by Carol Oates
Whatever it Takes by Sarah M. Glover
Clarity (A *Divinity* prequel single) by Patricia Leever
A Christmas Wish (A *Cocktails & Dreams* single) by Autumn Markus
Late Night with Andres by Debra Anastasia
Poughkeepsie (enhanced iPad app collector's edition) by Debra Anastasia
Poughkeepsie (audio book edition) by Debra Anastasia
Blood Eternal (A Blood Vine series single, epilogue to series) by Amber Belldene
Carnaval de Amor (*The Winemaker's Dinner*, Spanish edition)
by Dr. Ivan Rusilko & Everly Drummond

coming soon from
OMNIFIC PUBLISHING

The Hidden Races series: *Illumination* (book 2) by M.V. Freeman
The Embrace series: *Entwined* (book 3) by Cherie Colyer
The Adventures of Clarissa Hardy by Chloe Gillis
Where All Good Dreams Are Real by Jane Susann McCarter
The Ground Rules by Roya Carmen
Trouble Me by Beck Anderson

www.ingramcontent.com/pod-product-compliance
Lightning Source LLC
Chambersburg PA
CBHW020511120726
47904CB00003B/785